THEIRS TO WED

A Marriage Raffle Novel

STASIA BLACK
A.S. GREEN

D1719017

PREFACE

In the not too distant future, a genetically engineered virus is released by an eco-terrorist in major metropolitan areas all over the globe. Within five years, almost 90% of the world's female population is decimated.

In an attempt to stop the spread of the virus and quarantine those left, a nuclear war was triggered. It's still unclear who began attacking who, but bombs were dropped on all major US cities, coordinated with massive EMP attacks.

These catastrophes and the end of life as people knew it was collectively known as *The Fall*.

MAP OF THE NEW REPUBLIC OF TEXAS

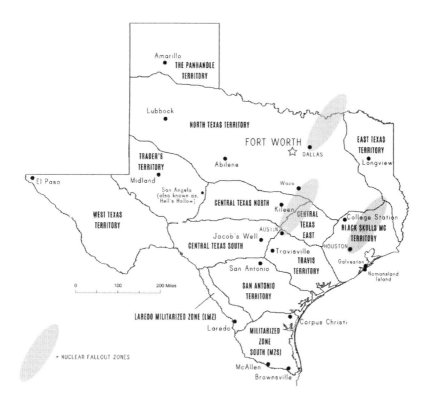

THE PANHANDLE TERRITORY

Amarillo

Lubbock

NORTH TEXAS TERRITORY

FORT WORTH

DALLAS

EAST TEXAS TERRITORY

Longview

TRADER'S TERRITORY

Abilene

Waco

El Paso

Midland

San Angelo (also known as, Hell's Hollow)

CENTRAL TEXAS NORTH

Kileen

CENTRAL TEXAS EAST

College Station

BLACK SKULLS MC TERRITORY

WEST TEXAS TERRITORY

AUSTIN

Jacob's Well

CENTRAL TEXAS SOUTH

HOUSTON

Travisville

TRAVIS TERRITORY

Galveston

San Antonio

SAN ANTONIO TERRITORY

Nomansland Island

0   100   200 Miles

LAREDO MILITARIZED ZONE (LMZ)

Laredo

MILITARIZED ZONE SOUTH (MZS)

Corpus Christi

* NUCLEAR FALLOUT ZONES

McAllen

Brownsville

CHAPTER ONE

LOGAN

"Piss off." Logan Washington shook his head at his supervisor, Phoenix ("Nix") Hale, as he drove the ancient four-by-four truck on the dirt road that cut through a field. He and Nix had worked side-by-side as part of the town's elite Security Squad ever since Logan arrived eight years ago from Austin (or what was left of it).

"I feel for you, Ghost. I do," Nix went on.

Logan glanced over, and his jaw went tight at the concerned expression that puckered the scar on Nix's face. They called Logan "Ghost" for a reason. With the exception of work, he kept to himself. It was better that way. For everyone. He forced his attention back to the road without acknowledging Nix's attempt at empathy. It didn't suit him.

The truck jumped as they hit a rut, and Finn swore from the back seat. "Take it a easy. There's no padding on these damn jump seats. You keep jolting me around like this and my balls are gonna be black and blue tomorrow."

Logan ignored him. Finn had been complaining for the last hour and the drive was only three hours long. It was early May, and they were out on a Scrapper run in the westernmost edge of Central Texas North. Closer to the border with Trader's Territory and West Texas Territory than Logan preferred.

Those bastards could be ruthless, especially if you ran into scavengers from Hell's Hollow, one of the most prominent townships and trading posts in Trad Territory.

Most of the best shit had already been scavenged right after the bombs fell eight years ago, but Graham, one of Nix's clan mates, always watched the satellite feeds. He swore the recent flooding had washed a biplane out into a clearing near here.

Since their own township, Jacob's Well, was one of the few places that had access to such technology after the EMP attacks, they had a good shot at being the first to reach the site. It was doubtful the whole plane would be worth hauling back, but if they were lucky, they could strip it for parts and start heading home before nightfall.

This all sounded good to Logan. Between Finn's complaining and Nix's constant hassling, he already had a headache the size of the New fucking Republic of Texas.

"Another woman could come to town any day now," Nix said, continuing to push the issue. "You should have put your name in for the girl who got here last week. When's it gonna be? At least put your name in next time. What's the harm?"

Logan didn't respond. He didn't see the point in answering stupid questions. He didn't put his name in the lottery box because he wasn't looking for a bride, or a clan for that matter; he was looking to be left alone. Nix was smart, so why was this so hard for him to understand?

"Well I'm sure never gonna miss a chance to put *my* name in," Finn piped up again from the back seat. "I haven't missed one since I turned eighteen, but I'm in the fifth tier so my odds are shit. But damn, Ghost," he punched Logan on the arm, and Logan glared at him in the rearview mirror. "You're in the first tier. I'd kill for odds like that. They've got to be like what, one in thirty?"

Again, Logan didn't answer, and the tension at his temples stabbed at him like red hot pokers. *Another good reason not to put your name in the box.*

Fuckin' Finn kept rambling. "But in a couple months...when I get that promotion you promised me, it'll mean moving up to the fourth tier. Just you watch. I'm gonna be married by the time I'm twenty-one and have me a litter of kids before I'm thirty."

Logan rolled his eyes but when he glanced over toward the passenger seat, Nix was staring intently back at him.

Logan returned his focus to the road. Okay, so calling it a road was generous. At this point it was more field than road—but every so often he'd make out ruts from where the road used to be, which told him he was still on track.

"Your woman..." Nix's voice was quiet. "Man, she's gone. You can't mourn her forever."

"Can't I?" Logan asked, and he meant it. He was thirty-eight. He and Jenny had been high school sweethearts. He'd been married to her for twelve years and now widowed for eight. But some nights he woke up just as raw as the day he realized he'd lost her. Some wounds were so deep, time didn't do shit to heal them.

Jenny. What he'd give just to see her again. He'd even take one of their knock-down, drag-out fights. He'd give his right nut just to hear her calling him names. "Logan, you stubborn ass!"

It didn't make sense that God would take someone whom the world so clearly needed. Whom *he* clearly needed. She had an IQ that was through the roof, curious, inventive, and so damn beautiful. Tall. Pale gray eyes that could always see right into the heart of him.

No, he had no interest in getting married again. And *no* interest in disrespecting his wife's memory with some stranger shoved in his life by a goddamn lottery. Not to mention, sharing a new wedding bed with four other men...? *Damn.* He knew the world was different and all, but some shit he'd just never understand.

Nix chuckled as if he could read Logan's thoughts. "I know. I thought the same thing, but it can work. Look at what I have with Audrey and my clan."

"Your wife is exceptional. No doubt, man," Logan said. "Jenny was, too. But what if something happened to Audrey..."

A low growl rumbled out of Nix's chest.

"Easy, asshole. But you just made my point. If something happened to Audrey, you think you'd jump into bed with the next woman who stumbled into town?"

"No," Nix growled, obviously upset at even the thought of it. Then he huffed out a loud exhale. "But you're hardly *jumping*. It's been eight damn years. A man shouldn't be alone that long. It's not natural."

"I like being alone."

"You'd like having your balls sucked more," Finn said, his head popping up between Nix and Logan.

"Jesus," Logan said, and he ran his hand through his hair.

"Like you know anything about it," Nix shot back at Finn.

"Well I'm *gonna*. Just you wait. Fourth tier. I'm telling ya, this is my year."

"If it's going to be anyone's year, it's going to be Logan's," Nix said.

Logan fought the pressure building in his chest. He knew from experience that Nix wouldn't let this go. His badgering had gotten worse and worse lately. It was time to shut it down once and for all.

"Fine."

"Fine?" Nix asked, blinking in surprise. "You mean it? You're finally gonna put your name in the box?"

"Yeah. I'll finally put a name in the box." He'd do it, too. As soon as a new woman came to town, he'd make a big show of it—bring Nix with him and get that ugly fucker off his back once and for all.

But Logan would never be writing his own name on a ballot. He'd already come up with an alias. *John Steinbeck.* He'd read his ancient copy of *The Grapes of Wrath* so many times the pages were barely legible. What could he say? Reading about the Depression cheered him up.

"Wow, just think if both our names were to get called," Finn said, leaning forward and getting in their space again. "That'd be awkward. Man, I'd like, see your junk cause we'd both be fucking our wife at the same time, right?" He turned to look at Nix. "Or wait. Do you just line up outside the bedroom or how—?"

"Jesus!" Logan shouted, and not just because Finn was a dumbass.

Logan jammed his foot on the brake, and the truck came to a skidding stop, nearly plowing through a rotted wooden fence.

"What the fuck?" Finn yelled, his body almost launching over the front seat.

Nix turned on him. "How many goddamn times have I told you to put your seatbelt on?"

Finn waved in front of them. "Don't yell at me. It's not my fault Ghost can't navigate for shit."

Logan's jaw locked. "Well maybe if we had a better map or directions I wouldn't be on a road that goes through a damn field and dead ends into a fence."

While Finn was still shouting and losing his shit, Logan went quiet. Then he turned around and jammed his hand over Finn's mouth.

Finn looked even more pissed, but Logan just hissed a long *shhhh* noise while not moving his hand from Finn's mouth. Then he made a motion to *listen,* and Nix immediately went on alert. It took Finn a little longer to catch on, but eventually he calmed down and settled. Logan closed his eyes to hear better.

The noise that had first drawn his attention sounded again and Logan's chest cinched tight.

"Is that a—?"

"Shhh," both Nix and Logan hushed Finn at the same time.

Then all three of them were quiet, and the sound came again.

Logan and Nix's eyes snapped to each other. And then they both shoved their doors open and started sprinting across the field in the direction of the noise.

In the direction of the high-pitched scream.

Logan was solid and well-muscled but not as bulky as Nix, so he ran faster. He jumped the fence like it was a hurdle and ran through the field before hitting the woods. Branches and nettles slapped at his arms and face, but he didn't slow down.

The shouting was louder now so he was going the right direction. *Hold on. Whoever you are, just hold on a little longer.*

When he came around the bend in the trees and saw the rocky embankment, he thought he was too late.

Two men—smugglers Logan would guess—stood over what looked like a pubescent boy, trapped on the ground by a thick meaty hand held at his neck.

"Hey!" Logan shouted, waving his arms over his head. The two men's heads shot up and looked his direction. "Yeah, you, you ugly fuckers. Why don't you pick on someone your own size?"

It was only as one of them raised a gun in his direction that Logan realized he didn't have any weapons on him. *Son of a bitch.* He'd heard the scream and just took off without thinking. He wasn't going to be any help to this kid if he ended up full of bullet holes.

Logan was about to dive into the bushes when the man holding the gun suddenly cried out in pain, arching and looking down at his foot.

Damn. The boy had shoved a wicked looking knife right through the top of his assailant's foot. The man stumbled and fell to the ground. His gun tumbled out of his hand at the same time.

The boy didn't waste a second. He scrambled for the gun, bashed the guy under the chin with it, knocking him out cold—all before the second assailant realized what was happening. The only conscious smuggler reached for the kid but—*Shit!*—the kid was fast. The smuggler's hand closed around air, then an explosive shot rang out, the sound vibrating against the rocks.

Logan was close enough to see the spray of blood before the second man dropped to the ground. Dead. Then the boy was up on his feet, the gun swinging back and forth between the unconscious smuggler with a knife in his foot...and Logan.

Logan's mouth dropped open. Not because there was a gun aimed at his chest. But because the boy wasn't a boy. It was a tiny woman, at least...Logan was pretty sure that's what he was seeing. Her hair was shaved close to her skull, and she was too skinny to have much in the way of breasts, but her eyes were dark, round and beautiful, and her hips... That was no boy.

"Who the fuck are you?" she shouted at Logan, gun still moving.

Yep. Not a boy. Logan put his hands up. "Just someone who wants to help."

She scoffed. "What do you think I am, an idiot?" She leaned over and, gun still trained on Logan, yanked her knife out of the smuggler's foot. He flinched and started to groan, coming to.

Logan took the last ten steps out of the woods onto the embankment. The woman kept her eyes on him the whole time as she leaned over and, using the knife she'd just reclaimed, slashed the smuggler's throat. Ear to fucking ear.

Holy shit.

Finn and Nix stepped out of the woods behind Logan. He held out an arm to keep them back. He didn't know who the woman was but she was lethal, that much was obvious.

She straightened her spine and turned in their direction again. Her face and dark stubbly hair was now covered in blood spatter. With the knife in one hand and the gun in the other, she looked like some sort of miniature avenging Amazonian warrior.

"I asked you a question," she bit out. "Who the fuck are you?" She jerked the gun to make her point that this was her show. "Don't make me ask again."

Logan's hands were already up, but he lifted them higher.

"Holy fuck, you *smoked* those assholes," Finn said excitedly "That was awesome. I mean, he was like," Finn made a choking gesture with his hand, along with accompanying gargling noise, "and then you were like, *whaaaaa*," Finn made a downward slashing motion, "and then, *boom*, you take him out. Fucking sweet."

The woman frowned at Finn, and Logan felt the urge to apologize. Nix took a step forward. "On behalf of Jacob's Well Township, I'd like to extend our warmest—"

The woman's eyes flared in recognition. "Jacob's Well?"

Nix nodded, eyes wary. "You've heard of us?"

The woman took a step toward them, and the gun wavered just the slightest bit.

"Jacob's Well," she repeated, her voice shaking. And then her eyes rolled back in her head, and she collapsed right where she stood.

CHAPTER TWO

RIORDAN

"You're going. Both of you. And that is that."

Riordan ignored his mother, scowled at his *perfect* brother Ross, then ran his spoon through the disgusting slop they called food around here.

Both of you. Always "both of you." Being an identical twin wasn't as awesome as people thought. Which was why Riordan was going somewhere all right—just not the same place his mother was talking about. Riordan was getting the hell *outta* this town.

He wouldn't plan his exodus to death like Ross would. No. Fuck that. He didn't mind taking chances. One day it would all get to be too much and he'd just pull the trigger. He'd pack some hunting gear, steal a truck maybe, then take off.

He'd go someplace where a man could really make something of himself. He'd thought about heading to Fort Worth and signing up for the Army, but shit, that kind of thing was more Ross's style. He didn't want to trade-in their mother's house just for another set of rules.

Don't stay out after dark, Riordan. Don't use that knife, it's too sharp, Rior-

dan. Come home right after school, Riordan. Why can't you be more like your brother, Riordan?

"Finish your stew, Riordan," said his mother, breaking into his thoughts. "It's got real meat in it, and you need the protein."

Riordan pushed the bowl away and slammed the spoon down on the table. "Jesus, Ma. I'm nineteen. When are you gonna stop treating me like I'm six years old?"

"Here we go," Ross muttered under his breath from where he sat at the table beside him. Ross scraped the bottom of his bowl like the good little boy he was, and Riordan shook his head in disgust.

"Maybe I'll stop treating you like a six-year-old when you stop acting like one." His mother put one hand on her hip and stared him down.

She was short and had the rounded profile of a keen-eyed bull terrier. And like a bull, she was prone to plowing down whatever obstacles lay in her path. Including her own sons. Sometimes Riordan thought she'd taken her survival from Xterminate as proof from the Almighty that she should always get her way. Especially since their dad had died not long after The Fall.

"Now. Finish. Your. Stew. And then you two need to march yourselves down to the town square to put your names in for the lottery. A new girl was just brought into town."

Riordan had heard about the knife-wielding wild woman that had been picked up earlier today. Apparently she was practically feral. She'd been brought into town covered in blood, head shaved, and skinny enough to barely count as a woman.

At least that's what he heard. It wasn't like he was ever allowed to be on the front lines of anything.

Riordan shoved his chair back and stood up. "No."

His mother's eyes widened. "What did you just say to me?"

"Riordan," Ross said, standing up with his hand out, obviously ready to play the mediator.

Riordan turned on him incredulously. "Grow up! You don't have to be so damn compliant all the time. What if your name gets called? You don't want to get married any more than I do."

"Ross will do what I say he needs to do," their mother said. "Because he's a good son."

Ross dropped his gaze to the ground.

"You know they don't give out merit badges for being a mama's boy, right?" Riordan asked.

Ross's eyes shot up with a quick murderous look before dropping again to the floor. Ross had always had his heart set on becoming an Eagle Scout. The world had gone to shit when they were twelve and even though the Boy Scouts of America no longer existed, Riordan knew Ross was still secretly working toward it. He was always such a dog with a bone.

Riordan would catch him pouring over all the old scout books and practicing knots or reading about what mushrooms would kill you, or setting up wilderness shelters from scratch. That was the perfect example of who his twin brother was—the kind of kid who loved rules and order so much he spent all his spare time following them to reach a completely pointless goal. So he made unofficial Eagle Scout? So...? Then what?

Riordan was done with all of it. Ma. Ross. Always being compared. Never good enough. D-O-N-E.

"Enough," his mother said like it was the last word on the issue. "You're both going to go down to the town square tonight." She looked Riordan in the eye like she was daring him to talk back.

He smirked but didn't say anything.

"Then you'll put your names in that box. Between the two of you, I've doubled my odds at having a son settle down. I could have a grandbaby by this time next year."

"Jesus Christ. A *baby*?" Riordan exploded.

Was she even listening to herself? They were *nineteen*. They were barely starting their own lives. Give them some time to live before saddling them with the responsibility of marriage and a damn family.

Actually, strike that. That was the kind of shit Ross might want—someday. But Riordan was gonna be a lone wolf forever, making his own damn way in the world. No one telling him what to do. Maybe he'd join up with some smugglers.

Or he could even leave the New Republic and head out West. New

Mexico or Colorado... According to the rumors, they were lawless territories that would be just the kind of place for a maverick like himself.

"Riordan Sean O'Sullivan," his mother came forward and grabbed his ear in an awful pinch, yanking him down so that he was eye-level with her five-foot-four frame, "I ought to wash your mouth out with soap for using the Lord's name in vain. Now. You will go to the square right this minute with your brother and you will put your name in that lottery box. Am I making myself perfectly clear?"

Riordan swallowed, shame and self-loathing rose up to choke him as he adopted the same posture as his brother, eyes to the floor. And then he did what he had done every day of his nineteen years on this earth. He gave in to the domineering woman who ran his life.

"Yes, ma'am."

CHAPTER THREE

MICHAEL

Michael sat on the edge of his bed and watched Ana, the woman who lived in the house next door, through the gap in his curtains. The sun had set about an hour ago but she had several oil lamps lit, so he had a perfect view from his garage apartment.

The first time he'd watched, it had just been through the tiniest gap and he'd only taken furtive glances. But as the nights and months progressed, he'd taken to leaving his curtains open wider and wider.

Because Ana? She left her own bedroom curtains *all* the way open, *as per usual*, and the lights on, *of course*.

For tonight's performance, she was wearing a red lace bra and matching panties cut high on her long legs. When she turned her back to the window, Michael sucked in a breath at the sight of her firm ass cheeks split by the red thong.

Ana was twice his age, nearly fifty, but you would have never guessed it to look at her. Sometimes he felt bad about watching, but never for long. She knew he was there. And she gave these shows just for him. They started shortly after she asked him about his clothes.

"*What's with the outfits?*" *she asked one day when they found themselves stepping out of their houses at the same time.*

"*The outfits?*" *he asked.*

"*Yeah.*" *She gestured at his body, drawing her hand through the air in a vertical line.* "*White tank top. White basketball shorts. You're like the sixth Back Street Boy.*"

"*Who?*" *he asked.*

She rolled her eyes. "*Never mind. Ancient history.*"

"*Oh.*"

"*So you're not going to tell me?*" *she asked.*

"*Tell you what?*"

"*What gives with the clothes? Every day it's the same thing. You must have a closet full of them.*"

"*Oh. I do.*"

"*And...*" *she said, prompting him to go on.*

Sensory processing disorder was not something Michael like to talk about. Not then. Not now. Not ever. There was enough disease, death, and loss in this world to trouble anyone with *his* lame issues. Besides, SPD was kind of a conversation stopper.

The short story was: Michael couldn't bear to be touched.

He didn't shake hands. He didn't go to the clinic. It was the reason he had this garage apartment instead of living in the men's dorms with everyone else—too much chance of being touched or jostled. After one too many panic attacks that ended up with him screaming on the floor in the fetal position, the Commander had taken pity on him and given him this place.

God, even the feel of most clothing was too much for him to handle for longer than a few seconds. How anyone could wear a wool sweater was beyond him.

The only thing he'd ever managed to tolerate for long periods of time were these tanks and loose basketball shorts because—one—they left most of his skin untouched and—two—they were made of one hundred percent silk, no scratchy tags, and no dyes, either. Basically, they were a whole lot of nothing.

Sometimes Michael felt like *he* was a whole lot of nothing.

His mama, *God rest her soul*, had always bought his "nothing" in bulk.

When he took a chance and explained all of this to Ana, she seemed more fascinated than pitying. He was grateful for that. To be seen and not judged, especially by a woman, he wanted that more than anything.

"No interest in a wife, then?" she asked.

He laughed out loud. "Loads of interest. Just no way to get close enough to consummate."

"So if a woman touched you...?" She took a step closer, and he backed up.

Ana was one of the women in town who'd elected not to enter the Marriage Raffle, an option for women who were either too old or for some other reason unable to have children. She'd come with her son, Danny, to the town so long ago both of them were practically pillars of the community. Especially considering the fact that Ana, like several other of the unattached women, became very popular because they shared their favors widely with many men.

Michael held up his hands in warning and took several more steps back. The idea of being one of the men who visited Ana's bed appealed to him, but it was impossible. "Best case scenario, I run. Worst case, I scream and bawl like a baby."

That's what Michael's father had called him: a big baby. "He'll never be a man," he'd said. "Helpless...crying...disappointing...baby..." Michael hadn't seen the man since he was ten but still his words banged around noisily in his head.

Ana glanced up at his window, the one that faced her house. "I hope you've got an old stash of dirty magazines in your room because, bless my soul, darlin', you've got to have some kind of outlet. If you don't, I know some men who have a whole stack in their closets."

"Nah," he said. "That's okay. I'm more of a three-dimensional-woman kind of guy." Ana's gaze moved over his shoulder to look at his bedroom window.

The window shows started shortly after that.

In no time, Michael became the virtuoso of voyeurism, not to mention, the maestro of masturbation. And he developed quite the sophisticated palate for both. At least he could handle his own touch. Thank God for small favors.

He was partial to the solo scenes Ana played, the slow strip teases. He'd work himself up, stroking, grinding against his palm as he watched her lower one bra strap, then the other... He could get lost in the arch of her spine as she unclasped the back... Then mesmerized by the shimmy of panties over sweetly rounded hips. When she'd turn and bend, dropping them to the floor and flashing her privates like a pretty pink petaled flower... *Poetry*.

Other times, one of her gentleman callers would join the show. The men never looked Michael's way. He didn't think they knew about their audience.

He often wondered how it would be, being a normal man and being with a woman like Ana. Or better yet, being one of the men chosen in a lottery. Having a wife of his own.

Tonight, Ana sat on the edge of her bed and spread her knees wide, sliding her hand down over her stomach. Her eyes locked on his. Or at least he thought they did—he only had one oil lamp burning on low.

But the next second he'd forgotten all about it because Ana was sliding her panties to the side and driving her finger into her cunt.

Michael stroked himself faster. Shit, she was so hot.

What would it be like to touch that pussy? To have his cock sliding in between those slick, wet lips?

A fucking fantasy, he knew, but still. What would it be like to have a woman like Ana, all his own...?

Right now, men were in the town square, putting their names in the ballot box for the lottery. Later, names would be called and a new clan would be created.

Michael would be there. Not because he'd put his name in the box. That was out of the question. No, Michael was a journalist. He covered the local stories only, so it was his job to cover the lottery for the *Gazette*. He'd take notes, consider the men who were chosen. He'd imagine himself in their place. Maybe later he'd wonder what it would be like to take their new bride home for the very first time.

He could do all this from the periphery of the crowd—away from the jostling and involuntary touching. He shuddered just thinking about it.

The bedroom door opened behind Ana, and a furry-chested warrior guy walked in. Michael recognized him. He had something of a standing appointment on Mondays.

A sly smile spread across his face when he saw what Ana was doing to herself. He came closer, bent and sucked on the side of her neck.

She tipped her head to give him more access and his hand slid down over her body until he replaced her fingers with his own.

This went on for a few glorious moments.

Michael was ram-rod hard. His ink-stained fingers moved swiftly over his cock, getting closer...closer...when the man suddenly looked up.

Michael froze. Had he been seen?

The man narrowed his eyes and scrutinized the parted curtains on Michael's window. Then the man slowly rose, took a few steps, and yanked Ana's curtains shut.

Michael exhaled with relief—though his orgasm was lost—and thought about the lottery again.

If he had a bride of his own? It would be one thing to share her with four other husbands. She'd still be his to wake up to in the morning. To talk to at dinner every night. To watch up close and personal while she stripped and one of the other husbands—

Too bad you'll never have that, freak. Always the voyeur.

Michael's hands clenched into fists and he jerked his shorts up.

Time to go do his job—reporting about the lives of other men living out what for him would only ever be fantasies.

CHAPTER FOUR

VANESSA

Everything happened for a reason. Vanessa believed that with her whole heart. She had to. There was no other way to explain surviving for as long as she had, all on her own out in the wilderness.

Luck.

Fate.

Karma.

Whatever you wanted to call it, Vanessa was one lucky girl.

Okay, so a lot of the time it was *bad* luck, but hey, she was still alive. That was more than most women could say. Her life had balanced on a knife's edge one too many times for her to believe in anything other than Fate being on her side.

Take the last twelve hours, for example. In half a rotation of the earth, she'd been almost recaptured by Lorenzo Ramos, one of the scariest human traffickers left in the whole of the Republic, held two of his crew at bay with their own weapons before giving them the only ending they deserved—aaaaaaaaand then she'd humiliated herself by fainting and needing to be "rescued" by some dudes from Jacob's Well.

She came-to in the back of their truck only to be driven the last hundred miles to the exact place she'd been *trying* to get to. Then when she got here, she was fed, cleaned up with actual soap and hot water, then brought to a very pink bedroom for a nap and was tucked into a bed that had—she still couldn't believe it—*pillows*. The soft kind with freaking feathers inside.

Suffice it to say, it was a lot for one girl to take in—even for Vanessa, who in her twenty-three years, had endured more than her fair share of shit.

Now it was late evening, and she was about to find out if all the rumors about Jacob's Well were true.

So far things looked promising.

Earlier in the day, the leader of Jacob's Well Township, Commander Wolford, and his exuberant daughter Sophia (whose bedroom she'd been given for the nap) told her the plan for her continued stay in Jacob's Well. They'd explained the necessity of the arrangement: a lottery to marry her off to five local men, which was when Vanessa'd cut them off, informing them that she already knew all about it.

"I know," she'd said matter of factly. "That's why I was heading this direction. I want to become a lottery bride."

Despite her isolation in the wilderness for the last eight years, Vanessa was well aware the world had changed since Xterminate had wiped out ninety percent of the earth's female population.

Women were vulnerable. She understood vulnerable. She'd lived that for *years,* both at home before the Fall and then afterward, alone and out in the wilderness. Didn't mean she couldn't protect herself, though. She knew all about that, too.

The Commander and Sophia had done nothing to hide their surprise at Vanessa's declaration. They'd obviously been told about the knife fight. Or maybe it was how she looked that had them pausing.

Vanessa passed a trembling hand over her head. She'd once had long, thick, chocolatey locks. Now it was shaved close, in some places *so* close you could see the nicks left on her scalp by her knife.

She'd shaved it out of necessity. Long hair was a stupid vanity when you were out in the wild and too often on the run. And she was determined to look nothing like herself after her last close call with Lorenzo... she shuddered even at the name.

She'd first run into the bastard six years ago. Back then, she'd camp off grid, but sometimes she found a group here or there to hook up with for a while. She'd been hanging out with this group that was camping out just past the badlands of the fallout zone east of Austin. There were several other women in the group and Vanessa had hidden in the trees for several days, watching, and only approached after seeing they were treated well.

No one knew exactly where the fallout zone ended and safe land and/or water began. There was a UT professor in the group who'd done some calculations based on the wind direction and speed on D-Day and he felt confident the area was safe.

It was back before the territorial control had been solidified by the various factions, when the war with the Southern States Alliance was waging and everything was pretty much chaos. So hiding out in an area others would stay away from sounded like a great plan to Vanessa.

They used an elaborate soil filtration system to clean their water, and hunters went out further east for meat and foraging, so Vanessa wasn't too worried about radiation poisoning.

What she should have been worried about, however, was the fact that most in the group were scientists, professors, and Austin hippy types.

When Lorenzo and his gang raided the camp a month and a half later, the inhabitants never had a chance. All the men were slaughtered immediately.

And the women, they were—

Vanessa clenched her eyes shut and took a deep breath.

She'd been spared only because she was a virgin.

Virgins were worth more at auction, you see.

What followed were the most hellish three weeks of her life. The things she saw... Her shudder worked its way down to her bones. She was dragged around with Lorenzo and his crew as they made their way to Nuevo Laredo. That was where the biggest and most lucrative slave market was.

Vanessa managed to escape the night before they arrived at the border.

But Lorenzo Bernal was not a man who forgave or forgot. Especially since she'd killed one of his men and severely wounded another as she escaped. Apparently, he took that sort of thing personally. Or maybe it was just the fact that he'd been bested by a woman.

He'd shot her as she ran away so—frankly—she'd considered them even. Okay...so she stole his truck technically *after* her shot her, but still. Why couldn't he just move on and forget about her?

Lorenzo Bernal was why she'd been forced to live off the grid for the last several years.

She found herself a nice cave by the Pecos River. She woke up every morning and did the grueling work of surviving another day. She talked to no one and avoided human interaction at all costs.

But then she got sloppy—ventured into a couple of trading towns to get seeds and to replace her broken and used-up supplies—and he found her again despite her disguise.

God, she was just so damn *tired*.

Every year she lost more muscle mass. She was getting slower and slower at skinning the rabbits she caught. She was sleeping longer and longer hours. She knew she couldn't keep up that kind of brutal existence forever.

Jacob's Well had been an extreme plan B, but as the months passed, it began to look more and more attractive.

Lorenzo's crew was only at most ten men strong. And he might be vengeful but he wasn't stupid. He was a vulture, picking at the bones of prey only after it was dead. He didn't walk into fights he wasn't positive he could win.

So no way he'd dare enter a well-governed township looking for her. Not to mention, slave trading was illegal now and the President had issued a price on his head.

Even if he was stupid enough to come into town, with five husbands devoted to her protection...

As soon as she'd heard rumors of Jacob's Well, she'd been fascinated. Traders talked about the town like it was a mythical place. An oasis outside of the rest of the war-torn, ruthless Republic. A place where peace and order ruled and women were treated like queens.

Queens who had to marry five men, sure, but still. Apparently there was a law in Jacob's Well that if you raised your hand to a woman, they'd cut your hand *off.*

The first time she'd heard about the township, she'd scoffed. Any time something sounded too good to be true, it usually was.

Even now—after having seen the place, met the Wolfords, and been treated so nicely—she worried she'd got it all wrong. Chances were, it was all a ruse. It would probably turn out to be just like Travisville where they lured women in with lies. Colonel Travis was an evil bastard who trafficked women in his territory right under President Goddard's nose, and nothing was done about it.

But the traders who talked about Jacob's Well were the real deal who usually saw beneath bullshit propaganda.

So yeah, she'd definitely been thinking about Jacob's Well.

When Lorenzo's two lackeys ambushed her at the river two days ago, well, that just accelerated her decision to make the plunge. She'd escape them, then high-tail it to Jacob's Well.

Men from Jacob's Well just happening to stumble on them and providing the perfect distraction so she could take Lorenzo's men out? What were the odds?

Fate was one tricky bitch, that was for sure.

So now she was here.

Tonight, they would have a lottery to choose her five husbands.

Vanessa felt her mouth go dry even as she lifted a nervous hand to her hair again. She immediately winced and looked away.

Obviously the whole chopping off her hair to disguise herself thing hadn't worked. And now she was left looking like she'd had a boxing match with a lawn mower and lost.

She hadn't exactly been thinking about beauty at the time—actually it was better if she was ugly. Her aim had been to come across as an ugly boy so when she went in to trade goods, no one would give her a second glance.

But now...

She'd looked in the mirror for about five seconds earlier today but it was enough to be permanently emblazoned on her brain.

She looked like something out of a horror movie. Her cheeks were gaunt and sunken under high cheekbones—one of which was lacerated, the other bruised to a deep purple. Lorenzo's bastards had gotten a few good hits in before she'd been able to turn the tables on them. Then there were her eyes, way too big and owlish in her face. She looked like some sort of wild animal, and...

God, was she really obsessing over how she *looked?* What the hell? She'd done what she'd had to in order to survive.

But there had to be more to life than surviving.

Right?

So yes, she really was going through with this. Normally she'd never be one to simply roll over and trust anyone, much less a *man,* to take care of her. Yet here she'd be putting herself under the protection of *five* men. But if she was being honest with herself (and honesty was something new she'd been experimenting with), she didn't think it sounded all that bad. In fact, it sounded fucking fantastic.

After so long on her own, beyond the safety issue, well, it would be amazing to finally belong to someone (or *someones*). To actually be loved ...? She could hardly imagine what *that* would feel like, but a family with all the trappings: a roof overhead, dinner on the table at six o'clock, anniversary presents this time next year... That would really be something.

Still... with the lottery she volunteered for now just minutes away, she had yet another flash of worry. She sat with Sophia Woldford in a room off the second-floor balcony of the courthouse, hoping against hope that she hadn't got it all wrong about this place.

Trust your gut, Vanessa. It's never let you down before.

Despite her gut telling her to relax, Vanessa glanced toward the exit, then back at Sophia, eyeing her suspiciously, looking for a crack in the pretty brunette's otherwise peaceful demeanor.

Vanessa sighed. Well...if she was wrong about these people, at least she'd scored a couple good meals out of it. That was something. If this all went to shit, she'd escaped worse jams. She glanced toward the exit again.

"I love that you're excited about the lottery," Sophia said.

Vanessa guessed Sophia was her babysitter, of sorts. If so, she wasn't doing a great job. It had been a piece of cake for Vanessa to convince her they should sneak out of the Commander's house and into the courthouse to watch the lottery first hand.

"*Well, the women* did *go to the lotteries in the beginning,*" Sophia had explained when they were still back in her pink bedroom. "*But the crowds got too rowdy, and Dad felt it was safer if the women didn't go.*"

"*Safer?*"

"*Oh no,*" Sophia had said, quickly reassuring her. "*I didn't mean it like that. Everyone here is really great. It's just all the guys in town get really invested in the process, you know? So much testosterone... It sure would be something to see.*"

Having sensed her opportunity, Vanessa doubled down on Sophia's romantic nature. "*It would sure put me at ease to see their enthusiasm first hand.*"

"*Would it?*" Sophia had asked, looking uncertain, but also very interested.

"*Most definitely.*"

"*Well...*" Sophia bit her lip and looked toward the door. "*Maybe we could...*"

"*What? We could what?*"

"*Well, if we took the back way past the mercantile—we could sneak into the courthouse through the delivery doors. That's where Dad usually officiates from —from the courthouse balcony. We'd have to do it before everyone gathers in the square.*"

So there they were, upstairs in a large room off the balcony hiding behind a couple of overstuffed couches pushed up near the far wall. The only other thing in the room was a stack of metal folding chairs.

Vanessa had learned a lot about Sophia in the two hours they'd been waiting. She was only a few months away from her own lottery and she was *very* excited about the prospect. If the lottery was a front for female slavery, the Commander had done a very good job hiding the fact from his daughter.

"I just really want a family of my own, you know?" Sophia said. "I know that's not really modern to say. But I never really wanted adventure or to go and see the world, not even when I was a little kid and that was still an option. I played with dolls and thought about my wedding and what I'd name my kids. I want a lot of kids. Aren't you excited at the chance to be a mom now?"

A mom? The idea had never crossed Vanessa's mind. In fact, babies had been the *last* thing she was thinking of late at night in the cave when she'd been sharpening her knives. But now...? Did she dare let herself imagine it?

Not that it would be an issue for a while—she hadn't had a period in years, she'd been so skinny and malnourished.

"Trust me," Vanessa said, shaking her head, "You're not missing out. Adventure isn't all it's cracked up to be. The quiet life sounds really appealing, and a family..." Vanessa trailed off.

Besides her and her mom, she'd never really had one of those. Not really. Five husbands had sounded like family enough, but would they want children, too?

She supposed...if she could put on some weight, maybe she'd start to get her period again... That would be good. It would be hard to have a family if her cycle never kicked back into gear.

She and Sophia stopped talking as soon as it got noisy outside in the square. Only moments later, feet sounded on the stairs and then the Commander was in the room with them, talking to another man, Vanessa had no idea who.

"How the hell does the lottery box go missing?" the Commander asked. "It's been guarded by men from your Security Squad you swore to me you trusted."

"I'm sorry, Commander. There was a bit of confusion when the box was brought to the courthouse. Apparently some of the men aren't happy with the new verification system. They got pissed at the delays and mobbed my guards. In the confusion, the box was lost."

"You lost the lottery box?" Sophia asked, popping up from her hiding spot behind the couch. "Daddy, what are you going to do?"

"Sophia?" her father sounded exasperated. "What are you doing here? And where's Vanessa? You didn't leave her back at the house alone, did you?"

"Of course not." Sophia sounded insulted. "She's here, too."

Sophia waved for Vanessa to stand up and Vanessa shut her eyes, her face scrunching. *Wow.* So, this was embarrassing.

She stood up slowly and, when she opened her eyes, saw the Commander shaking his head at his daughter. A big man with a scar running down his face stood behind him. He was one of the men who'd found her on the embankment yesterday, along with the handsome one and the young guy.

Vanessa glanced out the window. From the sound of the crowd outside, they were more than restless for the proceedings to begin.

"What are you going to do?" Sophia asked. "Postpone it?"

"No," the Commander said decisively. "We don't know who took it and that could be playing right into their hands. We'll just have to improvise." He paused a moment, his eyes going up and to the left like he was calculating something. Then he looked at Vanessa. "Pick a number between one and eighty-two.

She opened her mouth, and he held up a hand. "No, don't say it out loud." He walked close and leaned down. "Just whisper it in my ear."

Okaaaaay.

The number came to her quickly, without any thought. "Forty-seven," she whispered. It was the age her mother celebrated on her last birthday, just months before she died.

The Commander pulled back with a hard nod. "Thank you. Now, you two," he gestured at Sophia and Vanessa, "stay out of sight. Nix," he looked to the other man as he picked up a bullhorn from a chair near the door, "you're with me."

Sophia took Vanessa's hand and tugged her back around behind the couches again. They didn't crouch, but stood there while the Commander pushed open one of the double doors to the balcony. He and Nix slipped through it before shutting them firmly behind them. The doors were glass but had beige linen curtains running the length, held taut to the window by curtain rods on the top and bottom of the door.

Almost as soon as the doors shut, Vanessa was hurrying out from around the couches and toward the doors.

"Wait," Sophia called. "What are you doing? Dad said to stay—"

Vanessa rolled her eyes, then looked over her shoulder at Sophia. "Do you always do what Daddy says? Come on. It was your idea to come here in the first place."

Sophia bit her lip as if trying to remember if it had actually been her idea, then she started forward to join Vanessa at the door. "Okay, but don't move the curtains."

"I won't." Vanessa pushed the curtain the tiniest bit to the side so she could see out, then she grinned at Sophia. "*Much.*"

Sophia smiled back. Vanessa liked this girl, even more so when Sophia pulled her curtain back, too.

The Commander shouted orders through his bullhorn, and from the tiny bit Vanessa could see, the chaotic mass of men slowly organized themselves. It was messy at first and for several minutes Vanessa thought that, whatever the Commander was trying to get the men to do, it was never going to work.

But a few minutes later, rows began to emerge. Rows of five, five columns across. From her angle, Vanessa couldn't tell how many rows *deep* the crowd went, but it sure seemed like a lot. *Jesus*, how many men were there? And they'd all come hoping to be matched with her? Never before had she been the object of anyone's desire—well, apart from Lorenzo, but that was more financial and then vengeful.

When the square finally went mostly quiet, the Commander spoke again into the bullhorn. "By random lot, number forty-seven has been chosen. Where is group forty-seven?"

The formerly quiet crowd went wild again, shouting so loud it was deafening. Vanessa almost pulled away from the door, but she was too fascinated. This was the real test of how "civilized" this township really was. Would the men lose their shit and start fighting and rioting?

But to her shock, the rows of men only dissolved back into a formless mass that retreated to the edges of the town square.

This exodus left one group remaining at its center. They walked through the now open space, disappearing from Vanessa's view as they came closer to the balcony.

The big man with the scar, *Nix*, suddenly pulled open the balcony door, causing Vanessa and Sophia to jump back. He was smiling, as if the results of the lottery had satisfied him very much, but then he narrowed his eyes on Sophia.

"Oops," she said.

Nix's gaze slid to Vanessa, and his self-satisfied smile returned. "Think you can manage to stay put while I bring up the winners?"

Sophia laughed but then hurried back around the couch before her dad returned to the room.

The next couple minutes were a bit of a blur. But before Vanessa was really quite ready for it, the five men who were going to be her husbands had entered the room and stood staring at her.

They couldn't have been more different, well, except for two of them who looked like identical twins. At one end of the line was the tall, handsome man who'd first confronted her on the embankment. He was even *more* handsome now that her focus wasn't skewed by adrenaline. He had a strong jaw and a cleft chin. He was probably in his late-thirties, well-muscled, and tan like he often worked outside. Though he looked a little green at the moment—like he was about to be sick. Okaaaaaaay.

To his left was a slightly younger man, blond, blue-eyed, with classic movie-star good looks. For some reason, Vanessa got the feeling he'd been a frat boy in his former life. Right now his full lips were turned up in an amused smile as he looked her up and down. In fact, he actually laughed incredulously at the sight of her.

To *his* left was a lean black guy, more Vanessa's age, with curly brown hair, kind eyes, and a shell-shocked expression. He was wearing a silky white tank and matching basketball shorts, and he stood a step back from the other four.

To the left of him were a pair of twins. They looked barely out of high school. One wore his auburn hair parted and neat; the other's was unruly. They both had stocky, muscled bodies, and Roman noses. The one who was more well-kept looked terrified. The other looked... seriously pissed.

In fact... None of the five men looked excited to be there.

Um. Was this how it usually went? Vanessa's eyes flicked back and forth across the five. Part of the reason she'd wanted to come to Jacob's Well was to be part of a family, to be *wanted*. The way she'd heard it, winning the marriage lottery was a big honor for a man. Like, weren't they supposed to be celebrating?

Vanessa swallowed, and then she realized what was going on. *Of course. What did you expect?* she told herself. *You're tiny, insignificant, and on top of that...no great beauty. Not even on your best day, and you haven't had one of those in a while.*

And just like that, she was fifteen years old again. Her mother was sick, and her father—who'd left them when she was three to start a new family with his pregnant mistress—had come to help. Sort of.

From almost the moment he'd stepped in the door, he was busy looking at his phone. And after a few minutes, he said, "It's Cecily. I have to take this."

Cecily. His other daughter. The one from his other family. The one he loved.

After he hung up, he'd looked at Vanessa's mother briefly, just long enough to pull back in disgust at seeing the sores on her body... "I can't be here. I need to get back to my daughter."

His daughter. As if Vanessa was something less than that. How did a man reject his own flesh and blood?

"I'll come back first chance I get, okay?"

Vanessa nodded. She was strong. She had no choice in the matter.

Two months later, after witnessing the most horrific suffering imaginable, her mother died.

Her father had never returned.

And then the world went crazy.

The fires, the looting, the riots. There was rarely a day that went by without hearing gun shots. *Gun shots.* In their peaceful little Texas suburb.

Vanessa packed a bag and, in the middle of the night, ran to the car. She was lucky—at least for a while—because no one saw her. But when she got to her father's house, the luck ran out.

No one answered the door when she knocked. So she'd broken a window and recoiled at the familiar smell of death. She covered her nose and mouth with the inside of her elbow and raced up the stairs to investigate. She only found the wife upstairs. No dad. No Cecily. Did that mean...?

They said a few lucky women were naturally immune to the virus and sometimes the immunity ran in families. So was her half-sister immune too? Some genetic quirk passed down from their Dad?

In Cecily's room, the dresser drawers were open and empty. Which was when Vanessa realized the truth.

Her father had packed Cecily up and fled, without stopping to check on his other daughter. Vanessa wasn't even worth the ten-minute trip across town. He obviously hadn't wanted to be saddled with her.

And in the eyes of the five men standing across the room from Vanessa now, she saw the same apathy, if not downright dislike.

Her breath caught and she swallowed hard. Her hand went up to her awkwardly shorn hair, but then she yanked it back down, furious at herself and then at the men in front of her.

"Well, then," the Commander said, apparently getting the same read off their unenthusiastic reactions. "There will be a getting-to-know you period first, of course."

Vanessa understood from Sophia that none of the past getting-to-know-you periods had ever ended in anything other than nuptials. She had a sinking feeling she would be the first bride in the short history of Jacob's Well to be stood up at the altar.

And then Vanessa did the most honest thing she'd done in years. She put her head in her hands and cried. It was loud. It was messy. And those tears, like everything else about her, were not pretty.

CHAPTER FIVE

LOGAN

Logan had followed a gloating Nix up to the second floor of the courthouse, preparing to call bullshit on this whole thing. He'd planned to tell the Commander that he hadn't put his name in the box, that this Plan B pick-a-number bullshit was bogus, and that he wanted to forfeit his spot.

Even if he *had* been jonesing for a bride—which again, he was *not*, no way, no how—he couldn't marry the tiny, emaciated girl they'd rescued earlier. She might be fierce in a fight but she was barely a hundred pounds soaking wet. He'd crush her.

However, before he could open his mouth to protest, the girl who had been so badass out in No Man's Land began to tremble so hard he could see it from where he stood across the room from her.

"Well, then," the Commander said, frowning at Logan and the four others who flanked him. "There will be a getting-to-know you period first, of course."

Logan kept his focus locked on the girl and silently willed her to get her shit together. He'd watched her take down two seriously nasty smugglers. A girl like that didn't shake like a leaf just because of some stupid lottery.

"You've got to be fucking kidding me," muttered Camden Parker. Logan's jaw flexed. Cam had always been a pain in Logan's ass, all the way back from the days when Cam had been in the Security Squadron with Logan. He hadn't lasted long. He was unruly, insubordinate, and undisciplined. After picking one too many fights with his fellow Squadron-mates, Logan had personally recommended that he be removed from the Security forces.

Nix agreed and Logan still looked back on the day he'd personally had the honor of kicking Cam out on his ass with fondness.

Didn't seem like Cam's manners had gotten any better in the intervening years, either. He looked openly disdainful as he looked the woman up and down.

Ah, shit, now the girl was *crying*. The sound made Logan's heart drop.

The two boy-men—*twins*, he realized—started arguing amongst themselves. The more clean cut of the two was muttering, "I thought you said your plan was going to get us *out* of this."

Cam was now cursing under his breath. No word from the last one, who was dressed all in white.

Logan took a small step forward and the girl swiped angrily at the tears on her cheeks.

He took heart as she squared her shoulders and met him head-on. This had to be scary for her, but she'd be okay. They'd get this straightened out and then she could find a better match. Someone who would never fail her like he'd failed Jenny.

Logan, I have to go, said the memory of Jenny's frantic voice in his head. *You aren't getting better.*

He'd been feverish for days. To the point of delirium. He could barely get to the bathroom and only with Jenny's help. Still, he had enough brainpower to know what she was suggesting was insanity.

You aren't going anywhere, he growled. *I forbid it.*

You aren't in a position to forbid anything. You can't even get out of bed! I'm going.

No! Goddammit, Jenny, he wheezed, trying to catch his breath. *You've heard the news about Xterminate. They're saying the mortality for women who get it is over sixty percent! You aren't leaving this house.*

Oh but it's fine for you to risk your life?

Then he'd woken up only to find her gone, out on some hair-brained mission to try to get him medicine—at the height of the Texas Xterminate epidemic, during the worst of the Death Riots. And the news reporting had been wrong. The mortality rate wasn't sixty percent. It was *ninety*. Ninety percent.

He should have known what she'd do. She was so damn stubborn. He shouldn't have fallen asleep. He should have tried harder to convince her. He shouldn't have gone to that fucking hack of a dentist for a root canal—the tooth had gotten infected. Jenny had died because he'd gotten an abscessed tooth.

But no, that was a lie. Jenny had died because he was trying to save a fucking buck. She'd died because he wasn't strong enough to stop her. To save her.

So no, he wouldn't infect this girl's life with his presence.

They'd clear this up and then things could go back to the way they ought to be. He'd return to the silence of the little shack he slept in on the outskirts of town and when he had a shift, he'd come in and do his duty. It was a simple life and it was all he wanted. All he deserved.

Vanessa shook her head as if she still had hair to toss back. She didn't. She only had a quarter-inch of dark stubble over her perfectly shaped skull. Her eyes were large, dark brown, and round. Her body looked like a plucked bird, spindly with barely any meat on it.

"Someone get this girl a cheeseburger," Cam said and for once, Logan agreed with him. Something Logan sure as hell thought he'd never be able to say.

"Camden," the Commander snapped. "Never in the history of Jacob's Well have I seen five men behave so ungratefully. Do you know how many of those men out there would kill to be standing where you are?"

"Well let one of them take my spot then," Logan growled. It was time to bring this farce to an end. "I didn't put my name in the damn box."

The Commander, his daughter, and the girl all flinched. At his words? At his delivery? He couldn't tell.

"You didn't?" The woman—Vanessa, if he remembered right—asked, her voice sounding thin. She looked around at all of them. "Did any of you?" Her gaze finally settled on the fifth man, the one dressed in white who'd hung back the most. "Did *you*?"

"My name's Michael, Miss. And, no, I'm afraid I did not."

Vanessa took a deep breath like she was just managing to fight back more tears. It was the last thing he would have expected from the warrior woman he'd met earlier today.

Then again, Logan knew a little something about putting on armor to keep the world at bay. It looked like she'd finally set hers down—expecting Jacob's Well to be a safe haven—and then for shit to go so sideways on her...

Jesus, Logan thought, staring at Michael. He hadn't entered his name, either? What were the chances? Would there have to be a complete do-over of the lottery?

"If you didn't mean to be entered, then why were you even down in the square?" Vanessa asked incredulously, and the cry in her voice made Logan's heart constrict with pain. Were they all going to reject her? Shit.

"I'm a journalist. I only came to watch," Michael said. "But I got... sort of *chased*...into the crowd right before the groups were formed. Everyone was packed in so tight. There was no way out for me."

Vanessa didn't blink at his explanation. It made Logan think she was used to being chased—that maybe she understood the feeling of being trapped. He was racked by another wave of sympathy when he imagined how many times in the past her face had been as banged up as it was now. Being out there on her own for all that time...

Jesus Christ, even hardened Security officers only went out in groups of at least three when they went on Scrapper runs. When they ventured beyond their own territory or territories they had treaties with like Central Texas North, they took a full brigade of six to eight men.

But she'd been out there, all alone... ever since the damn Fall?

"You?" she asked, directing her attention now to Cam. He'd actually seemed really excited when their group was first called, but now he looked like he was sucking on a lemon.

"Camden's the name and, yeah. I put my name in the box." He was leaning against the wall, hands in his pockets. "But look, sweetheart," he pulled out a hand to gesture up and down at her. "You..." he trailed off, then looked to the Commander. "Look, this whole thing was fucked. The box was stolen and it wasn't even a real lottery. You should have a redo and then she can get someone, you know..." he shrugged, gesturing at her again like she was a piece of meat. "More suited to her."

What. The. Fuck. Did. He. Just. Say?

Logan fought the urge to punch the bastard in the throat, but the girl didn't seem surprised by his comment.

"And you two?" she asked the twins, her eyes narrowing. Logan couldn't tell if she was getting pissed, or about to cry again. Logan took a step closer to her. To do what, he didn't know—only that while he was poor husband material, these assholes might even be worse. He wasn't going to let any of them hurt her any more than they already had.

"We put our names in the box, but only because our mother made us," the first twin said. He, at least, was dressed like someone wanting to impress a bride. Hopefully he would give the girl the respect she deserved. "Ross," the kid said, pointing at his chest. "And this is my younger brother by two minutes, Riordan."

Riordan seemed to bristle at his introduction. He jutted out his jaw. "It was me, okay? I took a stand, and I did it."

"Did what?" the Commander asked.

Riordan turned a cool eye on him. "When people got all wigged out, protesting the new verification system you'd put in place double and triple checking people's papers, things started getting chaotic. I grabbed the opportunity and stole the damn box. Hid it in the bushes so mine and Ross's names couldn't get called."

Everyone but Ross stared at him with their mouths slightly open.

Riordan glanced around at all their faces, then he threw his hands up. "It wasn't supposed to work out like this. We're supposed to be home by now."

The Commander's face went red, like a thermometer ready to burst. His daughter covered her mouth, and Vanessa gripped the Commander's wrist for balance.

"YOU STOLE THE BOX?" bellowed Cam before anyone else had a chance to react. Within seconds, the room erupted into shouts and finger pointing. The accusations piled on top of each other creating an onslaught of angry voices and blame. *None of this would have happened if... I'm gonna fucking kill you! Get your hands off my brother! This is what happens when y'all mess with a system. You don't wanna mess with me!*

Logan didn't know who laid hands on whom first. But at some point, he felt someone push him from behind, and the next thing he knew, the girl—*Vanessa*—was standing in the middle of the fray, dodging blows with her arms outstretched to separate them. Fuck, she was going to get hurt!

"Stand back," she yelled and even though she couldn't have weighed a hundred pounds, they all fell silent. "What the hell is wrong with y'all? Have you lost all the good sense God gave you?"

Logan blinked. Then he fought a smile. Jenny used to ask him the same thing all the time.

"You!" Vanessa said, jerking her chin toward the windows.

Logan took heart that the warrior he'd met in the bush was back. He looked toward the unfortunate soul who was now the focus of her wrath: Michael, if he remembered correctly; the guy dressed all in white.

"I'll start with *you*." She moved out of the center of angry men and marched toward Michael.

The closer she got, the more panic showed on the guy's face. "Don't touch me!" he said.

"What the—?" Logan murmured.

"Relax," said Vanessa. "I'm not going to hurt you."

"I..." Michael closed his eyes and seemed to wince as if preparing for pain. "Just please... Don't get too close."

She stopped when she was only a foot from him. Then she calmly turned toward the Commander. "Sir, can I have a moment alone with my fiancés?"

But the Commander was shaking his head. "We'll just have to redo the entire lottery. Tomorrow, I'll—"

"Stop," Vanessa said sharply.

The Commander looked at her, the surprise obvious on his face.

"We will *not* redo the lottery."

"But this is obviously a disaster," the Commander objected, gesturing at the men. "And that one stole the box." He glowered at Riordan. "If anyone finds out, they'll think that it's okay to—"

"I don't give a shit about any of that." Vanessa slashed a hand through the air. "Everything happens for a reason. I take my luck as it comes to me. Now give me a minute alone with my husbands to be."

Husbands. Logan flinched at the word—he wasn't the only one—because she was clearly staking her claim. He would have protested, but his eyes were locked on the jagged scar across her bared shoulder blade. What kind of bastard would hurt such a tiny woman? He had the sudden urge to decapitate whoever'd done it. The bloodthirsty impulse startled him.

"All right," the Commander said, giving a slow nod as he looked back and forth between Vanessa and the men. "Sophia, let's follow up on Cam's earlier suggestion and see if we can find a late-night snack for Vanessa?"

Sophia gave Vanessa an encouraging hug, then she followed her father out of the room. When the door closed with a soft click. Vanessa slowly turned away from Michael to face Logan and the other three. "It appears we have a few things to learn about each other. Shall we begin?"

Logan bowed his head and wrapped his hand around the back of his neck. Jesus, what was he gonna do now? Something deep inside of him—a part of him he hadn't felt in years—was starting to stir the more he looked at Vanessa.

No. *No, no, no.* These feelings... They weren't real. It was just his guilty conscious getting sadistic all over his ass. There were plenty of hurt and traumatized women in this world. What was he going to do?

Suddenly swoop in to protect them like he hadn't been able to protect Jenny?

Right now, this tiny stranger was just an emotional surrogate for years of pent-up guilt. A convenient landing place for all the blame he shouldered. That's all she was, right?

Right?

CHAPTER SIX

CAMDEN

Camden Parker stared at the skinny, bald chick in front of him and shook his head. After all the lotteries he'd entered, year after year, chance after chance—eighty-nine of them to be exact—*this* was the one time his number came up? *This* girl?

He could hear his father's chuckle in the back of his head. *Looks about right to me. A loser for a loser.*

Cam clenched his jaw, breathing out hard.

Over the years, he'd heard his friends', acquaintances', and enemies' names called. But never his. Never fucking his.

Just a few days ago there'd been a hot blond who'd come in. But could he have won *that* lotto? Oh no, of course not. He had to get this half-starved stick figure. Jesus, she'd lost her shit and started crying almost the second they'd shown up. Was this what he'd waited all these years for?

At least the girl—Vanessa or whatever—was finally starting to show some backbone. Her voice was only a little shaky when she said, "Take a seat, gentlemen." She gestured at the folding chairs that were stacked against the wall.

When she realized no one was moving, she ordered, louder. "*Sit*."

Cam rolled his eyes. Being ordered around by someone who could be confused with a pre-pubescent boy was *not* how he pictured the first ten minutes with his future bride.

But then, everything about this lotto was bullshit. No way it should be counted as legit.

There still had to be time to talk the Commander into redoing it. Jesus, that idiot kid had stolen the damn box. That should disqualify him for a decade, not win him a spot as a husband.

Still, he didn't want to be a dick. Okay, he didn't want to be any *more* of a dick. So he sat.

Vanessa looked like she'd had a rough time of it recently, but then, it was the apocalypse. Everyone had problems. And Cam had had the short end of the stick too many times in his life to take this lying down. He'd sit through this meeting of hers, or whatever, and then go talk to the Commander one on one.

After five years in the military as a medic, surely that entitled him to some damn say in the matter, right? For serving his country and all that shit? He was a goddamned war veteran. Where was his damn reward already?

The twins sat down beside him on his left. He didn't know them, he just recognized them from around town, cause yeah, identical auburn-haired twins. Kinda hard to miss.

Then that Michael guy was at the end of the row on the other side of the twins. He was a weird fucker. Always kept to himself except when he was doing shit for the *Gazette*. And even then, he'd freak out if anyone got too close to him.

Cam had seen him lose his shit one time in the mercantile when old Mr. Perkins accidentally knocked into him and then grabbed Michael's arm to steady himself. Michael started screaming his damn head off and then he dropped into the fetal position. They had to close the store for an hour.

Cam shook his head. As if the wife weren't unimpressive enough on her own, no way did he want to be associated with that freak.

Parker men are supposed to be the best. To have the best. Too bad you're such a fucking disappointment. Do you know how embarrassing it is when people ask how my boy is doing and I have to tell them you failed out after one year of Berkley? Berkley! For fuck's sake, it's not even an Ivy League. But you still couldn't hack it, could you? No, I'm the only world-renowned neurosurgeon with a fucking idiot for a son.

Christ, at least you're not ugly. You can marry well. Just don't pick a whore or some average bitch. They say genius skips a generation, so there's still hope for the grandkids.

Cam shuddered and then caught sight of Logan Washington, sitting to his right. *Ghost*, they called him, as if he was supposed to be some kind of scary badass.

When Cam got back from the war, he tried to get a job in the Security Squad Because...why not? They had the best toys, they were respected around town, the pay was solid.

He would have done fine, too. He was quick on his feet, good with the weapons. He'd only been a medic in the war because his one year of medical school made him the most medically trained person around more often than not.

But Christ, he'd never had any intention of following in his father's footsteps, especially by pursuing a career in medicine.

So, yes, everything had been right on track to start his new career as Security Squadron badass.

Until Logan fucking Washington.

That man was born with a stick so far up his ass Cam was surprised he didn't choke on it. He'd taken one look at Cam and hated him on sight. Cam knew it was under Logan's recommendation he'd been kicked out.

So Cam had ended up working in the town's clinic. As little more than a glorified nurse. Oh how Dad must be laughing in his fucking grave. Cam could just imagine him leaning over his shoulder, critiquing his every move, making Cam second-guess even the application of a goddamn bandage.

Talk about ghosts... The ghost of Cam's father was one sick mother. Was it any wonder Cam sometimes got a little restless and short-tempered? Like this morning with that bastard who stole his ration card... Third strike his ass.

Bullshit. All of this was bullshit.

"Sorry if I'm not what any of you were expecting." The girl's words had bite and, of course, it was Cam she glared at as she said them.

"What the fuck did I do?" He threw his hands up. None of the other guys were any more excited about the situation, but he was the one who got singled out? Bullshit. Just like always.

She ignored him, her gaze moving up and down the line of guys sitting on either side of him.

"But I can assure you," she continued, steeling her resolve, "you aren't what I was expecting either."

"And what was that, sweetheart?" Cam asked, not bothering to hide his sarcasm. The quicker they got through this farce, the sooner he could talk to the Commander about fixing this whole thing and—

"For one," she bit out, "I wasn't expecting so many damn cowards."

Cam blinked. What—? Did she just—?

Logan's lips parted to speak.

"Cowards!" one of the twins sputtered. "You think I'm a coward?"

Vanessa turned on him coolly. "Aren't you the one who hid the box? Cowards hide. Brave men roll the dice."

Cam narrowed his eyes. So that one was Riordan. How the hell could she tell them apart?

Riordan scowled, but Vanessa was already moving on.

"I know I'm small," she said, eyes on the move again, flicking back and forth between all of them. Her face was hard now. The weakness she'd shown earlier was totally gone and Cam sat up a little straighter in his chair, especially when she continued in that calm, cool voice.

"I'm used to being underestimated. That's fine. I use it to my advantage. It's always given me the element of surprise."

She took a deep breath before continuing. "But frankly, I don't always win. I'm exhausted. The fact that I've survived this long..." She trailed off, her eyes going distant. Then she refocused on them, looking at Logan first. "I need you. All of you. *Whoever* you are. And that's what I'd like to find out."

She turned toward Michael at the end of the row and addressed him directly. "So I'll start with you. Why were you chased into the crowd?"

"Oh," he said, taken slightly aback. He looked to his right as if hoping one of the others could answer for him. "My...um...neighbor Ana... One of her, um, gentleman callers spotted me. He was looking to fight me, so I ran."

"Ana?" Cam turned on him. "Like fifty-year-old Ana who works in the mercantile?"

When Michael gave him a questioning nod, Vanessa asked, alarmed, "Is she married?"

"What?" Michael asked, eyes going wide. "No!"

"I thought you said you can't be touched," Cam said, confused. Ana was older, but she was still hot. He'd admit it. Cam had thought a few times about trying his charms on her but there always seemed to be some man or other hanging around her. Frankly, he didn't need the drama. He had plenty of magazines to take care of shit when the need arose.

And he just knew, deep down, one day his name would be the one called and he'd get to slip between the thighs of a real woman again. The kind he'd be proud to have bear his kids. To carry on the Parker line.

"I can't," Michael sputtered. "I don't." He shook his head vigorously. "She was only trying to be a friend to me." He blinked, then glanced at Vanessa nervously. "She understands."

"Exactly *what* does this woman *understand?*" Logan asked, jerking his chair in a quarter turn to face Michael directly.

Vanessa pulled her chair in closer, close enough to put her hand on Logan's arm. Cam didn't miss the way the "Ghost" sucked in his breath at her touch. From what Cam remembered, the guy had always had a hard-on for his dead wife. Wouldn't even talk or joke about chicks with any of the guys and got pissed if they gave him a hard time about it.

"Ana understands I can't be touched," Michael said, bowing his head.

"What?" Cam asked. What did that even mean?

"Hey," Vanessa said softly. "Hey. Look at me."

Michael raised his head.

"When I was in school, I had a friend who was on the spectrum. Do you—"

"It's not autism," he shook his head, "if that's what you think. Emotionally, I'd be the perfect husband. I mean, I'd try anyway. But physically..." He shuddered. "I can't be touched. You wouldn't under—"

"So, we won't touch." She lifted her hands in a hands-off gesture. "Maybe I don't understand completely yet, but I'm willing to learn. So. Will you still be my husband?"

Michael blinked. Then he looked to Logan, to Camden, and then to the twins. His eyes finally returned to Vanessa, almost disbelieving. "You'd be okay with that?"

"Would you?" Vanessa asked.

"Yes."

"Then that's settled." She turned to Cam with a scowl. "You're up."

Whoa, whoa, how had this suddenly turned on him? But fine. He crossed his arms. He didn't care what anyone in this damn room thought about him. He smirked at her. "Well, I sure as hell wouldn't want a wife I can't touch."

"I see." She gave him a dismissive look like she'd already sized him up. "You're the type who takes by force."

"What the fuck? No. Fuck, no!" Cam's chest swelled as he inhaled air noisily through his nose. "No woman of mine would need to be *forced*. I can assure you of that. What the hell do you take me for?"

"Nothing much yet." Vanessa shrugged and then shifted forward in her chair slightly. "Only that all this machismo thing you've got going on..." She waved in his general direction. "Is probably to make up for some deficiency in yourself." She glanced down suggestively at his crotch.

She fuckin' did *not*.

Camden narrowed his eyes, his heartbeat speeding up so fast he could hear it in his damn ears.

Why are you such a fucking failure? Do you know how humiliating it is to have such a goddamned embarrassment for a son?

He leaned in and stared her down, breathing hard. "You don't know anything about me, sweetheart. How many lotteries have you been to?"

Vanessa squirmed in her chair, for the first time since the tears losing a little of her composure. "This is my first. Obviously."

"This is my *eighty-ninth*. You see that many good women come and go, you start to get an idea about who you must be destined for. So pardon me, but a practically bald, half-starved weakling isn't exactly what I had in mind. You're going to have to cut me some slack if it takes me more than five minutes to wrap my head around that."

"Hair grows," Michael said, "and Vanessa's beautiful even without it."

"Maybe so," Cam said, and it was even sort of true. Now that he was looking at her closer up, well, she was bruised and cut up all to fuck, but her lips were the pouty kind that could give a man ideas. Not to mention she had thick, sooty lashes framing those huge doe eyes of hers.

Vanessa blinked as if she were surprised by his admission, so he went on before she could let it settle in. "But the woman I marry is supposed to be a force of fucking *nature*. One of a kind."

"Vanessa nearly decapitated that smuggler with her bare hands," Ross blurted out, and everyone, including Vanessa, turned to look at him. He swallowed hard and then bowed his head, addressing the floor. "At least that's what I heard, ma'am."

"Rumor," Cam said leveling his eyes back on Vanessa.

"I saw—" Logan started to say, but Vanessa had already leapt from her chair. In one motion, she pulled the knife from Logan's belt and threw herself at Cam.

What the—Cam didn't even have time to get his hands up. —*Fuck!*

She slammed into him, toppling him and his chair backwards. The impact knocked the wind out of him. He was still gasping for air when he finally got his bearings, looking up to find Vanessa straddling his hips.

With the damn knife at his fucking throat.

Holy.

Mother.

Fucking.

Shit.

This, he could work with.

With his looks and this killer instinct of hers, they'd have gorgeous, badass little warrior babies. Suck on *that*, Dad, you motherfucking asshole. *And rot in hell while you're at it.*

"Don't feel bad," she winked at Cam, flipping the blade and running the dull side along his jaw as if she were giving him a shave. "I told you, most people underestimate me."

He grinned at her. Turned out fate might have finally done him a solid after all. It was about damn time.

Cam's grin grew even wider and he chuckled. "Got it, sweetheart. Won't be making that mistake twice."

Looked like he was getting fucking married.

CHAPTER SEVEN

ROSS

Ross was terrified by the tiny wild woman. *Impressed*, yes, certainly. But terrified. Nothing about today was going the "right way," and his dad, God rest his soul, always said, "In all things, there's the right way, or the highway." He was the one man who showed Ross the "right way" to do just about everything.

Riordan never listened, of course. Riordan was all about making a splash, finding the shortcut, catching the spotlight. If Riordan was the hare, then Ross was the careful tortoise. A tortoise who knew that the right way in *this* situation was supposed to be sweet smiles, longing looks, a couple weeks of respectful courtship, all leading to an Irish Catholic marriage in a church with a chaste kiss.

Jacob's Well had never had a Catholic priest, though it had a pastor of sorts. Sure he was stoned most the time, but he could usually remember enough of the traditional marriage ceremony to stumble through it credibly.

But good Lord, would *none* of the protocols be observed with this courtship and marriage? It made him feel off-balance.

"*Dude*. Is she a big enough force of nature for you now?" the guy in white asked the guy on the floor. *Michael*, Ross thought, trying to learn everyone's names. And *Camden?*

"Yep. And she's clearly one of a kind, too," Camden said with a smirk. "I was just checking." Then he winked.

"Jesus," Logan muttered.

Ross agreed with Logan—*Ghost*; a man he knew to respect even before today. How did this Camden guy have the gall to wink at a young lady who was holding him at knifepoint? He was so completely arrogant. Did Vanessa *like* that trait in a man?

Ross wrung his hands. What if he was too boring to run with these people—even with his own brother? Good Lord, the wild woman had barely *looked* Ross's way yet. It was as if she already knew he was all the things Riordan called him: *Mama's boy, dork, nerd, loser.*

It was quite possible that, if Ross didn't do something fast, Vanessa would forget he was even in the room.

Vanessa pushed herself up to her feet and handed the knife back to Logan, handle first. Ross thought it was gracious of her not to mention how easily she'd disarmed him. If she liked the kind of politeness she showed Ghost, Ross saw his opening.

He quickly stepped forward, linked his arm through hers, and escorted her back to her chair, holding the metal backrest while she sat so it didn't move on her.

It did the trick. She seemed surprised at first, like she didn't know what to do when he took her arm. But when she looked up, she seemed to appreciate his chivalry after all. And good Lord, the way she *looked* at him. Her eyes were so dark, so round, so beautiful... He sucked in a deep breath.

"Your story next," she said, breaking into his thoughts. "What's with you and your brother?"

"Um..." Ross glanced over his shoulder at Riordan, whose mouth was still hanging open, even as he sunk back onto his chair. Ross knew his brother well enough to know that all the anger he'd been feeling earlier had drifted away. *Of course* Riordan would be jazzed by Vanessa's action-hero display. She was exactly Riordan's type. He might not have wanted a wife when he walked into this room, but he was obviously warming to the idea.

"We came to the lottery," Ross said, "because our mother insisted. She wants..." He cleared his throat. "Grandbabies."

Vanessa's neck jerked back, and the pretty shade of pink in her cheeks quickly faded to pale.

Shit, that was obviously the wrong thing to say. Leading the courtship with talk of procreation, pregnancy, and childbirth wasn't the likeliest way to a woman's heart. Christ, she was so tiny. Could she even carry a child?

"But we don't!" Ross said quickly, trying to recover. "At least not yet, ma'am."

"Oh. Well... All right," she said, "And it's *Vanessa*."

"We have things we want to do first," Ross explained.

"Like what?" she asked.

Ross looked back at his brother again. Vanessa's curiosity seemed to have placated him even more.

"Like adventure," Ross said.

Logan leaned forward. "And you don't think *marriage* is a big enough *adventure*?" He sounded almost angry.

Ross swallowed hard. Why did he keep saying the wrong thing? He knew Ghost had once been married. Clearly he knew what he was talking about and Ross felt instantly chagrined. He knew nothing. He was so out of his league.

"I'm sure it is...sir," Ross said. "In fact, it's completely new territory for us. We don't even know—"

"Don't," Riordan said, voice cutting. Ross looked back at his brother but Riordan's eyes were on Camden, as if preparing to defend himself.

"You don't know what?'" Vanessa asked.

Ross ducked his head, then swung back to face Vanessa. "We don't know how," Ross said, ignoring his brother's warning. He whispered the rest, though he didn't know why, because everyone in the room could obviously hear him. "To consummate a marriage, I mean."

"Speak for yourself, asshole," Riordan said, sitting back in his chair and crossing his arms over his chest. "I'm sure it's not exactly rocket science."

"Oh, like *you've* had sex, *Rior*dan!" Ross said, his own irritation breaking through, and Riordan shot him a killing look. "Might as well admit it now. It's gonna be embarrassing enough when they figure it out for themselves." Ross jerked his chin in the other three men's direction.

"That's nothing to be embarrassed about," Logan said, but Camden's look of superiority begged to differ.

Michael merely shrugged and added magnanimously, "Y'all are only...what? Twenty?"

"Nineteen," the twins said in unison.

"See?" Vanessa said. "Plenty of time to learn. I'm sure Logan can teach you how."

"What?!" Logan asked, and Ross could have sworn he saw him pale.

"You've been married before," she said. Ross glanced at Vanessa. She was new to town. How did she know that?

Vanessa dipped her head to gesture toward Logan's left fist. "You have a tan line on your ring finger. You only took off your band recently. What happened?"

Ross would have been impressed by her keen observation skills, but he was more focused on Logan's clenched teeth, and the line of muscle that flexed along his jaw. Looked like Ross wasn't the only one who had a problem with blurting the wrong thing today.

"You know what happened," Logan bit out.

Vanessa swallowed and gave him a single nod of acknowledgment. "How long ago?"

"Eight years."

Ross could see the emotion building in Logan. It was the sign to step back. But Vanessa pressed on and maybe she was right to do it. They'd have to talk about it eventually, right? Wasn't that how marriages worked? You had to talk about things?

"And you only *just* took off your ring?" Vanessa asked.

Logan frowned.

"You still love her," she said matter-of-factly.

Ross held his breath. The subject of Logan's first wife was common knowledge around town, but very few people dared broach the subject. This felt like dangerous ground to Ross. Everything in him cautioned to step back, keep quiet, change the subject. Abort, abort, abort!

"Jenny—" Logan said, and Ross heard the tremble in his voice. God, he was going to go there. He was going to talk...right there...in front of strangers. Ghost never talked.

"She was my *life*. She was everything I ever wanted. None of you can understand that." Logan glanced wildly across their faces. "None of you understand what it means to have your heart ripped from your chest and then to be forced to march around this earth without any life left inside of you."

Ross glanced at Vanessa. She seemed to be holding back more tears. What would she say? What on earth would be the right thing in this moment?

"She sounds amazing," Vanessa said as her eyes got thick with moisture. "I would have liked to have known her."

Logan stared at the floor unable to say anything more. Ross let out a breath. She'd done good, he thought.

"I admire your devotion to her," Vanessa said.

Logan's head jerked up, and his eyes blazed with fury. *Oh, no...*

"Will you teach me what that feels like?" she asked.

"Child..." His stare sucked all the oxygen out of the room.

"I've never seen that kind of love for myself. My father abandoned us when I was a little girl. I've been living alone since my mother passed. No one to even share a meal with. No one to care about me... And maybe it's not the same, but I know loss, too."

Ross was conscious of everyone shifting uncomfortably. They'd all lost at least someone since the Fall. He didn't know anyone who hadn't.

"I don't expect you to feel the same way about me as you did about her," Vanessa pressed on, "but even a *hint* of what that feels like would be the most beautiful thing I've ever had."

"Child, stop," Logan said, his voice warning her not to take this any further.

Ross reached out tentatively and touched Vanessa's shoulder hoping to make her stop. She didn't.

"I'm *not* a child. I'm a woman. A woman who needs you. *All* of you and whatever you're able to offer. I know I'm not much but..."

"Damn, woman," Riordan said, getting out of his chair. "You're *plenty*. At least you're not boring. You're the most interesting thing to hit this town in years."

"Listen to him," Ross said. Vanessa turned her face toward Ross, and he drew the back of his hand gently down her cheek. "You're more than plenty."

"And you're badass," Camden added with a smirk. "Don't forget badass."

"Plus scary beautiful," Michael added, coming forward.

Logan hung back, and they all turned to look his way. The man's face was twisted in pain, and his fists were balled at his sides.

"What do you say, Logan?" Vanessa pleaded. "Can we all be a family? *Please?*"

CHAPTER EIGHT

VANESSA

"No!" Logan roared, jerking back. "I can't. I'll give you whatever protection you need, but I won't get married."

"You *can't*? Or you *won't*?" Vanessa asked. She thought she'd been on a roll. She'd thought she had made some headway, breaking past Logan's armor of grief and survivor's guilt.

She was wrong. And in her head, the bubble popped. She wasn't going to get her happily ever after, after all. At least not with *this* beautiful man. Why was she so surprised?

Before Logan could answer her questions, the doors to the conference room swung open. They hit the wall with a bang, and the Commander stood there looking grim. "Enough talk. Where do we stand? Is the new Clan Washington ready to make it official?"

"Washington?" Vanessa asked, as the Commander and Sophia reentered the room.

"My last name," Logan growled, his voice sounding tight. "I'm the highest ranking."

"Vanessa Washington?" Vanessa said, testing it out.

"I said, 'No!'" Logan bellowed. He got to his feet and tossed his metal chair across the room.

"Jesus!" Cam blurted out. "Easy, man."

Logan stalked across the room and out the door. Vanessa watched him go, not understanding where she'd gone wrong. Still...there was time to salvage something. She squared her shoulders and cleared her throat, turning to face the four remaining men.

The Commander had the same idea. "What about the rest of you?" he asked. "Ready to make it official?"

"I'm in," Cam and Riordan both said together, then they glared at each other.

"I already said yes," Michael said.

"It would be a privilege to marry a woman as strong as you," Ross said.

Vanessa let out a sigh. It wasn't perfect. But it was more than she'd ever had before. Soon she'd have a home with a roof, food in the icebox, a real bed, and someone (some*ones*) to take care of her.

And she'd be *safe*.

But... How long did it take to plan a wedding? If it took too long, they could change their minds. Logan had already rejected her. The others could do the same. She couldn't let that happen. She didn't need a fancy wedding dress, or flowers, or engraved invitations. She didn't have anyone to send them to, anyway. All she needed was to get to the altar before what was left of this beautiful fantasy *poofed* away like all of her other dreams.

"*Tomorrow*," she said. "I want to get married tomorrow."

Sophia shrieked and clapped her hands. "Shay got married just as quickly. Oh, I do love a wedding!

Vanessa would have asked who Shay was, except she was busy racing toward the French doors to the balcony. She flung them open and rushed to the railing just in time to see Logan striding across the square.

She gripped the rail and leaned out, yelling with all the volume she could muster. "Tomorrow, Logan!"

Logan stopped short. He lifted his head but didn't turn around.

"I'm getting married tomorrow, and if you're half the man I think you are, you'll be there!"

Vanessa thought she saw his shoulders lift as if he were taking a deep breath. Did that mean he was going to say something? She waited. But he never turned around, and a second later, he picked up his pace and strode out of the square, disappearing into the darkness.

CHAPTER NINE

VANESSA

By morning, Vanessa was dressed in a floor-length white gown with a foot of train. It was long-sleeved to cover her scars and made from some kind of synthetic silk that made Vanessa remember a floor-length negligée her grandmother used to have hanging in her closet.

In addition to the dress, Sophia had made a wreath of bluebonnets to place on her head like a crown.

When she looked in the mirror this time, she didn't have to flinch away. With the light dusting of makeup Sophia had powdered under her eyes and across her cheeks. Well, maybe she was even sort of... pretty?

She shut her eyes and breathed out hard, turning away from the mirror. Sophia had gone to check on the pastor, leaving Vanessa alone in what Sophia called the "bride's room." But Vanessa was going to suffocate from claustrophobia if she stood in this tiny broom closet of a room waiting for another second.

Right before she opened the door, though, she heard voices from the corridor outside. She recognized them immediately.

Camden, Michael, and the twins were arguing. She would have been fine with the arguing if she'd heard Logan in the mix.

She didn't.

"Any sign of him?" Commander Wolford asked.

"How the hell could he skip out on us?" Cam said. "It's bad enough embarrassing Vanessa, but now he's making me look bad, too."

Suddenly Vanessa didn't feel so pretty anymore. Her whole heart seemed to shrivel into a small, dark pellet.

"How in the hell is he making *you* look bad?" Michael asked.

"Everybody knows he kicked me out of the Security Squadron. They'll think he's skipping out because he doesn't want to be in a clan with me."

Vanessa cracked the door and peered into the corridor.

"Oh so you're going to make this all about *you?*" Riordan said with a sneer.

"*I* know it's not," Cam said. "He's being a little bitch about marrying Vanessa. But it doesn't matter what I know. I'm talking about what people will *think*."

"Logan will show," Ross said. "I know he will."

"And what do you know about it, *Riordan?*" Cam asked.

"*He's* not Riordan," Riordan said, taking a step forward, obviously offended. "*I* am, asshole. He's Ross."

How could Cam not be able to tell them apart? If he couldn't pick up on the subtle differences in their faces, it was obvious that Ross was the one who'd combed his hair.

"Same difference," Cam shrugged.

Riordan threw a punch, but Cam caught him by the wrist.

"Not the same," Riordan bit out.

"We're nothing alike," Ross added.

"And don't you forget it," Riordan warned, jerking his hand free.

Cam just smirked, smoothing down his suitcoat and Vanessa shook her head and closed the door again.

Children.

She was marrying *children*.

They wouldn't act like this if Logan were here.

But he wasn't, was he?

She lifted a hand to her forehead. What was she getting herself into? She'd been so sure yesterday. She'd met them and they were all so big and strong. And fate and luck and all that... all that *bullshit*.

Because maybe there wasn't any big plan. Maybe she'd just survived as long as she had because life was fucking chaos. So far she'd always managed to land on her feet—but like a cat who'd used up its nine lives, maybe her luck had finally run out.

If she couldn't make a go of it here she didn't know where else she could. She'd meant it when she'd told her would-be clan she was exhausted. She was weary down to her bones and running on empty. She had been for a long time now.

She slumped against the door.

The guys were still at it outside.

"The ceremony was supposed to start five minutes ago," Michael said. "Vanessa is going to be wondering what's happening. Maybe we should start without Logan."

"We wait," Cam said. "We have to wait for the press to get here anyway. They're running late."

"The press? Like the newspaper?" Ross asked. "Why?"

Newspaper?

A film of nervous sweat slid between Vanessa's small breasts. She didn't want pictures. This was already humiliating enough as it was.

Sure the make-up helped a little but she knew she was still a wreck. Then there was the issue of the missing groom. She was hoping to make a fresh start here and you could only make a first impression once.

Not to mention that the last thing she needed was her face captured on camera. What if one of those newspapers made it out of town and Lorenzo saw it?

Yeah he only had a band of about ten and probably wouldn't dare come after her in a well-fortified town like Jacob's Well—one of the many reasons she'd chosen to come here in the first place—but Jesus, she didn't need to be tempting fate any more than she already was.

Because the truth was, she wasn't just staying for the protection.

She... she wanted it all. She wanted a family. She wanted to be loved. She wanted to know what it felt like to have a man to love her so deep that even if he lost her, he'd wear her ring for years afterwards because that love lived on even after *death*.

And wanting anything that hard, God, she knew how stupid it was. She'd spent her whole childhood wanting her Dad's love. Would she spend her adult life the same way?

"That's how it's done in civilized society," Cam said. "A write-up in the paper, with a picture. I asked some people from the *Gazette* to come."

Vanessa heard Michael sputter. "Did you think I might have wanted some say in whether my co-workers were here in a professional capacity?"

Cam ignored Michael's question. "Don't any of you have anything nicer to wear?" It sounded like he half-way hoped the answer was no.

"What?" Ross said. "This shirt is clean, and the pants are well-repaired."

"Vanessa's lived out in the wild," Riordan said. "She's going to like someone who looks more rugged than a slicked back ass clown. Where'd you even *get* a tuxedo?"

"Wouldn't you like to know," Cam said, and Vanessa could hear the sneer of superiority in his voice.

"Well," Riordan said. "At least *I'm* not dressed like the angels of the NBA."

Vanessa sighed. He must be talking about Michael. Why did Riordan have to take a shot at *him*? Michael hadn't done anything.

"Suck my dick," Michael snapped back.

"Everyone, stop," Ross sounded appalled. "This is a church. This is our wedding. A little decorum, please."

"I didn't think anyone *could* suck your dick," Cam said.

Michael didn't come back with anything more, and Vanessa cringed in empathy at his apparent mortification. She needed to get this wedding going before they tore each other apart.

Thankfully, an out-of-tune piano began to play the wedding march, and everyone in the corridor went silent. A few seconds more, and the door to the bride's room cracked open, revealing Sophia. She was in a lavender dress with a single flower in her shiny brown hair.

"Ready?" she asked.

Was she ready? God no.

"Yes," said Vanessa, shaking her head fervently. It was best to get unpleasant things over with quickly. Skinning a possum? Taking a dip in the river to get clean in winter? Take a deep breath and rip off the band-aid. It was the only way. "Let's hurry."

"Take your time," Sophia said, reaching up to readjust the crown of flowers on Vanessa's head, smiling so wide it looked like her face was about to split. "After all, you only get married once. You have to enjoy every moment of it."

Vanessa attempted a smile. It probably came off more as a grimace, but Sophia didn't seem to notice.

Sophia spent forever fiddling with her train behind her until Vanessa couldn't stand it anymore. "Okay. I've enjoyed all I can out of this moment. Let's get on with it. Any sign of Logan yet?"

She glanced over her shoulder just in time to see Sophia's happy expression falter. "Not yet," she said, eyebrows knitting together.

"All right. Then let's go," Vanessa said, eyes forward. It was fine. So she'd have four husbands instead of five.

Hadn't she just been admiring the love Logan had for his first wife? Now she was going to fault him for it?

She blinked hard against the emotion biting at her eyes as she opened the door and then strode out. The hallway was empty now.

Sophia directed her down the hallway and over toward the back of the church's sanctuary.

Two middle-aged men playing the role of ushers opened the double doors into the crowded sanctuary.

Sophia gave Vanessa's hand a squeeze, then she headed down the aisle first. She only glanced back once to make sure Vanessa was really following.

As soon as Vanessa stepped on the flower petal strewn path, the tinny piano started playing the bridal march.

Talk about surreal.

Her eyes immediately flicked to the end of the aisle where four men stood waiting for her. Four. Not five.

Vanessa's stomach sank. Which was stupid. She knew he wouldn't show.

She locked her jaw. Just rip the damn band-aid off. Get through this and then start her new life with her new family... whatever that meant.

She was only vaguely aware of the people in attendance as she continued down the aisle.

Nix was one of the few who stood out, seated in the back row with a stunning redhead and several other men. Nix looked agitated as he kept his eye on the door to the church.

Vanessa also noticed a short, stocky woman seated on the aisle. She had a rounded profile and small dark eyes, which she dabbed at with a handkerchief. Everyone else was a blur.

As she reached the front, Vanessa couldn't bring herself to make eye contact with her soon-to-be husbands. It would only remind her of the one who wasn't there.

The pastor stood between two tall candlesticks with flickering candles. He was frowning and when she got close, he leaned in like he wanted to get a better look at her. Except he wasn't looking at her face.

"Someone messed up your hair," the pastor said.

Vanessa reached up self-consciously to touch her head.

"Jesus, Jonas," said Michael and only then did Vanessa notice that the pastor's pupils were seriously dilated.

Wait. Was he *high*?

The day had already started off with a bang, what with her fiancés' bickering and Logan turning out to be a no show. A baked pastor did nothing to boost Vanessa's flagging confidence.

Pastor Jonas then turned to squint at Cam. "Hey, I remember you. You're the one who almost got tossed out of town for fighting. Would've been your third strike."

Vanessa looked at Cam. *Third strike?*

"That was nothing," Cam said, neck reddening as he waved a hand. He looked to Vanessa. "It was nothing. It wasn't even my fault. This guy stole my ration card and—"

"Okay, then," Pastor Jonas cut off Cam's flood of justifications as he looked down at the big book in his hands. "Let's see, how does this go again...?"

He flipped back and forth through the book, as if trying to find the right page. "Fuck, now where did it go?"

"Church!" Ross whispered loudly at the same time as several people in the audience gasped.

The pastor didn't seem to notice, though. He was already moving on in a booming voice. "We gather here today to celebrate the wedding of Vanessa, Michael, Camden, and..." He paused, looking between the twins, "which one are you again?"

"Riordan," Riordan said quickly, getting ahead of his brother.

"And Ross," Ross added.

The pastor scrunched his brow. "Where's the fifth?"

"Here!" roared a new voice from the back of the church and a wave of relief swept through Vanessa.

He'd come.

Logan had come.

Vanessa turned around to beam at him but then her eyes widened in horror. What the— She tossed the flowers Sophia had given her to hold to the floor and dashed down the aisle to him. He was bloodied with a swollen cheek and eye.

"What happened?" she cried, barely stopping herself from throwing her arms around him.

Which was dumb. Freaking idiotic. She barely knew him. It was probably the idea of him more than the man himself she'd let herself become attached to in such a short time. But still.

Seeing him bruised and bloody made her chest ache in a way that was foreign. Like a ghost pain from a lost limb. She just hadn't had anyone to care about in so long she'd forgotten what it felt like.

"Nothing. Now let's do this." Logan took her elbow and practically dragged her along with him to the altar.

What the—

"Are you kidding me?" Vanessa looked at him incredulously. "It's not nothing. You look like you got hit by a Mack truck."

"Just perfect," Cam muttered. "This is going to look *so* great in the papers."

As soon as they got back to the alter, Pastor Jonas started up again. "You have all come today to share in the commitment these people make to each other..."

"Who did this to you?" Ross hissed under his breath to Logan.

"It doesn't matter."

"Where is he?" Riordan asked. "The guy who jumped you. I could probably take him."

"To offer your love and support to their union..."

Logan gave Riordan a look that said he was less than impressed. Vanessa tried to focus on what the pastor was saying but her soon to be husbands had apparently decided her wedding was the perfect time to chat it up.

"Marriage is a permanent union," Pastor Jonas stated, oblivious to everything. "Until death do you part."

"No way, kid," Cam smirked Riordan's direction. "If anyone wants to mess with this clan, I'll be the one who straightens them out."

"God help us," Michael muttered.

"The six of you will no longer live for yourselves alone. You will belong to one another. An unbroken circle. You must trust, love, and respect one another."

"Is that right?" Riordan asked. "And who the hell are you? Oh, I forgot, you're a *nurse*, right?"

Vanessa held her breath and tried counting to calm herself down. Why weren't they listening to the pastor? Fine, he might be stoned, but he was still making good points. Trust and respect. The other one she didn't expect, but goddammit, they could try showing a little respect.

"If you've got something to say to me, just come out and say it," Cam said, bumping his chest against Riordan's.

"For the love of God, people, we are in a church!" Ross yelled. "We are at the altar. We're supposed to be getting *fucking* married."

"Ross!" yelled the short, stocky woman who'd been crying earlier. "Language!"

"Save it, ma," said Riordan.

"Enough," Logan all but roared and everything quieted. The pastor. The other husbands. The whispering congregation.

Logan glared at Cam, Riordan, and Ross. "Are you boys or are you men? Because standing right in front of us is a good woman. And she deserves to marry *men*. If you can't be that to her, then get the hell off this altar. Right now."

Vanessa held her breath. He'd stood up for her. Demanded respect. No one had ever done that for her before. Ever in her whole life.

Cam looked to the floor like he was ashamed. Riordan's jaw went tight. He didn't seem to like anyone telling him what to do but he glanced at Vanessa and then gave a quick, tight nod. And Ross, well, Ross was staring at Logan like he was the best thing since sliced bread.

But no one moved. No one left.

Holy crap. This whole thing might actually work. This was the first time that she really, truly believed it.

The pastor went through the rest of the short ceremony. The I do's were said with seriousness and solemnity, and the rings exchanged.

What Logan had said had really sunk in.

At least Vanessa thought so, until Pastor Jonas announced, "You may now kiss the bride."

At first things were fine. The pastor gestured toward Logan. "As the head of Clan Washington, Logan, you go first."

Vanessa watched the vein in Logan's throat bulge, but he stepped forward and before Vanessa could even appreciate what was happening, he bobbed his head down and pressed the briefest, most chaste kiss on her lips.

She blinked and it was already over and Logan had pulled back.

She didn't have long to overthink it, either, because Cam and Riordan were shoving the others out of the way in their rush to get to Vanessa next. Riordan pushed Ross out of the way, and Ross stumbled into Michael, who let out an earth-shattering scream.

At the same time, Cam reached Vanessa first, tugging her toward him and away from Riordan. In the same motion, he dipped her backwards like he was going in for one of those old Hollywood smooches.

"Cam!" she gasped, and not just because he'd spun her body off balance and was now closing in for a kiss.

"What sweetheart?" he asked, lips only centimeters from hers.

"Fire!" she squeaked, squirming in his arms.

"I know, sweetheart," he grinned. "I feel it too."

"No, you idiot," Logan yelled. "You lit her dress on fire!"

"What?" Cam's eyes widened as he looked behind her and saw what they meant. When he'd spun her so dramatically, her arm was flung out at an awkward angle, hitting one of the tall candlesticks.

The candle tipped out of its socket and landed on the train of her dress. The old fabric went up like a torch, blazing up toward the back of her legs.

Get it off, *get it off*. Vanessa screamed and tried uselessly to yank the dress down and off her as heat singed the back of her legs. There were yells and shouts from all sides.

And then a body slammed into her from behind, taking her to the ground.

Camden, she realized, as they hit the floor and he immediately started rolling with her, slapping at the flames until the fire was out.

They both lay there heaving together. Vanessa blinked as she looked at the large section of the back of her dress that had been totally melted away, the edges blackened. Cam's face was sooty, and his tuxedo a mess.

Ross, Logan, and Riordan swarmed Cam and Vanessa to see if they were okay.

All the while, the camera flash bulbs burst, filling the room with exploding blossoms of clear white light.

CHAPTER TEN

MICHAEL

Michael couldn't stop staring at Vanessa for the entirety of the short ride home. After they arrived at their new little ranch-style house, she hurried inside and down the hall to the master bedroom to "freshen up."

The other guys started chattering but Michael barely heard them. He couldn't stop staring after Vanessa.

She was so beautiful. Even malnourished and battered. He winced just thinking about it. Every time he looked at her cuts and bruises he literally felt nauseated. How could anyone do that to her?

He'd always been too sensitive. That was his mom's word for him. Dad's was *pussy*.

More than anything, he wanted to fold Vanessa in his arms and hold her close, assuring her that they'd protect her and nothing else would hurt her.

Too bad you're a screwed-up freak.

He could never offer her a comforting touch. Never bandage up a scrape or push back a stray hair from her face.

Never kiss those tempting pink lips of hers...

"This is it?" Cam's voice broke into his thoughts. "Isn't it a little...small?"

"What were you expecting?" Ross asked. "The *Taj Mahal?*"

"The Taj Ma-*what?*" Riordan asked, rolling his eyes. "Quit being such a know-it-all."

"No, I just thought they always gave clan families really nice houses and this is just..." Cam scanned the house, disappointment clear in his face.

Michael thought the place was nice now that he looked around. Normal. Homey. The furniture looked comfortable and there was even a leather couch in the living room.

It had been a long time since Michael had a home. A real one anyway. The garage apartment didn't count.

"So how are we gonna do this?" Cam asked. "Do we all go in there at once? Or like, take turns, or what?"

"Jesus," Logan swung around from where he'd been staring out the window.

"What?" Cam asked, flinging his arms out. "It's a valid question."

Logan heaved a breath out.

"We should let Vanessa take the lead," Michael said.

"Well if we're going in turns, then it only makes sense for someone with experience to go first," Cam said.

"Bullshit," Riordan said, taking a step toward Cam.

"Let me guess?" Cam smirked at Riordan. "You think the youngest should go first? Well sorry, kid, this isn't like some school field trip. A woman needs to be primed before you go in and—"

"So I learn," Riordan said. "She can teach me how she likes to be touched."

"Would you idiots shut up?" Logan hissed. "Are you forgetting how we found her? Or how she flipped you on your ass and even managed to disarm me, a trained security officer? You think a woman learns that kind of self-defense for nothing?"

"What do you mean?" Ross asked.

The nausea was hitting Michael again. Hard.

"He means she might have been..." Michael couldn't even finish the sentence.

"Oh shit." Cam ran a hand down his face.

"What?" Ross asked, looking around at them all.

"That if she's had sex, it might not have been consensual," Logan said, through gritted teeth. His fists were balled like he wanted to hit something even thinking about it.

Both Ross and Riordan's eyes widened with horror.

"Let me go talk to her," Michael said. "I'll ask her what she wants to do. I'm not a threat," he gave a somewhat humorless laugh. "I can't even touch her."

Logan was already nodding and seeing him, Ross started nodding too.

"Sounds like a good idea," Ross said.

Michael turned around without a word and headed down the hallway to the master bedroom at the back of the house.

Even though he'd volunteered, the butterflies attacking his stomach combined with the nausea that already had his insides churning weren't amazing for his confidence. But he'd faced more terrifying things in his life.

After one especially bad meltdown when he was ten—on a school field trip to a local museum—his parents had gotten into a huge fight. Dad had accused Mama of coddling him. He said if she didn't let him raise Michael the way a man ought to be raised, then he was done. He was leaving.

Mama told him to pack his bags.

Michael didn't leave the house much after that. Mama let him do online school and things were good. Well, as good as they could be.

He even had friends. Good ones. He'd spend all day online, talking over a phone app to his friends and gaming when he wasn't in school.

Not being able to touch anyone barely seemed like a disability at all. He did everything by voice command so he didn't even have to touch the laptop keys if he didn't want to.

He didn't leave the house from the time he was fifteen until he was twenty-two. He did freelance writing gigs here and there to help Mama out with the bills. He even had an online girlfriend for a while.

They broke up because he found out she was "dating" a couple other guys in their group of friends. But still. Life was good.

Until it all fell apart. Mama got sick. All the women got sick. People outside started going crazy.

Then Mama died. A couple months later, the lights went out.

No more computer.

No more internet.

No more nothing.

And he survived that, hadn't he? He never thought he'd be able to take that first step out his front door after eight years never leaving the house. But he had. He'd done that and he'd gotten to Jacob's Well and he'd even become a reporter at the *Gazette* where it was his *job* to go out into the world and interact with people on a daily basis.

So going in to talk to his new bride on their wedding night was nothing compared to that, right?

Right?

His hand was on the doorknob and pushing the door open, so there was no turning back now. Which was usually the way it worked.

Like learning to swim—jump in the damn deep end. You figured out how to swim or you drowned.

He hadn't drowned yet.

He knocked on the door as he pushed it open. He didn't peek around the door until her soft voice called, "Come in."

When he came in she was sitting on the edge of the bed, her hands plucking nervously at the bedspread.

She was only wearing a tiny little camisole and itty bitty sleep shorts.

Michael swallowed hard, fighting the stiffy growing in his shorts.

"Hi," she said, laughing a little awkwardly. Then she tilted her head, looking behind him. "Um. Where's everyone else?"

He cleared his throat. "That's what I'm here to talk to you about. I'm sort of an ambassador."

Her eyebrows went up and Michael felt stupid. *Ambassador?* God. "I just mean, we wanted to— Or well, we didn't want to—" Goddammit, could he stop putting his foot in it? "Overwhelm you." He finished lamely.

"We thought maybe well, if you'd had any bad experiences and didn't want to, you know," he gestured at the bed, "um, do anything right off the bat. That's okay, because, you know, we would never force you to, or expect anything you weren't—"

"Oh, no! You didn't think... *No*, Michael." She stood up and went to grab his hand, but he yanked it away just in time.

"Oh," she stopped and pulled her hands back to her chest. "Sorry." She sat back down on the bed.

Michael felt the back of his neck heating up. God he was such a freak. She was apologizing to *him*?

But the next second she went on, "No, no one has ever..." Her eyes went distant and then she shuddered

"But they tried," he said, feeling the anger bubbling up.

"Sure, they tried," she shrugged, trying and failing for a smile. "Most didn't live to try twice. A couple got close and survived." Her eyes got that faraway look again and Michael got the feeling that she wasn't with him.

"But you got away?" Michael asked, hating whatever memory she was reliving. He wished so much that he could reach out and touch her. Hold her. Anything to bring her back to him.

His voice seemed to do the trick though. Her eyes met his again. "One burned down my shelter. Another stole my goat. You know how hard it is to live in a world without cheese?" She said it like a joke but her smile didn't reach her eyes.

Michael had spent most of his adult life watching from the outside in. If there was one thing he was good at, it was reading people.

Michael shook his head. "So you're untouched?" He needed the reassurance of hearing it out loud one more time.

Blood rushed into her lovely face. "I hadn't even been kissed until today."

Michael's mouth popped open. How was that possible? A girl who was both exciting and sweet, delicate and aggressive... She was an intoxicating combination of everything sexy and she had to be only, what, twenty-four or twenty-five at most? How had she not been kissed senseless every day of her young adult life?

"So was that your only objection?"

"Oh. Um. Well we also didn't know if you wanted to set up, like, a schedule. Or if you'd rather... we could come all together. But not if you don't— You know, just whatever you'd prefer."

Her eyebrows went up at his words. Shit. Had he said something wrong?

"Well what I want right now..." she trailed off, her eyelashes dropping for a moment before her eyes flicked back up to him in a way that had him sucking in a breath. "is to look at you. All of you."

Her words shocked Michael right out of his thoughts. "Wh— *What?*"

She blinked those big brown doe eyes at him again. "You are my husband, aren't you?"

"Yes, but..."

"Michael. I won't touch you, I promise." Looking into her eyes, he trusted she was telling the truth. And he also saw the honesty there when she said, "but I'm curious. I've never— It's never been safe to— I've always wondered what a man looks like... down there." Her cheeks colored and Michael realized he wasn't the only one nervous here.

And what she was asking... his cock immediately went stiff in his shorts.

And she was being brave, so he could be too. Even though sweat beaded up on the back of his neck as he clarified, "You want me to strip for you?"

She shrugged one narrow shoulder. "Would you mind?"

Michael stared for a second, then he realized this was karma for all the times Ana had stripped for him and he'd passively watched. Now the tables were turned.

"Where do you want me?" He fought a nervous smile.

"Over there," she said, gesturing at the windowless wall across from where she sat.

Michael walked to the wall, feeling all the hairs on his arms stand on end. "Here?" he asked, turning to face her.

"Yes, now take off your tank."

Michael looked down, crossed his arms and took the hem in his fingers. He breathed out then slowly pulled it up and over his head.

The shirt dropped to the floor and Michael clenched his fists at his side.

He could feel Vanessa's gaze on his skin as sure as any touch. But unlike a touch, there was no pain. His cock was no longer at half-mast but pointing due north and demanding her attention.

Vanessa bit her bottom lip. "Keep going." The words came out as a breathy gasp. Which only had his cock hardening more.

"Damn, woman. Are you trying to torture me here?"

Vanessa looked surprised at his words. And then a small, pleased smile took over her face.

Which had him hurrying to slip his hands under the elastic waistband of his shorts and shove them down over his ass. More goose bumps flittered over his arms as the silky material slid down his legs. Once they were at his ankles, he kicked them off.

And then he stood there.

Naked.

Absolutely exposed.

Vanessa's wide eyes flicked left and right and up and down. Before settling and zeroing in on his cock.

Shit. She wasn't saying anything. Why wasn't she saying anything?

Did she like what she saw? Was she freaked out by it?

His abs tensed and his heavy cock bobbed as Vanessa stood again. He didn't realize he was backing up until he ran into the wall.

"I won't touch you," she whispered, sounding fascinated. Her gaze never once strayed from his cock. "I just want to get a closer look."

Michael knocked his head back against the wall but only for a second, because he couldn't take his eyes off her.

"You're beautiful," she said, dropping to her knees.

Holy shit. Did she know what she was doing? He'd never had a girl in this position before but he was a guy and had been around back when there was internet so yeah. Having a girl on her knees in front of him? *Shiiiiiiiiiiiiiiit*.

"Do they all look like that?"

"Mostly," he managed to get out. God, he could feel her warm breath on his *balls*. He was gonna die. He was seriously three freaking seconds from spontaneous combustion.

"If I can't touch you, can you touch yourself?" She did that thing where she looked up at him through her lashes.

"Yes," he ground out through his teeth.

She finally seemed to notice just how much of an impact her actions were having on him.

"Then do that," she said, blowing a stream of warm air across the head of his cock.

"*Fuck.*"

More than anything in the world, he wanted to beg her to suck his cock into that teasing mouth of hers.

But what if the small bumps on her tongue were too rough? Or if her lips didn't feel as soft as they looked? He couldn't handle having one of his freak-outs right now. Not in front of his beautiful wife. Especially not right now when everything she was saying and doing felt *so* damn *good.*

"Show me how you touch yourself," she whispered and he couldn't hold back another second. He reached down and took himself in hand.

God. He couldn't help groaning at the relief his hand provided and the friction of rubbing himself up and down.

"Now let me see you," he growled. "Show me how *you* touch *yourself.*"

"Oh." She pulled back in surprise, looking up at him from the floor. As much as he liked her in that position, he wanted to see her bringing herself pleasure. In fact, he couldn't think of anything hotter in the whole damn universe.

"Vanessa," he groaned. "Please." He pulled on his shaft, squeezing and rolling the tip and then dragging back down again.

She went back to the bed and pulled off her T-shirt. She was braless, and though her breasts were small, they were definitely *there.* Round and firm despite the fact he could count every one of her ribs.

"That's right, beautiful," he gasped. "Now those little shorts."

"You, too," she said. "Don't stop."

Michael didn't need to be told twice. He fisted his cock and stroked it.

"Good," she said. "Just pretend it's me doing that."

"This is not...what I...came up here for," Michael said, though he was already starting to pant. This might not have been his intention walking into the room, but now that they'd started, he needed to see her come. God, he needed it more than he'd ever needed anything in his whole life.

Vanessa slipped her shorts off but left her soft pink cotton underwear on. Michael was just about to tell her to take those off too, but then she reached up and cupped her breast in her hand. He felt the tingle race down his spine.

"It's not?" she asked, squeezing herself.

Michael groaned and pushed his cock through his fist again. "They're not going to be happy with me."

"Well, I am. That's what counts, right? And if we can't touch, then we'll need something special just between us."

"I... God..." Yes, She was perfect. So perfect. He'd never been in the same room with a woman when he worked himself to climax. Seeing her there... So close... Breathing in the scent of her... Seeing her eyes spark with lust... Watching him... Fuck!

"When everyone else comes in," she said, "and that's what I want —no nights, no schedule, just all of us together—I want you there, too. This isn't five individual marriages. It's one big one. And you're as big a part of it as anyone else." Then she bit her lip again, a small frown creasing her forehead. "Will that be hard on you? Watching them?"

Michael grunted. "A little."

"Then that's why we'll have these special times just for us, too."

Vanessa still had her thin cotton underwear on, but when she spread her legs and opened herself to him, Michael got a look at the darkening spot between her legs.

He was making her wet.

Him.

Just the sight of him aroused his bride, and she was soaked. She hadn't even touched herself yet.

Well enough of that.

"Stick your hand down your panties. Rub your clit and stick a finger inside yourself."

She blinked at him. Maybe she was surprised by the growl in his voice. But she obeyed and fuck did that make him even harder, something he wouldn't have thought was possible a second ago.

Her breath hitched and her chest arched outward the slightest bit almost the very same moment her hand disappeared down her underwear.

Michael imagined the pale of her hand against the wet, pink folds of her pussy. He could tell the moment she slipped her finger inside herself.

He was about to tell her to take the underwear off too, but God, holy— Was she—? Already?

Her forehead scrunched and the leg bracing on the ground went stiff as a tiny, high-pitched cry escaped her throat.

She was coming. She'd barely even touched herself and she was already coming.

Holy sh—

He stroked up and over the crown of his cock, then thrust his fist down the shaft.

"Michael," she cried. "Come with me!"

He grunted and his hips shot forward just as long thick ribbons of cream spurted all over the floor, soaking the shorts he'd kicked off in front of him. He only barely missed Vanessa's bare feet.

"Wow," she said, then she slapped her hand over her mouth, giggling.

Michael was mortified. He'd come in record time, *on command*, and nearly all over his bride. She didn't seem to mind though. She seemed more amazed than horrified. "It's like one of those special effects in old movies."

Michael bowed his head and laughed at himself. "That's me," he said. "*Special*."

He bent to pick up his shorts, then realized what a mess they really were.

"Here," she said, retreating to the bathroom. She came back with a very pink, very frilly robe. "I think Sophia must have brought this for me."

"You expect me to put that on?" Michael asked.

She shrugged. "It's clean. It's dry. And best of all," she wagged her eyebrows, "it's silk."

Aha. How well she already knew him. Then he grinned broadly when he got it on. It barely made it all the way around him. He imagined the other men's reactions to his new look when he returned to the study with his report.

He blew Vanessa a kiss, wishing it could be a real one, and promised to be right back.

He wasn't disappointed by the guys' reactions when he walked out to them, either.

"What the fuck!" Camden said. "Tie that thing a little tighter, dude. I don't need to see your junk."

"Were you lying to us?" Ross asked.

"You had sex with Vanessa?" This from Riordan, his face all but green with jealousy.

"Relax," Michael said. "I didn't touch her. And neither has anyone else."

"What?" Logan asked. "She told you that?"

"She was never raped." Michael grimaced just saying the word. "Though not for lack of anyone's trying it sounds like. She's tough as hell. And you," he said still addressing Logan. "You were her very first kiss."

Logan's eyes went round as an owl's as he reached up and touched his mouth. Then he turned away and walked over to the window, back to them.

"So why are you wearing that pink shit?" Camden asked. "Where are your clothes?"

"What happened is going to stay just between Vanessa and me." Michael had decided that on the short walk back to the living room. "All you need to know is she wants all of us."

"Yes, but who does she want first?" Riordan asked.

"All of us. No assigned nights. She says she's married to us all, so it's all of us she wants."

"At the same time?" Ross asked. "How is that even possible?"

"Has she lost her damn mind?" Logan asked, turning momentarily from the window to glare down the hallway at the bedroom.

Michael didn't appreciate his tone. "Actually she seemed perfectly rational. And what our wife wants, she gets."

That was the other thing he'd decided. Vanessa was wonderful. Amazing. Perfect. What she'd just given him—not just a pity peep show, but a woman looking at *him*, wanting *him*.

It was everything. Fucking everything.

He'd move heaven and earth for that woman.

"I'm not interested in seeing all of your man meat on display," Cam said.

"Then keep your eyes closed," Ross said, striding down the hallway.

"Yeah man. Where's your sense of adventure?" Riordan asked, smacking Cam on the shoulder before following his brother.

Michael hurried to slip in front of the twins. Then he put his arms out to block the hallway, barely even considering the fact that one of them might run into him. Touch him. He was too concerned about his new wife.

"Whoa, whoa, whoa," Michael said. "No one's going in there with their egos or boners blazing." Shit, could Vanessa hear him from the bedroom? He didn't know how thick the bedroom door was. "Did you dumb fucks miss the part where I said she's a *virgin*?" he whispered.

"We didn't miss it." Logan strode across the living room from the window and then he pushed through the men clogging up the hallway. Michael jumped aside before Logan could plow into him. "And we'll take it as slow as our wife needs. I'll make fucking sure of it."

And with that, Logan pushed open the door to the bedroom.

CHAPTER ELEVEN

LOGAN

Logan took the lead and pushed the door open for the same reason he'd decked that motherfucker at the bar outside town earlier this afternoon who was talking shit about Vanessa.

Because she deserved better.

She was a good woman. A helluva good woman from the little he'd seen. And she deserved more on her wedding night than a couple of fumbling boys barely turned nineteen and that undisciplined hothead Camden. Logan hadn't liked Camden back when he was in the Security Squadron and the years since certainly hadn't done anything to endear the man to him.

Michael seemed like a good enough guy but he couldn't even touch their wife, so what the hell good was he?

No, if Logan wanted to make sure Vanessa was safe, both physically and emotionally, he'd have to take the damn lead.

Which all seemed well and good until he opened the door and—

Topless.

She was topless.

He felt gut punched at the sight of her on the bed.

Because not only was she topless, but she wasn't wearing anything except for the flimsiest little pair of cotton under-nothings.

And her legs went on for-fucking-*ever*.

But it was where those legs came together that had his eyes riveted —where her fingers played up and down the edges of her panties at the apex of her thighs.

She saw where he was looking, too.

And then she leaned back on the bed and, even though from ten feet away he could see her whole body was shaking, she opened her thighs wide in invitation.

Logan literally staggered, the wave of lust hit him so fucking hard.

His traitorous cock went hard as stone in two seconds flat. She was — Jesus Christ, he didn't think—

Wasn't she supposed to be, he didn't know— Virgins were supposed to be *shy*, weren't they? Okay, so he hadn't been shy when he was a virgin but girls were different, right?

Jesus, he realized how bad that sounded the second he thought it.

"You're beautiful," Ross breathed out, seeming to recover from the same stupor Logan was in.

"Gorgeous," Riordan echoed.

And even though she'd spread her legs for them, her cheeks flushed at the twins' words. The sight had Logan's cock going even harder. Because in spite of all that she'd lived through, and he knew he couldn't even begin to imagine it all, she was still innocent. How on earth had she managed it? It was fucking incredible. *She* was incredible.

And then Jenny's image flashed in his mind. For the first time in how long, Logan couldn't even remember.

But even as his stomach soured at the thought of how he was betraying Jenny, his cock stayed just as hard.

There's no way Jenny could have survived. She's dead. It's time to move on.

Nix's voice. Everyone's goddamned voice.

Eight years. When are you going to let her go?

"They're right, sweetheart," said Camden, the first to move toward the bed. "You don't know how lucky I feel to be here tonight. We've waited for this moment for a long time, but—"

"*But* we're willing to give you whatever time you need," Riordan interrupted, shooting a dark look Camden's way.

Camden just took it in stride. "*But* Michael tells us you're ready for us now? Is that right?"

"That's right," Vanessa said. She'd been looking around at all of them, but her eyes settled on Logan. He didn't look away though God knew he should.

Was it a question or an invitation he saw in those big brown eyes of hers? Not that he knew how to answer either.

"Good, sweetheart," Cam said. "How would you like to do this?"

"Well..." Vanessa drew out the word. "I've recently discovered that I like to watch."

She sent a quick smile Michael's direction and the quick shot of jealousy that swept through Logan made him want to put his fist through a wall. What the fuck was happening to him?

"Watch?" Riordan looked disturbed. "Um, I'm not doing anything with any of these guys. I mean, Ross is my *brother*."

Vanessa laughed, and her eyes darted to Michael again, like she wanted him to explain.

"She wants to watch you all undress," Michael said. "But, sorry, guys. I don't think there are any more pink robes to go around."

So she'd had Michael undress for her. And she'd liked it. She was a virgin but whatever her experiences had been after The Fall, it looked like they hadn't turned her off of sex. In spite of her fidgeting hands, she looked curious. Flushed. Excited.

Logan's cock strained in his jeans and he gritted his teeth.

You're just here to make sure everything goes smooth. Not to get your dick wet.

"You heard her," Logan turned to the other men. "Get your clothes off."

Riordan immediately reached behind his neck and pulled his shirt over his head. His jeans were unzipped and down around his ankles before his shirt hit the floor.

The last thing Logan wanted was to be checking out another guy's junk, but he needed to know what Vanessa would have to be working with, and—*Jesus Christ*. Riordan was hung like a fucking horse.

Logan swung around to look at the other twin who was folding his clothes and carefully laying them on a small chair in the corner of the room. And dammit, his dick was just as huge as his brother's.

What did you expect, dumbass? They're identical twins.

Shit. They'd split Vanessa in half if either of them tried fucking her with those damn things. Okay, so they were out of the running for first dibs tonight. And Michael couldn't touch her.

Which just left Camden.

Great.

Logan's favorite person.

Camden stripped without a word and stood there as proud as a damn prize stud strutting closer to the bed, where Vanessa had scooted back to make room for them.

A quick glance showed that at least Camden was a more manageable size, though still larger than Logan would have preferred for Vanessa's first time.

He'd have to do, though. Because even though Logan's own cock was narrower than Camden's, if a little longer, he had absolutely *no* intention of getting anywhere near the woman he'd just married.

Between the other four—Logan glanced at Michael standing against the wall, okay, well, *three*—husbands she had left who could touch her, she'd have plenty to keep her hands full in the bedroom. The twins were still officially teenagers for Christ sake. No doubt they could run circles around her and exhaust her every night all on their own.

No, there was no need for him to become physically involved with her.

He'd protect her. That was what he'd vowed to himself as he stormed into the church this morning. God knew he had enough black marks on his soul already. He wouldn't add failing Vanessa to the list. No matter how much it killed him to look but not touch.

"Oh my God," Vanessa whispered, her eyes flicking between Riordan and Ross's cock's. "Will they fit?"

"Shh," Logan said, immediately moving to her side. "Just lay back, baby. We'll go slow and get your body ready. Nothing will happen that you don't want to."

Vanessa reached out and grasped Logan's hand, but she looked at all of them when she said, "But I do. Want to."

Logan gulped hard and, not taking his eyes off the courageous woman in front of him clipped out, "Riordan, on the bed, head between Vanessa's legs. You're going to learn how to eat our wife out. Ross, get close to watch what he's doing because you're next."

Cam didn't say anything, for once, and Logan was glad. If he had, Logan might not have been able to get his next words past the lump in his throat. "Only after she's ready, Cam, you can be the first to make love to our wife."

Still Cam didn't say anything, he just nodded vigorously and came to sit on the bed beside Vanessa's head, opposite Logan.

"Boys," Logan addressed the twins, his voice hoarse, "pull her underwear off."

Ross grabbed the flimsy fabric at one hip and Riordan took the other side. Ross started to efficiently yank it down her thigh and Logan shook his head.

"Gently. Every touch is part of the seduction."

Ross looked at him with wide eyes. "Seduction? But we're married."

Jesus, was the kid serious?

"Yeah and if you wanna stay that way you better learn how to seduce your wife," Logan growled.

Ross just nodded like an eager student so Logan guessed his heart was in the right place. He was just genuinely clueless.

"Like this," Logan said. He leaned over and gripped Vanessa's hip, kneading her flesh in his fingers.

Jesus Christ she felt good. Logan's eyes dropped closed and before he could stop himself he leaned over, pushing the kid out of the way.

He ran his nose up the inseam of her thigh and then, oh Jesus, to the apex where her aroma— He felt her stomach flex and her legs start to tremble.

He bit down on the top hem of her underwear and dragged them downward. As he did, even more of her scent was released and his nose skimmed right over her curls.

He reached up with his hand to take over for his teeth and dragged her underwear the rest of the way down as he opened his eyes.

His breath rushed out in one great whoosh as he yanked the panties off her left leg and then grabbed her thigh and shoved it roughly open against the bed.

Exposing the fucking promised land.

Her pussy was pink and the lips glistened with her arousal. Logan spread her thighs open even wider and he could see all of her—the swollen bud of her clitoris. The opening hidden behind those drenched lips.

Dive in. Lick up every ounce of that honey. Let her feel your thick fingers inside her, stretching her while you suck on her clit and bring her to climax after climax—

"Logan," Vanessa gasped. "*Yes.*"

But as if her words startled him out of a dream, Logan yanked back from her, blinking hard. What the fuck—?

He was breathing so hard his chest moved up and down like a goddamned old timey bellows. And his cock, Jesus Christ, his cock. He knew he was already weeping precum.

He jacked off sometimes like any guy but these days it was only once every couple weeks and more out of habit than anything. Just cleaning out the pipes. And he always, *always*, thought of Jenny while he did it.

So what the fuck was his cock doing reacting to another woman like this?

"Riordan," Logan snapped. "Lick up her sweetness. Now."

Thank fuck Riordan didn't need to be told twice. He moved between Vanessa's legs and after only a moment's hesitation, he extended his tongue.

He licked up her cunt in one long swipe that had Vanessa shuddering beneath him.

Obviously encouraged by her reaction, Riordan did it again. Licking her like she was a damn lollipop.

Logan was still breathing hard. Taking her scent inside him with every breath. And with every breath, fighting the impulse to shove the kid out of the way and devour her himself.

He ran a hand through his hair and then grunted, "All right, now suck on her clit."

Riordan paused, questioning eyes shooting Logan's way even while his tongue was still extended.

"She's not a fucking popsicle," Camden said, smirking as he leaned over Vanessa's chest and teasingly licked just the tip of his tongue around her nipple. She hissed and arched into him.

"Here." Logan's hand shook with restraint as he reached back toward Vanessa's spread thighs. And the second he made contact with her flesh, he couldn't help the moan that rumbled up his throat.

He also couldn't help rolling his middle finger around the swollen nub of her clit.

She squealed in response, one hand going to the back of Camden's head, pressing him more firmly to her breast.

And her other hand—Jesus, her other hand grasped Logan's with a passionate desperation that telegraphed her pleasure so clearly he couldn't help giving her clit another circle.

"This is her clitoris," Logan whispered to Riordan, barely able to get the words out. "Sucking on it will drive her crazy."

And then, before he could stop himself, Logan licked his lips and dragged his fingers through her drenched sex down to her sweet virgin hole. "And dip your fingers in here." Logan's voice was little more than a rasp as he pushed his forefinger inside Vanessa.

Her hot flesh closed around his finger and suckered onto him so fucking tight. Jesus Christ, oh fuck, she was—

Riordan dropped back down and started sucking on her clit.

Logan should pull his hand back. Riordan could do this part.

Instead Logan pushed his finger in deeper, turning to watch Vanessa's face. And he was rewarded.

He thought her face was flushed before?

It was nothing to the two crimson spots high on the apples of her cheeks. Her mouth dropped open in helpless gasps, and her eyes went wide, her eyebrows almost at her hairline. She looked down her body, eyes flicking from Camden mercilessly sucking on her breasts to Riordan and Logan working her cunt.

But it wasn't until her eyes met Logan's that her gasps turned to high-pitched squeals of ecstasy.

She was close. Jesus she was close.

Had he ever— She was *so* responsive. He dragged his finger in and out of her pussy and he could see the reaction on her face at his every move. And when he slowly worked a second finger inside her, stretching her even more?

Her breathy squeals became one long cry as she arched against Camden and her stomach and leg muscles went tense.

She was coming and Riordan kept sucking her clit noisily through it. She squeezed Logan's hand so hard he thought he might lose circulation but he didn't care. Jesus, he didn't care. He was on the edge himself and he didn't even have a hand on his cock.

Just watching her was enough—

Fuck, she was so magnificent.

She was— Logan blinked, his thoughts careening crazily.

She was—

Not Jenny.

The thought should have had him yanking his hand back from her hot, young flesh. But it didn't.

Because another thought was singing a siren song almost as loud:

She was... *his.*

Vanessa was his. That's what she was.

"I think you're ready for me, sweetheart," Camden said, moving from her berry-red nipples to kiss her long and deep.

Logan finally withdrew his fingers from her sweet depths, but he didn't move from where he leaned beside her in the bed. She was still clutching his hand, after all.

Chaotic thoughts warred in his head.

Jenny.

Do you take this woman as your lawfully wedded wife?

Vanessa.

You will belong to one another. An unbroken circle. You must trust, love, and respect one another.

"All right, sweetheart," Camden said. "Can you feel me?"

"Yes," Vanessa breathed out. "Michael? Logan? Are you with me?"

Logan's attention snapped back to Vanessa, everything else in his head quieting at the sound of her voice calling his name.

"I'm here, baby," he said, squeezing her hand back. He glanced down only briefly to where Camden was feeding his cock into the pussy that only moments before Logan had been stretching and preparing.

He turned back to Vanessa's face and saw a virgin's anxiety in her features.

"You don't have t—"

"I want it," she repeated what she'd said earlier. "But Logan, will you kiss me?"

In that moment, he would have done anything for her. Anything to help her final transition to womanhood go as smooth as possible. For her to find pleasure in this moment instead of pain.

He looked Camden's way one last moment and warned, "Slow," in a deadly voice.

"I swear, I won't hurt her."

It was the most solemn Logan had ever seen Camden, so, satisfied, he turned back to Vanessa.

He cupped her cheek. Jesus, she seemed so fragile against his big hand. Too small. Too breakable.

So at first he just dropped the lightest kiss on her lips.

Yours were the first lips she ever kissed.

In her entire *life*.

You were her first.

And you will be her last.

Logan brushed the errant, troubling thought away. He was just here to make her wedding night go smoothly. That was all.

Just this one night.

Just this one kiss.

He closed his eyes as he took the kiss deeper. Drawing her tongue into his mouth and teasing the tip of it with the tip of his own tongue.

The gasp he drew from her made a satisfaction he couldn't explain roar from somewhere deep inside him.

And then she hiccupped and her breathing sped up.

Logan knew it wasn't only from his kiss.

Camden was breeching her.

Had he reached her maidenhood?

Logan laid fully down beside her and drew her as much as he could into his arms while she still lay open to Camden.

But Logan was there, holding her and trying to drug her with kisses as Camden took what she'd determined would be taken tonight.

When she cried out, Logan wanted to rip the other man's heart out of his chest for ever causing her pain.

Thoughts like that wouldn't do Vanessa any good.

So he just kept whispering, "Baby, you're doing so good. You're so beautiful. That's right, baby. You're driving us crazy. You're doing so good. You're perfect."

When kissing her didn't seem to be enough distraction, Logan dropped a hand to play with her breasts, circling and pinching lightly at her nipples.

And Camden for his part was taking it slow.

He didn't start moving his hips until Vanessa's breathing came back to something resembling normal and even when he did, he was unhurried. Slow and steady.

Logan kissed from her lips down to nuzzle against her neck. He nibbled on her ear until she was turning her head and begging for his lips again.

And soon, even though it felt like decades, her little gasps of pleasure returned.

Except this time, they were accompanied by the bed thumping the wall with Camden's every thrust.

"Look, baby," Logan whispered. "Look down at him fucking you."

Logan kissed around to the sides of her breast so she could see down her body to where Camden's cock was disappearing inside her. Logan knew it was only right to give them that moment.

Camden moved and took her mouth while he continued fucking her.

Logan pulled back even more, now only connected by the hand she still held. He closed his eyes, unable to watch now.

Camden was her husband.

The husband who could give her all the things Logan couldn't.

He could give her *everything*—including his whole self.

He wasn't a ghost.

It was time for Logan to go.

He squeezed his eyes shut even harder against the need pulsing in his cock and the draw of the woman who now bore his name.

None of that mattered.

Go. It's time to go.

He'd done what he'd come here to do. He'd helped her through losing her virginity and the men had all behaved admirably. Even Camden.

"So fuckin' tight," Camden gasped between kisses. "Sweetheart, I'm — *Ohhhhhhhhhhhhh.*"

Vanessa had wrapped her legs around Camden's hips and she pulled him even tighter into her as he came.

Logan would have gone but she wouldn't let go of his hand.

She kissed Camden again and let out the sweetest little giggle.

And it all sent a spear through Logan's goddamned heart.

It wasn't jealousy this time. No, it was knowing that he'd never experience another moment like this. He'd never allow himself back into this bedroom. It was too... too *much.*

People called him Ghost because they didn't understand. He just lived life simple these days. It was the way he needed to be. He didn't mix much with people and tonight was the perfect example of why.

It got... messy when you let yourself get involved. Emotions and memories and...no, he just didn't do messy.

He remembered a church service from back in the day when he and Jenny went to those things. The pastor went on and on about how the word *holy* meant 'separate.'

So living separate from people wasn't a bad thing. It was holy, even. Like the monks. He was a modern day monk, that was all.

And monks didn't do... whatever this was tonight. Monks didn't get married and monks didn't get hard-ons that could break down brick walls.

Monks were disciplined.

They lived by a code.

They lived separate.

They were *holy*.

So Logan was about to pry his hand away from Vanessa's in spite of her death grip when she said, "Okay, Riordan, now you. And Logan, should we try a different position? Maybe, what do they call it? Doggy style? Like where he takes me from behind?"

Doggy— Did she really—

And just like that, every single ounce of self-control Logan was barely clinging onto fucking *snapped*.

Maybe it was hearing 'doggy style' come out of her mouth. Maybe it was the fact that she even knew the term in the first place.

But the nail in his coffin was when she flipped over like a fish and got up on her hands and knees, swaying that lovely ass in the air.

Riordan's eyes had gone bright and he started to move behind her but Logan shoved him out of the way at the last second and grabbed Vanessa's hips.

"Jesus, woman," he hissed, massaging one of her ass cheeks and then giving it a smack. With that sharp sound, eight years of repressed urges slammed into him. He lost hold of who he was, who he'd vowed to be, everything he knew. With the sound of that slap, Logan Washington was like a man possessed. If he could have been on the ceiling looking down, he wouldn't have recognized himself. In the back of his mind, he knew all of this, but he didn't fucking care. Not one bit.

She let out a little cry but by the way she pressed her ass back against his dick, goddamn, she liked it.

His woman was dirty and even though she'd just been fucked, she wanted more.

Logan grabbed his long cock and put it between her thighs until he was running his shaft against the lips of her sex.

"That's right, baby," Logan said, chest heaving. "Soak my cock with your pussy juice. Slick me up real nice."

She cried out—he didn't know if it was from the feel of his cock rubbing against her cunt or from his dirty words.

His cock pulsed from the contact with her most intimate fucking place. "That's right, baby. You love having another cock between your legs, don't you? You fucking love it."

He pulled his dick from between her legs and then grabbed her ass cheeks. He shoved his cock in the crack between them and smushed her ass around it until he made a tunnel of flesh to fuck without actually penetrating. As far gone as he was, he still couldn't allow himself that pleasure.

Jesus *Christ* that felt good. She was so damn hot. He hadn't allowed himself even the smallest amount of friction before now, but her hot fucking body, and the way she wriggled against him— Fuck. It was so—

He smacked her ass again.

"Ross, rub her clit," Logan ordered, eyes never leaving her sweet ass. She was skinny, too skinny, but like her tits, she still had enough ass to count. He mashed her ass cheeks in between his hands as he fucked them more vigorously.

"Riordan. Move up the bed. Vanessa, baby. I want you to suck his cock. I'll tell you how."

"Yes," she cried, hips moving back against Logan even more frantically now that Ross was working her clit. He was a quick study. Good.

Logan ran a hand down her spine as Riordan sat at the head of the bed and fed the tip of his cock into Vanessa's mouth.

Fucking hottest, dirtiest thing Logan had ever seen.

And that was what Logan wanted. To dirty up their sweet little perfect angel. To make her so fucking dirty and for her to come so goddamned hard she never forgot exactly who it was she belonged to.

Riordan was huge and Vanessa was soon gagging around him.

Logan smacked her ass again. "That's right, baby. Don't be afraid to gag on him. If it's too much, though, you can stop."

Vanessa only grabbed the root of Riordan's fat cock in her fist and bobbed lower on it, though.

"That's it, baby," Logan growled as Riordan's head tipped against the wall and his eyes rolled back in his head.

"Suck him hard," Logan kept on ruthlessly. "Don't be pretty about it, either. I want your drool dripping down over his balls. I want you to feel him at the back of your throat. Maybe not tonight, but one day soon, you're gonna learn how to swallow him all the way down. Yes, even those twin goddamn pythons. You'll be swallowing them like a fucking pro, baby."

"Jesus, Washington," Cam muttered. "What's got into you?"

His question should have made an impact, but Logan was too far gone.

Vanessa made ecstatic noises around Riordan's cock, her hips bucking more wildly than ever as Logan directed Ross to continue working her clit.

She was giving herself over to it.

To him.

To his command over her.

He grabbed her flesh and fucked her ass cheeks more furiously than ever. Jesus but he wanted to sink inside her. He wanted it so damn bad.

He reached down between her legs and stuck a finger in her cunt, that sweet haven he wouldn't let himself bury his cock in.

She was more drenched than ever.

He smacked her ass with his other hand. And then he took the finger in her cunt and dragged it up to the most forbidden spot of all. Time to dirty up their woman a little bit more.

She jumped the second his finger made contact with her sweet rosette.

"That's right, baby. I know my dirty little girl wants her asshole played with. Have you ever stuck your finger up here when you touch yourself?"

"Logan," Michael warned, but Logan didn't acknowledge it.

Vanessa shook her head without losing purchase on Riordan's cock, and Logan felt a surge of excitement quake through his chest.

Another first he'd be taking.

Taking.

Stealing.

He didn't care. He wanted it fucking all.

What would it be like to fuck her there?

A shudder ran down his spine and he pressed his forefinger, slick with her wetness, into her tight asshole.

She was so tight and clenched, his finger wouldn't go in at first.

He massaged her ass cheek.

"Shh, baby. You're doing so good. Let me in." He rubbed down her spine again. "Let me in, baby."

And at his words, she relaxed just that little bit so he was able to pop his finger inside her anus.

Oh Jesus, yes.

He grabbed his cock with his other hand. The barest friction wasn't enough anymore. He gripped himself in an iron fist, jerking up and down so roughly on his shaft it was on the edge of painful.

Just like he fucking deserved.

He yanked back down hard on his cock as he pressed his finger further up Vanessa's ass.

Your wife's ass. You've got your finger up your wife's anus. And you fucking love it.

Precum flowed out the tip of his cock and he painted it up and down the crack of Vanessa's ass, all around the spot where his finger disappeared.

"Shit. That's right, baby," he hissed. "You're doing so good. Sucking his cock like you were fucking born for it and riding my finger all up in your ass. Look at Ross, baby. I don't think he's gonna last much longer while he watches you sucking his brother. Ross, move a little up the bed so Vanessa can see you fucking your hand while she sucks off Riordan."

Ross whimpered. While he'd been fingering Vanessa's clit, he'd been jacking himself off. More and more frantically every minute. Logan could tell he was right on the edge of coming. Riordan too. Maybe it was a twin thing.

Almost as soon as Ross had moved so that Vanessa could see him— that is, if she strained, looking to the left while her mouth still stretched around Riordan's impressive dick.

Less than two minutes later, both Ross and Riordan were shouting out their release. Logan fucked her ass with his finger even more furiously and looked over her shoulder to see Riordan's cum spilling out of her mouth and down the sides of his cock.

She hungrily sucked and licked at it and her body clenched around Logan's finger because she was coming too and holy fuck, it was too much—

Logan grasped his shaft harder than ever and his hips jackknifed forwards and backwards. "Jesus," *thrust,* "fucking," *thrust,* "*Christ!*" *thru-uuuuuuuust.*

His cum shot across Vanessa's cheeks in a glorious arc of cream, painting her ass with his essence.

Blinding.

...

Full.

...

Perfection.

...

And then Logan blinked. And saw Vanessa underneath him, her back heaving with exertion. And his still hard cock nestled between her ass cheeks. With his finger buried up her anus.

Oh Jesus.

No.

What had he just done?

He pulled his hand free and then he backed down the bed. Away from Vanessa. Away from all of it.

He'd just stolen pleasure that should never have been his to take.

He'd vowed to *protect* Vanessa and instead he'd— He'd come in here and he'd— He'd—

"Logan?" Vanessa's voice was drowsy as she glanced over her shoulder.

But Logan couldn't even bring himself to look at her. He'd already fucked things up bad enough.

Punishment.

That was all a selfish, ruinous bastard like him deserved.

So he turned and fled the room like the coward he was.

CHAPTER TWELVE

VANESSA

One Month Later

Vanessa had been married for a month and nothing was going according to plan. She was supposed to come into town, enter the lottery, and for once in her life be part of a family that *wanted* her.

She shook her head at herself as she pulled on her jeans, using the belt because they were still too big on her.

No, the plan was to come here and get married so you'd be safe from Lorenzo. So, mission accomplished, right?

She frowned and sat down on the bed, raking her hands through her hair. It had grown half an inch since she'd been here so that now she resembled a newborn chick, with soft fluff that stuck straight out on all sides.

She stood up again, jaw set.

She was being ridiculous.

Every day for the past eight years had been a struggle fighting for her life and now she was going to sit here crying over the fact that her love life wasn't all she wanted?

Boo hoo.

So what if Logan hadn't ever come back to her bed after that first night? If he wanted to sleep down the hall and spend half his time working night patrol at the Security Squadron, well, good for him.

Riordan, Ross, Cam, and Michael still slept in the master bedroom each night.

If the sex was a little... less than spectacular, well, that was fine too.

Sometimes she came. Sometimes she didn't. It was just that, well... Ross often seemed at a loss for what to do with her. Whereas Riordan treated sex like a full-on contact sport. Especially when he and Cam were both in bed with her at the same time.

Sometimes she felt like an object they were using in a never-ending game to one-up each other. Who could fuck her longer or make her come more often, that kind of thing. She swore, they might as well start making notches on the damn bedpost.

She'd overheard them the other day taunting each other about it.

"You up for tonight, Thing 2?" Cam said. He'd taken to calling the twins that. Thing 1 and Thing 2. Because maturity. "Cause that rutting like a pig technique you were working last night was less than impressive. Good thing I was around to give it to her like a man."

"Shut up, old man. You worried your arthritis is gonna act up and you'll throw your back out? That why you gotta talk shit before the game?"

"I'm only thirty-three, you little fuckwad."

A chuckle from Riordan. "Hey, I'll even let you go first. Age before beauty, right? Just think, I'm about to enter my prime and you'll be... middle aged. Hope Vanessa doesn't mind saggy, limp-dicked old men."

"Say what you want, but I'll be the one who'll have Vanessa screaming from the rooftops while you're still trying to sort out her clitoris from her clavicle."

Vanessa wanted to yell at them that they were both idiots and that she faked her orgasms half the time no matter which one of them it was.

But she still had hope that this was just an adjustment period. And after the sex, when she snuggled up between their firm bodies, it really was quite lovely.

And that was the kicker, wasn't it?

The happiness she longed for was so close, she could almost taste it.

If only Logan would stop being so stubborn and come back to them— If only Cam and Riordan could put aside their differences and work together—

If only.

And then there was Michael.

Oh Michael.

That first night everything had seemed so promising. He could watch while she made love to the others and touch himself and be just as much a part of the family as any other husband.

Except for the fact that it wasn't working out like that.

She squeezed her eyes shut remembering last night. Riordan had been fucking her—she usually didn't like to be so crude about it, but there was no other word for what he'd been doing. He'd had her legs up, ankles by her head, and he was banging away at her like he thought he could get an Olympic medal for endurance fucking if he kept at it for long enough. It was doing absolutely zero for Vanessa but she thought, maybe if she looked over at Michael, she could make that connection and feel an emotional link there.

But Michael's gaze was locked on where Riordan entered her. And though he pumped his cock up and down, it wasn't lust she saw in his eyes. His brows were drawn together and he looked half-mesmerized, half-devastated.

In the first couple weeks, Michael got off work early and hung around Vanessa every chance he got. But as the month wore on, she'd felt him pulling away more and more. She'd have to be an idiot not to figure out why.

It was killing him. Watching the others take her and only being able to look but not touch.

Even though at least once a week she made sure to give him a private show, just him and her, it wasn't enough. Not nearly enough.

And this week when she'd invited him to come home for lunch, *just the two of them*—what had been their code for their special times together—he'd mumbled some excuse about having to work without meeting her eyes and then hurried out of the room.

She glanced out the window and the light that had been pouring in what felt like moments ago was now shadow.

Crap, what time was it?

She got to her feet and scrambled to pull on her socks and shoes. All this time sitting here wool-gathering, she was gonna be late. Audrey had invited her over for a girl's afternoon and she hated to be late. If there was one solidly good thing about her time here in Jacob's Well, it was the female friendships she'd formed. The women were so welcoming. It was like nothing she'd ever had before.

As soon as she got her shoes on, she hurried to the bedroom door and pulled it open, all but running through it without even looking.

"Van— No!" Michael shouted, jumping back from the other side of the door.

But it was too late.

She'd been in so much of a rush, her momentum kept her barreling forward. She ran into Michael's chest and out of instinct, her hands went to his forearms to catch her, or him, she didn't know.

What she did know was that he screamed, "Don't fucking touch me!" and yanked back from her so violently she stumbled and fell to her knees.

And then he stood there above her, his entire body shaking and his eyes wide with horror—she didn't know if from her touch or from seeing her on the floor.

They both froze there for a beat.

One.

Two.

Three.

"Michael—" she whispered but he just shook his head back and forth violently and then spun on his heel and ran down the hallway.

"Michael, wait!"

He didn't stop.

She got to her feet, wincing at what would probably be bruised knees, and hurried after him. But the front door was slamming before she even got to the end of the hallway.

"Dammit," she yelled, kicking the back of the couch. Which only gave her a sore toe in addition to her sore knees.

She scrubbed her hands down her face.

Just give him a little time to cool off. Tonight after she got back from her time with the girls, she'd talk to him. They'd find a way to work this out. They had to.

She glanced at the schedule posted on the wall. They all worked such different hours and shifts, it was the only way to keep things straight. Even she'd gotten a job working a few afternoons a week at the school, teaching a survivalist course.

It looked like tonight was one of the nights all of their schedules would align so they'd get to have dinner all together, a rare occasion. Even Logan was off work. As to whether he'd show up, well, that was anyone's guess. When he wasn't at work, he seemed to spend all his time at Donovan's, the bar outside of town.

Vanessa sighed as she grabbed her keys, locking the door behind her.

Then she headed down the street to Audrey's house. The day was hot—shocker—but Audrey's house was shaded by several big oaks and with the windows open, it felt like a little oasis. Cooler than Vanessa's own house, especially when Sophia handed her a glass of lemonade with—

"Holy crap, is that ice?" Vanessa breathed out, holding the cold glass up to her cheeks, first one and then the other. "Oh my God, I want to marry this glass of lemonade."

Audrey laughed. "I know, right?"

"Shhh, Dad pulled some strings," Sophia said, ushering Vanessa into the living room where Drea, Shay, and several other women sat chatting. "Don't tell anyone about it. But some of the engineers in town just managed to hook up solar panels to what used to be this little Italian place."

"Okaaaaay," Vanessa said, not following.

"Not the whole place," Audrey clarified. "They're just routing power to the big walk in freezer in the back."

"Oh my God," Vanessa said again.

"Right?" Sophia said. "Come on in. Look, Camilla made bread pudding."

Vanessa smiled at her and she immediately looked down. She'd met Camilla before but the woman never said much. Vanessa had heard her story from Sophia, about how she'd been married to five abusive men who worked for Arnold Travis. Even thinking his name made Vanessa shudder.

She'd always stayed clear of Travisville but Lorenzo traded regularly with the man, and he wasn't running guns or stolen goods. Like Lorenzo, Travis specialized in the underground flesh trade.

So Vanessa felt sympathy for the quiet woman, having escaped that hell. She went over and sat down on the open spot on the couch beside her.

"Looks delicious, Camilla."

"Thanks." She flashed a shy smile Vanessa's way.

"Damn, girl," Drea said, looking Vanessa up and down. "You should take two pieces of the pudding. Are those boys stealing all your rations or what?"

"Drea!" Sophia exclaimed.

"What?" Drea said. "Are you not seeing what I'm seeing?" She gestured at Vanessa's body. "She looks as skinny as the day they brought her into town. I thought they were supposed to give you clan families extra rations."

Vanessa crossed an arm over her stomach. Damn. She knew she hadn't been putting on weight like she should but she didn't think it was so obvious.

"Anyway," Sophia said, glaring Drea down. "Camilla's helping me at the Food Pantry a couple days a week."

Drea shook her head but then introduced the other woman sitting on the couch by her. "This is Kylie. She's new to town too."

Kylie was beautiful. She had the kind of curves Vanessa couldn't help but be envious of. Along with long hair so dark brown it almost looked black.

"Hi," Vanessa said, reaching out a hand to shake. "I'm Vanessa.

Great to meet you. I can't believe I missed news of your lottery. Is Sophia helping you plan the wedding?"

Kylie shook Vanessa's hand but her face shuttered at the question and she let go quickly. "No. I had the option of staying free, so I took it."

Vanessa frowned, and she looked to Sophia and then Drea, each of whom had opposite expressions on their faces at Kylie's pronouncement.

"I don't underst—"

"I had an ectopic pregnancy when I was really young, okay," Kylie said, face hard like she expected a fight. "It ruined my tubes so no babies for me."

"If you can't get pregnant, then there is a loophole in the lottery law," Audrey explained gently, a hand on Kylie's shoulder. "You have a choice as to whether you'd like to enter a lottery, or if you'd rather…"

Kylie's eyes flashed Vanessa's way. "Or if you'd rather take random dick whenever you feel like it. Which I'd much rather do than be shackled to five dudes for life. You got a problem with that like all those other bitches in town?"

Vanessa shook her head no, lifting her hands up. "No, no problem."

"The whole system is barbaric," Drea said, and Vanessa could tell she was gearing up for one of her rants. "We aren't fucking cattle. We should be treated with resp—"

Sophia rolled her eyes. "Yeah, yeah, here," she shoved a plate Drea's direction. "Why don't you do something useful with your mouth for once and eat some bread pudding?"

Drea glared Sophia down. "Someday, Princess, you're gonna wake up and realize that you can't just blindly swallow everything Daddy says as gospel. I *really* hope I'm there to see it."

Sophia rolled her eyes again, with even more exaggeration. "Oh please. It just kills you that there are actually good men out there. You'd love to just hate them all. But my dad's one and take a look around this room." Sophia gestured at Audrey, Shay, and Vanessa. "Three women here are happily married, so that's *fifteen* good men. Sixteen, counting Dad. Sort of shoots holes in your whole all-men-are-evil theory, huh?"

Vanessa busied herself with scooping out a portion of bread pudding. She agreed that her husbands were good men. As for the happily married part, though...

"How's it been going, Vanessa?" Audrey cut in, obviously trying to diffuse the tension between Sophia and Drea. "Shay was just telling us she's finally settling in and whipping her men into shape."

There was light laughter from all the women and Vanessa looked up, pasting what she hoped looked like an appropriately cheerful smile for a newlywed bride. "Oh it's going great. There's all those personalities to get used to, you know," she waved a hand. "But it's great. *Really* great."

God, how many times could she say *great* in the same breath? *Kill me now*, she thought.

Sophia clapped her hands like a little girl just presented with a pony. "Oooo, I can't wait for my lottery! It's just two months away now. I already have my dress picked out. And Rebecca is going to play the flute at the reception. She used to play in the Austin Philharmonic, you know? And Shay, you've been making remarkable progress with Jonas. If you keep it up, he'll probably even be sober for my wedding!"

"Oh my God, do you even hear yourself?" Drea asked, thudding her forehead repeatedly into her palm.

"You know," Sophia cocked a hand on her hip, "if you made even the *smallest* effort to be pleasant, people wouldn't run the other direction when they saw you coming. I literally saw Mrs. Morris do an about-face the other day when she saw you go into the General Store in front of her."

"Oh, because being *pleasant* is my whole job requirement as a female, right?"

"Ladies!" Audrey said, hands up, stepping in between the two women. "Love you both, babes, so how about we take it down a notch? We have iced tea, sweet treats, and Sophia, you offered to trim our hair, right? We thought we'd all have a little spa afternoon. So let's *relax*, kick back, and enjoy ourselves. Okay?"

Sophia's eyes were still flashing as she looked Drea's way but she huffed out a breath and stepped back, crossing her arms over her chest. "Of course. That's what I want, too. Just don't expect me to touch that rat's nest." She gestured at Drea's dreadlocks.

"Like I'd let you anywhere near me with a sharp implement."

Audrey looked exasperated and Drea held her hands up and offered a quick, "Sorry," to the room before sitting down on the chair furthest from Sophia. "Look, *relaxed*. I'm relaxed."

"Oh, don't stop on my account," Kylie said, spooning off a big bite of bread pudding. "This is the most entertainment I've had all week."

Everybody laughed at that and the mood lightened.

"All right, so who's up first?" Sophia asked, moving over to the dining room table where she had scissors and several other hair-cutting implements all set up.

Tentatively, Vanessa raised her hand. "Do you think you could do anything with, well," she gestured up at the uneven, furry mop on her head, "*this?*"

"Step right up!" Sophia said. "Sophia's beauty parlor is officially open for business."

————

Several hours later, Vanessa was hugging all the women goodbye in Audrey's foyer.

"Thank you again, Sophia." Vanessa's hand went to her hair. It was all she could do not to run back in and check the mirror again.

Sophia had turned the goofy puff ball on her head into a sleek pixie cut. Then Sophia had gone on and on about how with Vanessa's high cheekbones, she now looked *model chic*. That girl could make a snaggle-toothed hippo feel beautiful, Vanessa would swear.

Both Sophia and Drea had such big, strong personalities, Vanessa suspected that if only they could get past their differences, they'd be fast friends. Then again, that was a big *if*.

"It was great to meet you, Kylie."

"You too," Kylie gave Vanessa a warm hug.

Vanessa blinked, a little startled by the woman's easy affection. After going so long without human contact, an afternoon like today was something of a revelation. *Friends*. What a crazy concept.

The whole afternoon had put her in a much more cheerful frame of mind. Being around such strong, powerful women—it made her feel like she could do anything.

So she'd run into a few snags the last few weeks. So what? It was still early days. She and her clan could still figure this out. There was time.

With honesty, openness, and a little elbow grease, they could make a marriage out of this whole thing yet.

She jogged up the steps of her own porch and grabbed the door, full of optimism. Only to find the door locked.

Well that was strange. The twins should have been home already. Cam too. And Michael...

Her stomach dropped, thinking of her run-in with Michael earlier.

She'd accidentally come close to touching him a few times before. Nothing like what happened earlier, but still. He'd always just brushed it off and everything went back to normal. She never treated him differently. He knew how she felt about him, right? Right?

She pulled her key out of her pocket and unlocked the door.

When she walked into the house, it was quiet. As in, completely silent.

She frowned. "Hello?" she called. "Anybody home?"

No response. What on earth? She looked at the schedule by the door. Nope, she hadn't misread it earlier. Everybody was supposed to be home. Hours ago.

The sun was dropping low in the sky, maybe an hour and a half from sunset. It was late summer, so that meant it was probably around eight-thirty.

"Hello? Ross? Riordan?" She walked into the kitchen, then to the back door. Maybe they were all out back cooking? Usually only one of them went out at a time because it got so hot. But when she looked out back, no one was standing around the cook circle. No kindling had been set, it was just as clean as it had been after clearing out the embers from this morning's meal.

Okay, seriously, what was going on?

"Cam?" she called, walking down the hall. "Logan?" Were they washing up?

But there was no one in any of the bedrooms.

She walked back out to the living room, baffled. Had all their respective jobs needed them to work overtime, just by coincidence. Or were they together for some reason? If they were, why hadn't they left a note?

She looked again to the board but it looked the same as it had when she left.

Just when she was going to throw her hands up and start considering alien abductions, the front door opened.

"Cam," she exclaimed hurrying over to him. He was in scrubs and he looked exhausted. "Thank God. Where have you been?" Okay, dumb question. He'd obviously been at work. "Do you know where everyone else is?"

He stood up straighter and looked around. "The twins aren't here?"

"No. Why?"

He blew out a breath and his head dropped back. "Ugh, those *idiots*."

"What?"

"We all got home a couple hours ago and they got into it saying we needed more meat. So they thought it'd be a great idea to go hunting."

"What?" Vanessa's mouth dropped open. "But— But—" She was at a loss for words for a full ten seconds. "That's what the town has the professional hunting party for!" she finally got out.

"Yeah well, they felt like we haven't been getting enough protein." He dragged a hand through his hair. "You aren't gaining weight. It's worrying all of us."

Oh no. No no no no. Ross and Riordan went off all half-cocked because of *her*? She thought of the box she'd buried at the back of the closet. Her secret box. The one she hadn't been able to get rid of no matter how many times she'd tried to convince herself she didn't need it. And now the twins were...

"Still, it's no excuse to go running off to the Neutral Zone like a couple of—"

"The *Neutral Zone*?" she gasped. "Like between here and Travisville?"

"I told them not to go," Cam growled. "I would have tied them to the damn porch if I had to, but I got called away on an emergency C-section. Mrs. Gonzalez had the twins and I couldn't stall. I came back as soon as I could."

Audrey put a hand to her stomach. "I think I'm going to be sick." She knew exactly how dangerous the neutral zone could be—Colonel Travis's men were vicious. Hadn't they stopped to think that they weren't the only one's who'd come up with the bright idea of hunting in the neutral zone? It was probably crawling with smugglers and poachers skirting the edge of Central Texas South.

"We have to go after them." The second she said it, she started to feel calmer.

Okay, first things first. She'd need a pack. Some rations. A blanket because she'd probably end up spending the night out—

"Are you crazy?" Cam grabbed her elbow as she tried to move past him toward the coat closet where they kept the camping equipment. "It's almost sundown. You can't just go after them."

She jerked her arm out of Cam's grasp and glared him down. It was her fault they were out there. No way was she going to let them get hurt or...

"I'm going," she said, voice icy. "Either you come with me, or you get out of my way."

CHAPTER THIRTEEN

ROSS

Three Hours Earlier

Riordan was in a bad mood the second he walked in the door after work. But that was nothing new. Riordan had been in a bad mood for a decade, it seemed to Ross. Longer, maybe.

"What the hell are you doing with Dad's crossbow?" Riordan asked, wiping his sweaty brow and going straight for the water jug they kept on the kitchen counter.

Ross barely glanced up from the bag he was packing. Okay, he had his compass, map, the bow, provisions in case he was out longer than he intended to be, and of course, water. Then he had the wilderness survival kit he always had packed as part of his Eagle Scout training, along with the first aid kit. No matter what he faced out there, he'd be ready.

Ready for everything except his brother's interrogation.

Ross tried to skirt around Riordan but Riordan just got in his way. "Where do you think you're going?"

"Hunting, okay? I'm going hunting."

Riordan narrowed his eyes and Ross sighed. "Vanessa's not gaining enough weight. The tiny bit of meat rations and few eggs we get a week aren't cutting it. I want to go get something more substantial for her."

The plan had come to him while he'd been up on the Ruiz's roof hammering down new shingles.

Vanessa had changed everything.

Ross hadn't known life could be like this. She was kind and funny and caring. She didn't talk down to him even though she was almost five years older.

Then there was the bedroom stuff. It wasn't every night but often enough, she'd pull that silky nightgown off over her head and pull him, Riordan and Cam to her after the lights were off.

And the way she touched him—God, he'd thought that first night was good. But it was nothing to the way it felt to sink into the warmth of her hot, wet—

"That hard-on mean you're thinking about Vanessa or how impressed Ghost will be if you manage to bring back a possum or rabbit like a good little Boy Scout?"

Ross huffed out a frustrated breath and shoved the map into his pack before closing it. "Do you always have to be such a douche?"

Riordan shrugged. "Just sayin'. It's pathetic the way you drool for Ghost's attention when he clearly couldn't give less of a shit about any of us."

"That's not true," Ross couldn't help firing back. "And stop calling him that. Logan's not a ghost." Ghosts were dead people. Like Dad. Ross shuddered even at the thought.

Riordan just smiled smugly, knowing he'd hit a sore spot.

Then Riordan downed a huge cup of water, slammed it empty on the counter, then clapped his hands loudly. "Okay, so where are we going on this little adventure?"

"What little adventure?" Cam asked, coming in the front door.

"We're going hunting."

"No," Ross said, "*I'm* going hunting."

Riordan scowled at him. "Look, I know you love being the center of attention, Mr. Perfect, but you're going to have to share the glory this time. I'm coming with you."

What—? Riordan baffled him sometimes.

Ross never went out of his way to be the center of attention. He didn't like attention, actually. What he mainly felt was afraid. Afraid of losing people he loved. Afraid of things slipping away. Afraid of failing people when they needed him.

Like Vanessa. He was supposed to provide for her. But she was still so skinny and gaunt. He wasn't doing his job. What if she got sick? Small as she was, what if she didn't have enough strength to fight off even the flu? The thought terrified him so much sometimes he couldn't sleep at night.

So today he'd decided to do something about it.

"You know hunting's regulated in the Territory," Cam said. "And poaching's illegal. Don't be stupid." He went to pour himself some water. "Fuck it's hot out there."

"Oh poor you," Riordan snapped. "Working inside at your cushy nursing job while we bust our asses all day outside doing manual labor."

Cam lowered his glass, clearly pissed, but Ross broke in before the two could start going at it. "Hunting isn't regulated in the Neutral Zone." He swore those two could barely stand to be in the same room as each other. And he thought *he'd* had a volatile relationship with his brother. Sheesh.

Cam just looked from Ross to Riordan and then back again. "Jesus, you two really are Tweedledee and Tweedledum. You looking to go get yourselves killed? They caught three smugglers coming into the Territory on the edge of the Neutral Zone just this month. And they were all armed to the fucking teeth."

"Fine." Riordan shrugged. "We'll take Logan's gun."

Whoa, hold up. Ross wasn't trying to put anyone in danger. "Maybe we should go by the licensing office and apply for a hunting license," he said uncertainly.

Riordan scoffed. "Don't let this asshole get in your head. It takes weeks for a license to go through. Vanessa needs the meat now."

He turned to Ross. "We'll be fine. He's just trying to scare you. Before all this I was planning to take off West. I was going to face way worse than the edge of the Neutral Zone. I'm ready for anything we face out there. Which will probably just be cacti and if things really get exciting, a snake or two."

"For fuck's sake," Cam said, "Don't be fucking—"

But a knock at the door cut him off. "I'll be right back." He pointed his finger in Riordan's face. "Don't go anywhere."

Riordan rolled his eyes and made a jacking off motion as Cam left to get the door.

Ross dropped his head into his hands.

"Be right back," Riordan said, then jogged out of the room.

Cam came back first, obviously in a rush. "They need me at the clinic, I have to go. You're a smart kid, Ross. Stay home. Promise me you will. For Vanessa's sake."

Ross didn't say anything. He didn't know what the right thing to do was.

After a long moment of silence, Cam just shook his head. "What the fuck ever. I tried. You two are grown ass men."

Then he turned and headed out the door, muttering under his breath and shaking his head the whole way.

Right as the door slammed, Riordan walked into the kitchen holding Logan's Glock with a huge smile on his face. "Locked, loaded, and ready to go."

"Jesus, put that thing away."

"Keep your panties on. I know what I'm doing with it." He tucked the gun into the back of his pants. "You might like playing with bows and arrows, but Dad taught me to shoot. Plus I got more practice last year when I did that semester of practical training with the Security Squadron."

Ross nodded uncertainly and swung his pack over his shoulders. Well, if they were just *borrowing* it... Still, as he followed Riordan out the door, he had a feeling he was going to regret this.

———

Ross glanced at the horizon and the setting sun and then back down at his map. They left home in the late afternoon and had spent the last two hours hiking. "Maybe we should head back and try again tomorrow."

"Jesus Christ, this was your idea in the first place. And now that there's the slightest hint of adventure, you wanna turn tail and run? You think Logan would turn back just because it was getting a little bit dark?"

Ross's jaw set. He usually considered himself a calm, peaceful guy. But no one could get under his skin like his brother.

It hadn't taken Ross long to realize that planning an expedition on paper, and doing it for real, were completely different things.

Their arms were scraped and burning from nettles, and their backs were sore from walking in stooped positions through the rough underbrush.

Even Ross's feet hurt.

The depressing truth was that for all their talk, neither he or Riordan had been more than ten miles from their home in Jacob's Well since they arrived seven years earlier. They'd lived comfortably. They stood in line for rations and bought their clothes at the General Store.

Ross stopped, yet again pulling out his compass. Ross squinted at the dial in the fading light. It was an heirloom from their late father, and it was still one of his most cherished possessions. Their father hadn't given Riordan anything but his temper.

Ross had the crossbow with a quiver of broadhead arrows strapped to his back. He'd felt like a legitimate hunter when they'd headed out, confident in his skill. But with each bird that they flushed out of the brush, he realized he'd never actually shot at a moving target before.

Riordan's attitude wasn't helping, either. Or the fact that when Ross said go left, Riordan went right. He'd started saying the opposite just to keep them on the right track. They'd been hugging the border to Central Texas South. Cam's talk about smugglers had rattled Ross more than he'd like to admit, so he figured sticking close to their home Territory was the best bet.

"Why do you have to do that?" Ross asked. "Pick on me like that?

And be so damn ornery all the time? We're out here for the same thing. To help Vanessa."

"Of course I want to help Vanessa. You think you're the only one that cares about her?"

"That's not what I s—"

"Just because I don't want to follow your bullshit rules every step of the way doesn't mean I care any less. Besides, the deer aren't following your stupid compass. They're just wandering around. It's fine if we wander too."

"You ever think it might be good to know where we are so, I don't know, when we want to head home we know where to go?" Ross couldn't keep the sarcasm out of his voice. Usually he tried not to stoop to Riordan's level but he was hot and he was tired.

Riordan rolled his eyes. "Stop being overdramatic. You're so obsessed with doing things the *right* way. Jesus, you must be constantly constipated having that stick up your ass all the time. Have a little imagination. Live a little."

"Besides, we've been walking west." Riordan pointed at the sun. "So we go back east. Worst case scenario we head north and hit the Blanco River and follow it back to town. It's not rocket science. If you'd take your eyes off that damn compass for three seconds, maybe we'd actually find something to fucking shoot."

"Maybe if you'd stop talking so much and making such a damn racket," Ross whispered, "we'd find something to shoot."

He was really not in the mood to stand here and have Riordan go on and on about imagination and what it meant to *live*.

Ross knew plenty well what it meant to live. It meant not fucking dying. And if following rules meant he felt a little safer, so what?

Riordan smirked, shaking his head like Ross was a child. "All I'm saying is that great men never made history by coloring inside the lines or following the rules."

"I'm not trying to be a great man or make history!" Ross tossed his hands up. "I'm just trying to feed our wife. So how about we both shut up and try to find some damn deer, sound like a plan?"

Riordan just huffed out a sardonic laugh. "The shutting up part sounds great to m—" He cut off mid-word, his eyes going wide.

Then he laid his index finger vertically across his lips and pointed silently into the thick oak forest, mouthing, *Hog.*

Ross looked in the direction Riordan was pointing then nodded. There, off in the distance, was indeed a hog. It wasn't in the northwesterly direction Ross had wanted to go, but if they could get a quick kill, it wouldn't matter.

Ross checked the breeze and positioned them so it was in their face. Hogs had good noses but shitty eyesight. If they were lucky, they could sneak up on it.

Quietly, they crept through the brush, following the path of rounded hoof prints and listening as the snuffling and rooting sounds grew louder. They finally had a good view of the large, hairy sow digging in a patch of mud by the base of a broken fence.

Ross pulled the crossbow off his back and quietly placed his foot in the stirrup. He pulled the string back until it cocked. When he had that right, he loaded an arrow into the barrel and tried to ignore the pounding in his ears.

Follow the front legs up, Ross went through the instructions he'd memorized from the book Dad gave him. *Then strike mid-chest.*

He brought the crossbow to his shoulder and steadied the bow. He exhaled slowly, taking his aim. Then, the second before he could pull the trigger, a loud *boom* sounded from beside him. Followed by ear-piercing squeals.

What the—

Riordan was standing beside him holding the gun out.

"Well don't just stand there!" Riordan yelled. "It's getting away!"

Riordan ran in the direction of the fleeing pig, a heavy blood trail in its wake. For a second, Ross could only stare. Oh, God...the blood. He choked down the urge to vomit and raced after his brother.

Twenty minutes later, they were tired. It was dark. But they found their prize. She was sizable—at least one hundred and fifty pounds. She'd feed the clan for weeks.

That was, if not for one *teensy* logistical matter they hadn't adequately considered.

"How do we get it home?" Riordan asked.

Ross bristled, as irritated with the question as he was with Riordan for shooting the damn pig when he had a shot perfectly lined up. Maybe if Riordan would have just let him take the shot, they wouldn't have had to chase the damn sow all over creation and wouldn't be who the hell knew where.

Not to mention the other problems.

Should they butcher it here and wrap up the meat? Try to make some sort of litter and drag her dead weight home? It would probably take them all the next day.

One other problem... The longer Ross stared at their kill and the bloody wound on its shoulder, the more lightheaded he was getting.

He turned around to cover the fact he was about to have the dry heaves. What kind of hunter got sick at the sight of blood?

He never had a chance to find out because right then, a raspy voice filled the darkening woods.

"Thanks for supper, boys. I was starving. And that loud gunshot letting me know exactly where to find you was mighty helpful too."

CHAPTER FOURTEEN

LOGAN

"Thank God, you're home, Logan," Cam said as soon as Logan walked in the door. "You can talk some sense into her."

Logan frowned when he saw Vanessa tugging the straps of a hiking backpack over her shoulders. The damn thing looked heavier than she was.

"What's going on?"

Cam quickly explained and Logan couldn't keep a lid on his temper. "They did WHAT?!"

"Exactly," Vanessa said. "Which is why we have to go after them. It's almost dark out and who knows what trouble they've gotten themselves into already."

"You aren't going anywhere," Logan snapped, running a hand through his hair. Goddammit.

The whole reason he'd married Vanessa in the first place was to watch over and protect her. Bang up job he was doing at that.

He hadn't even noticed she wasn't gaining weight like she should.

And if he hadn't come home to grab some more script for the damn bar, she would have gone off into the Neutral Zone!

But Jesus, none of it had gone like he planned when he'd headed to the church the morning of the wedding.

He'd never meant to fucking touch her. But he had. And the wedding night... Jesus, it haunted him.

Even sleeping down the hall in the same house was enough to keep him up at night. Especially knowing the twins and Cam were still enjoying her body every time the lights went out. In the mornings, they'd all have such smug, satisfied fucking smiles on their faces. The ridiculous jealousy was so thick sometimes he thought he'd fucking choke on it.

Jealous of *boys*.

So he spent as many hours as he could out of the house and when he had to be home, he kept his eyes off Vanessa as much as possible.

But now that he actually looked at Vanessa, *really* looked, Jesus Christ, they were right. She was little more than skin and bones. They had dinner together most nights, at least four times a week. Logan might not look at her straight on but surely he would have noticed if she wasn't eating. No, all the bowls were empty when dishes were done at the end of the night.

But what about breakfast and lunch? Vanessa always packed their lunch and they were always full. Stew. Bread or cornmeal. Sometimes bits of jerky. Occasionally an orange

The twins and Logan had to all weigh up to two hundred pounds with as big and built as they were and that required a lot of calories. Was she skimping on her own meals to give them more?

"If those idiots had concerns, they should have come to me and we could have discussed it as a clan."

"Because you've been around so much lately," Vanessa snapped, eyes furious. "And don't tell me what I can and can't do. I spent eight years out there. I know how to survive better than any of you."

Logan took a step toward her until they were toe to toe. "You are *not* going."

She laughed. Laughed right in his face.

"What authority do you think you have over me? It's the twenty-first century, buddy. Husbands don't get to tell their wives what to do. And even if they did, you barely count as a husband. You haven't even consummated the vows."

That was a low fucking blow, and by the flicker of regret in her eyes, she knew it, too.

It didn't stop her from lifting her chin and pushing past him, though.

"Goddammit," he swore, turning to look after her.

"Well what the hell are you waiting for?" Cam asked. "We have to go with her." He strode after Vanessa.

"Fine," Logan growled. It looked like apart from physically restraining her, there was no stopping their wife. "Just let me go get my—"

"Gun?" Cam asked. "Oh, did I forget to mention those geniuses took your Glock?"

"Son of a—"

"Come on," Cam said. "If we don't hurry, she's gonna leave us in the dust."

Logan growled out several more swear words as he watched Vanessa disappear out the front door. The very sight sent his heartbeat racing so loud he felt seconds away from a heart attack. Sweat beaded at his temple.

No. No, she couldn't leave.

He couldn't let her leave.

He had to stop her—

He had to—

And all of a sudden, he wasn't standing in the clan house and it wasn't Vanessa he was watching walk out the door.

"Logan, stop being so goddamned stubborn."

He was stubborn? Jenny thought he was being stubborn? "It's just a little infection. The fever will burn it off."

"That fever is going to fry your brain, and the ibuprofen isn't working."

He opened his eyes and looked up. She loomed over where he lay on the couch, her hands on her hips. Never a good sign.

Logan groaned and closed his eyes again. "So now you're a doctor?" The words came out raspy, and he gasped for breath. Damn. Now it was affecting his lungs? How could a little tooth cause so much trouble, abscessed or not?

"Don't cop an attitude with me, mister. I may not be a doctor, but I got more good sense than you've got in whatever brain cells you have left. You wait any longer, and you're going to be dead."

"It's just a little—"

She kicked the foot of the couch, and Logan felt it in his spine. "Infection. Yeah, I know. And that little infection has probably already spread. Burying a husband is not what I call a good time."

Logan grimaced. There were more new burial mounds in Austin than he cared to count, but they were wives, mothers, girlfriends, and daughters buried under all that dirt. Nothing was going to happen to him. He was going to beat this, then he could be the strong one again. He hated to see her worrying.

"Listen," Jenny said, exhaling and obviously preparing to play her last card. He could feel the determination brewing up in her, the way she lifted her chin... "I've heard of a clinic in San Angelo."

San Angelo? Was she crazy? San Angelo was a four hour drive away. "What about the penicillin tea you were talking about making? Have the oranges started growing mold yet?"

Jenny didn't listen. She kept on talking. "This clinic has a supply of penicillin —the real kind—and the doctor's not charging an arm and a leg for it. Yet..."

Logan winced against the pain and turned his head into the couch cushions. "I'm not going to San Angelo."

"Of course you're not. You're in no condition to travel. I'm going."

Logan's eyes snapped wide. "You sure the fuck are NOT!"

Jenny leaned down and got in his face. "You can barely get to the toilet to piss. You think you're going to stop me?"

Logan tried to push himself up. His body felt like it weighed a metric ton. "Jenny, I swear to God, you set one foot outside this house—"

"And you'll what?" She folded her arms. Damn this woman.

"I've kept you safe and quarantined inside this house for months, and the virus hasn't touched you. I'm not worth the risk. You're not going out there."

"You are the only risk worth taking. You are my husband. I love you. And I will fight for you, Logan Washington, until I stop breathing."

Logan pushed himself up to one elbow, and his head spun. "Which is exactly what will happen. I forbid you to leave. You heard what they said on the radio. The mortality rate is now sixty percent. You are not risking those odds."

"Oh, but it's fine for you to risk your life?" she asked. She marched to the kitchen and started slamming around the pots and pans.

"It's just a damn tooth. Get me the pliers. I'll pull the damn thing out myself." Logan got himself to a sitting position and he swung his feet over the side of the couch, placing them on the floor. Or, at least he thought he had. He couldn't actually feel the floor. He stood, stumbled a few steps. His head seemed to separate and float away from his body. The next thing he knew, the floor was racing up toward his face. He didn't even get his hands up to catch his fall.

Jenny screamed, and Logan felt the floor vibrate as she fell to her knees beside him. "Are you all right? Jesus, honey. Are you okay?"

Logan jerked away from her touch, grumbling. "Make me the tea. I'll be fine."

Jenny didn't respond right away. He waited. He expected her to say something. She was never happy unless she got the last word. But she rose silently to her feet and walked away.

Logan crawled back onto the couch and, a few minutes later, Jenny returned with the tea. He swallowed the disgusting concoction and fell asleep. When he awoke, he didn't know how much time had gone by. The house was silent and on the floor beside the couch, in a place where he couldn't miss it, lay a note from Jenny.

She was gone. She risked her life for him. And she never came home.

And the mortality rate was higher than sixty percent. So much higher. It was *ninety* percent. And she'd just walked out the door.

The fucking kicker of it all?

The goddamned penicillin tea worked.

Within two days, he was up and walking again. He waited a week and a half for her to come home, agonizing every fucking day about whether to go after her or stay and wait for her to return. What if she came back and he was gone?

But after ten days of waiting, he couldn't fucking stand it anymore. The virus took more women every day and the Death Riots were only getting worse. Day and night, nightmarish visions of what could be happening to Jenny flashed through his head.

Jenny had taken the car, but Logan was desperate. He stole a neighbor's truck and made his way on the clogged roads toward San Angelo.

It took him a week and a half to get there. Gas stations all along the way were shut down. They'd run out of gas and weren't getting restocked because refill tankers feared rioters. Occasionally Logan would see a battalion of National Guard, but they were few and far between.

After his truck sputtered out, Logan covered the last fifty miles on foot.

Finally he got to San Angelo and the city looked like hell on earth. Thick black smoke filled the air from fires that burned freely—one entire strip mall was in flames. On another street, Logan saw a guy hawking men and women who were locked in a long row of cages behind him, like some sort of human kennel.

Logan had run across the street and thrown up, both at realizing what human beings were capable of and at the fact that Jenny might have come here.

Jenny was all that mattered, though, so he put his head down and after a day and a half of asking around and following dead end after dead end, he finally, *finally* tracked down the only dealer in town who supposedly sold penicillin.

There was no clinic like Jenny had talked about. Just a small mouse of a man covered in tattoos with a mustache and bloodshot eyes.

And he'd been out of penicillin for weeks.

The dealer remembered Jenny though. He said he'd tell Logan what he'd told Jenny, but only for a price.

Logan offered him everything in his wallet—four hundred dollars—but the man wasn't interested. He'd laughed and said money wasn't worth the paper it was printed on anymore. No, he wanted Logan's gold watch.

It had been Logan's father's, but Logan took it off and handed it over without hesitation.

"North Austin," the guy said, taking a long drag on a cigarette as he lifted the watch close, slowly examining it. "Little pharmacy in Pflugerville."

He dropped the watch on the counter and grinned. "I'm feelin' generous. The thought of reuniting true lovers and all that shit. So I'll give you the address... If you give me your shoes."

Logan wanted to punch his fucking face in but he bit his rage back.

"This the same address you gave Jenny?"

The guy nodded, smarmy grin still on his face.

Logan gritted his teeth and took off his shoes, slamming them on the counter. They were nothing too fancy. Just a pair of Nikes that he'd bought before the world went to shit.

"Nice doing business with you."

The guy scribbled an address on a Post-it Note and Logan marched out of the shop in just his socks. He didn't fucking care. He'd crawl on his knees back to Austin if that was what it took to get home to Jenny.

But two days later, D-Day happened.

Austin was wiped off the map.

Between Xterminate and D-Day, he knew Jenny was gone.

Because he'd failed her.

Over and over again.

She'd died because of him.

So there was no way in fucking hell he'd let another woman under his protection walk off into danger without him by her goddamned side.

———

Logan, Cam, and Vanessa headed out of town on their two-up ATV, following the hunting path. Vanessa sat beside Logan. Cam stood on the back end, hanging onto the roll bar. Michael was nowhere to be found. Vanessa said something about having a misunderstanding with him earlier in the day but there wasn't time to hear any more about it.

They took the wheels as deep into the woods as they could, and then they had to continue on foot. Logan had a rifle he'd borrowed from Nix slung over his shoulder.

When Vanessa tripped over a tree root, Logan caught her in his strong arm, quickly righting her on her feet.

"You should go back to the four-wheeler. Wait for us there," Cam said.

"Cam's right," Logan said. "We'll take it from here."

Vanessa made an outraged noise. "Did we not cover this back at the damn house? Which of the three of us survived in the wilderness for years at a time?"

Logan only barely bit back the retort on the tip of his tongue. They were *twice* her size. If they ran across a bobcat, it could swallow her in a single damn bite.

"There, look," Vanessa said, pointing her flashlight at a muddy spot near a broken fence. The sun had just set and Logan didn't know how she'd even spotted it. But the closer he looked, he saw what she meant. The dry grass was stained a dark reddish brown. It wasn't mud like he'd first assumed. "That's blood. They must have got something."

"All right," Logan said, walking closer, "assuming it *was* them. But there's no drag mark. The animal must have run."

"You don't think they would have followed it deeper into the neutral zone, do you?" Cam asked, looking out at the large expanse of land to the east. The same direction the blood trail went.

"Would *you* follow it, Vanessa?" Logan asked.

"Yes," she said, eyebrows pinched with worry. "If I was hungry or desperate enough."

"Then they followed it. Come on."

They hiked for another half hour when they noticed the smell of a campfire.

Logan held a hand up for them to stop and put a finger to his lips. Both Vanessa and Cam nodded that they got the point. No talking.

Logan crept forward, the others right behind him.

It could be the twins. If they'd caught up to the animal, they might have decided to butcher it on the spot. The meat wouldn't keep long without ice.

But as they neared a small clearing, it was quickly apparent what had happened. A hog's skin and innards were burning on the fire while an enormous man with an eye patch over his left eye hunkered over the carcass.

And right behind him?

Ross and Riordan were both gagged and tied to a large oak tree.

Ross's eyes look haunted in the firelight, and Logan soon understood why.

The smuggler had dumped his pack—likely filled with weapons, judging by those the Security Squad had previously intercepted—and he was still butchering the hog, describing his work in detail.

"You gots to take off the front legs," he said, as he drove through them with his axe. "Tough work. It'll be tougher when I get to the two of y'all. A man's innards don't smell the same on the fire, either. Bacon's just as good, though. Y'all look like good eatin'.'"

Vanessa made a small pip of a noise, and Cam slapped his hand over her mouth.

They hadn't come as heavily armed as the smuggler, but Logan had the rifle, and Vanessa and Cam both had hunting knives. Logan felt confident he could get the upper hand with a little wit thrown in.

"Cam. Cause a distraction at the other end of the clearing. Get him to move away from his weapons. Then I can hold him at bay while you untie the boys."

"*I'll* get the twins untied," Vanessa said.

"No fucking way," Cam said.

"*What?* Why?" she asked.

Enough. Enough was *enough*.

She was reaching to pull out her knife but Logan stopped her, cupping her cheeks in his hands. Jesus, she was so tiny. His hands practically engulfed her.

"We don't risk you, that's why," he hissed. "Don't you get it? You mean too much to all of us. If something happened to you, you think Ross could live with himself? Or Riordan? Would you do that to them? Without any one of us, the clan goes on. But you're the glue. You hold us together."

Vanessa's eyes searched his back and forth. "You're wrong," she whispered, her voice barely audible as she shook her head. "It's you. We haven't been right since you left us."

Her words hit him like a sucker punch. Jesus.

He pulled her head down and pressed a quick kiss to her forehead. "Go back to the four-wheeler, baby. Please. For me."

When he pulled back, her lips trembled like she was fighting back emotion, but she nodded.

With that assurance, Logan nodded at Cam, who crept around the perimeter of the clearing. Logan waited to see what he'd do and, even though he was expecting something, he flinched right along with Ross and Riordan when a bush started to rustle. Christ, he was feeling so jumpy. It wasn't like him.

That's because it matters. These people are important to you.

"Who's there?" the smuggler asked, standing up. Jesus, he was colossal. He had at least six inches on Logan, and that was saying something.

The smuggler grabbed a flaming stick from the fire and stalked toward the sound, holding the torch in front of him for light. Before he got too close to where Cam lay hidden, Logan charged into the clearing and raised his rifle. "Stop!"

The smuggler stopped, then turned slowly, arms out.

"You've taken something that belongs to me," Logan said.

The smuggler chuckled. "Everyone's a scavenger out here in the bush. You want one of the hams? Fine by me. I can't carry it all back anyway."

"I was talking about my boys," Logan said, tipping his head toward the tree.

"Your—?" The smuggler glanced toward the auburn-haired twins as if he'd momentarily forgotten about them.

"Those boys are my family," Logan said. "And I don't take kindly to anyone who fucks with my family."

Cam entered the clearing from behind the smuggler and moved to the tree to untie the boys. When he cut through the ropes, they both fell forward onto their hands and knees.

"Tie him up," Logan said, directing Cam, while the twins struggled to get to their feet.

Cam made short work of it and as soon as he was done, Logan leaned his weapon up against a tree.

Ross and Riordan clawed at the dirty rags that gagged them and looked back and forth across the clearing as if they were searching for something.

"Relax, boys," Logan said. "I'll save the tongue lashing till we get home."

Then he saw the smug expression on the bound smuggler's face—right as Riordan finally got his gag off and yelled, "Behind you!"

Logan swung around right in time to see a second man snag the gun from the smuggler's pack and cock it. He aimed it straight at Logan's head. "Everyone, line up!"

Logan's heart hit his gut.

Another fucking fatal mistake.

He'd just led them all to slaughter. Was Vanessa far enough away? Please God let her be halfway back to the four-wheeler by now.

What if these animals find her, too?

She'll die.

Just like Jenny.

And it will be your fault again. Oh God. What had he done?

Logan, Cam, and the twins lined up in a straight line at the smuggler's orders. Logan's mind raced. He could lunge for the gun. Even if he got shot, Cam and the twins would still have a chance. If they moved quick enough. It would really only work if he could signal them what he was planning. Cam was former Security Squadron, he might pick up on it.

"What should I do, Jack? Plow them all down together, or make them watch their *family* go down one at a time?"

"NO!" Logan yelled, but it wasn't at the smuggler.

Vanessa dropped from the trees right over the smuggler's head, landing on the man's back like a spider monkey.

One second, she held a knife at his neck. The next second, a long scarlet ribbon split across his throat. His eyes and mouth opened in shock, and then he sunk to his knees.

Vanessa landed gracefully on her feet while blood spilled from the smuggler's neck. Another second, and he face planted onto the saturated ground.

Even though it wasn't the first time he'd seen her kill someone, for a second, Logan was just as shocked as the rest of his clan.

Ross's eyes rolled back in his head and he fainted.

More than shocked, though, Logan was furious. He'd told her to go back to the ATV. She'd fucking promised. What was she—

Movement off to his left had him swinging around right in time to see the first smuggler taking advantage of the momentary lapse in everyone's attention to yank away from Cam's grip and start running into the darkness, hands still tied together.

Vanessa saw it too. And with the same lethal swiftness, she grabbed the gun that had fallen from the smuggler's hand. She obviously knew how to handle it, holding both arms out, one hand on the gun's handle and the other underneath, bracing it.

She lined up her shot.

"Vanessa," Logan yelled, lunging forward and shoving her arms down the second before she squeezed the trigger.

"What are you—" she started but Logan was done. So beyond done.

"What the hell do you think *you're* doing?" he yelled. He yanked the gun from her hands and her mouth dropped open like he was crazy.

"He's getting away!" she shouted, looking after Jack.

"You think shooting him in the back is the answer?" Logan shoved the gun in the back of his pants.

"He's a fucking *cannibal*!" she shouted, shoving Logan in the chest.

Logan grabbed her wrists and pulled her close. Her words only reminded him of how dangerous it had been for her to come back for them. "Which is why you should have never come back in the first place!"

Her mouth dropped open. "I saved all of your lives, you stupid oaf. You would have died!" She yanked her wrists, struggling to get free, but Logan wasn't about to let her go.

"I had a plan. You should have trusted me."

She stopped struggling for a moment to scoff. "What plan?"

"I was going to rush him. The others could have used the opportunity to get the gun and—"

"You would have let him shoot you," she whispered, a sharp contrast to her furious shouting moments before.

"It probably wouldn't have come to that," Logan said. "I probably could have gotten the gun away from him and—"

She ripped one of her wrists out of his grasp and then slapped him hard across the face. "How fucking dare you?" she shrieked, back to full volume. "You're mad at me for coming back when I had a plan to save us all that wouldn't get anyone hurt and—"

"You didn't know it wouldn't get you killed," Logan shouted. He let go of her wrists and grabbed her shoulders, giving her the slightest shake. "When will you get it through your head? You're too important. You're— You're—"

"What?" she asked, eyes searching his as she grabbed the fabric of the front of his shirt and went up on her tiptoes so she could get right up in his face. "What am I?"

"You're my fucking *wife*."

He wrapped his arms around her and yanked her close enough to feel all of her against him, warm, solid, and alive.

And then he gave into what he'd been wanting ever since he left her bed four weeks ago.

He kissed her so hard she'd feel it into next week.

CHAPTER FIFTEEN

VANESSA

Logan's devouring kiss was like a strike of lightning.

Shocking,

Electric.

Life-changing.

Vanessa groaned into his mouth and lifted her arms around his neck. Then she hopped up, wrapping her legs around his waist.

He caught her, one hand going under her ass, squeezing as he strode with her to one of the nearby trees.

They passed Cam as they went and Logan broke from her mouth only long enough to toss Cam the gun from the back of his pants.

"Anyone approaches, you shoot first and ask questions later."

Then his lips were back on hers. Consuming her.

He could have *died*. He'd been about to do more than risk his life. Charging at that psycho would have gotten him—

She ran her hands through his hair, nails scraping his scalp until she grabbed the sides of his head and dragged his head back from hers.

"Swear to me that you'll never think about doing something so idiotic ever again."

His eyes burned with lust and fury. "Just like you promised to go back to the four-wheeler?"

"Goddammit, why do you have to be so—"

"I know," he said, then cut her off with a kiss.

Oh God, she thought. They shouldn't be doing this. Not now. They needed to get the hell out of here. That one-eyed smuggler... *Jack*... He was—

But she couldn't bring herself to let go of Logan as their tongues dueled and he pressed her back against a tree.

Oh *God*, she could feel his hardness through his jeans. Her breath hitched and he kissed her harder, his hand moving from her ass up to squeeze her breast and then back down to her ass again.

Then he was unwrapping her legs.

She couldn't help whimpering at the loss of contact, but the next second, she felt his hand at the button of her jeans, and the bolt of heat that shot through her sex almost had her coming on the spot. Did this mean— Was he finally going to— Out here of all places?

She wasn't going to second guess it, though. She needed it. God, did she need it. She'd almost lost him.

She'd recognized Nelson. He traded regularly with Lorenzo, and Jack had been part of his crew back when she'd escaped. That eye patch Jack was wearing? She was the reason for it.

Jack had been on guard duty the night she'd escaped. He'd underestimated her. He came close, playing with one of his knives, describing in detail which cuts of meat he liked best, just like he had been with the twins. Which cuts of *human* meat.

He came so close, she'd head butted him, which had startled him into dropping the knife. One thing she'd say for Jack—he kept his knives sharp.

She sliced through the rope tying her hands and then, when Jack lunged for her, she stabbed him in the eye with his own knife.

Too bad she hadn't finished the job—back then or tonight— because to see Nelson about to— She shuddered, remembering how he'd held the gun at Logan's head. And Jack...that fucking psychopath...

He'll report back to Lorenzo. He'll tell Lorenzo he saw you.

But that was a worry for another day. If he was out here with Nelson, that meant he wasn't one of Lorenzo's crew anymore, so it would take him time to track Lorenzo down.

None of that mattered now.

Logan was alive and in her arms.

She was safe. Logan was alive. They were all alive. Alive, alive, *alive*.

Vanessa pushed Logan's fumbling hands away, yanked her belt free, then shoved her pants down. He was doing the same with his jeans.

The second she kicked off one leg of her pants, he grabbed her leg and hiked it around his waist.

He pressed her against the tree and she felt him—oh God she felt him. So hot and hard, right at the entrance of her sex.

There was a moment, the shortest moment where his eyes came to hers. He was breathing so heavily his huge chest pressed into hers with his every breath, and God, she loved the friction against her breasts.

But it was what she saw in his eyes that had her insides turning liquid. She saw the fear he'd had for her—the abject terror at the thought of losing her. There was lust, too, and just so much emotion, she was overwhelmed.

Also she saw a question there: did she want this?

"Yes," she whispered, reaching up to cup his face. "God, *yes*."

His face transformed then, lust burning away everything else in those expressive eyes of his. He reached down, grabbed her ass with both of his hands, squeezing and kneading her flesh.

And then he lunged forward, taking her with one powerful, sure thrust.

Vanessa cried out in pleasure and fullness. She ripped her shirt off over her head, undoing her bra with her next breath. Then she wrapped her arms around his neck so tight he might have trouble breathing.

She didn't fucking care. She needed to hold on to him with everything she had. She lifted her hips back and then dropped them down in rhythm with his thrust.

"Deeper," she cried. "Oh God, harder, Logan. Harder."

He wrapped one arm around her back to brace her so the tree bark wasn't so abrasive—he was so considerate in everything, even this animal haze of lust—and the other under her ass.

And then he let go of every inhibition.

He slammed into her over and over and fucking over. He kissed and suckled and bit at her neck and breasts. He growled filthy things in her ear.

"I'm gonna fuckin' destroy this cunt. This cunt is fuckin' mine, you hear me? Fuckin' *mine*. You're gonna walk funny tomorrow and every time you feel that soreness between your legs you're gonna remember this. Me right now. Fucking every other thought out of your head."

"Yes," she cried because it was the only thing she could say. "Yes. Yes, yes, *yes*."

In the quiet of the evening, apart from the smugglers' crackling fire, the slap of Logan's balls against her ass seemed to echo across the night.

Her orgasm rose so sharply all she could do was wrap her legs around him more tightly and hold on for dear life.

He must have felt it because his thrusts became even harder and more frantic. "Baby. Oh fuck, Vanessa. I— You—"

The pleasure rose.

Higher.

Then higher still.

Oh God, she'd never— Surely it had to—

But no, the wave crested even *higher*.

"Logan!" she cried as the blinding light burst outward.

He bit down on her shoulder and she dug her fingernails into his scalp as the light pulsed. One heartbeat.

Two.

Three.

Four.

Her and Logan, together in the light.

Annnnnnnnnnnnnnnd exhale.

The wave crested and dissipated, but she wasn't ready to let go. She stayed wrapped around Logan's body, breathing him in. She wasn't alone and she wouldn't let him run.

Even if he tried, she wouldn't let him run again. Not after this.

"Vanessa," he murmured, dropping the gentlest kisses up and down her neck. "My sweet, perfect Vanessa."

That was when the tears came.

He wasn't running.

This was real.

Still, she clung to him, face tucked into the crook of his neck, too afraid to break the spell.

"Well, okay, then," Cam said from behind them. "Looks like that's settled."

Logan chuckled against her neck. "We gotta get cleaned up and head back to town."

She shook her head, face still buried in his neck, because she couldn't bear to look in his eyes and know if Cam was right. Were things really settled?

Logan finally pried her away, cupping her cheeks. "Baby, look at me."

It was only after he said it that she realized she had her eyes squeezed shut. She opened them hesitantly.

He chuckled again. "Where's my Amazonian warrior? Fearless, jumping into battle without a thought for her own safety?"

"She's not real," Vanessa whispered. "She's pretend. I'm scared all the time, can't you see that? I'm always scared shitless."

He stopped smiling, sober as he met her gaze. "You don't have to be scared any more. I'm here."

"Are you?"

She saw him wince at the question, but she wasn't sorry she'd asked it. She needed to know, once and for all. Was he in or was he out? Because if he was in, it was time to be all in.

He understood what she was asking because he took his time answering, and when he did, it was with appropriate gravity.

"Yes." He expelled a heavy breath. "I can to let the past go. You and this clan are my future."

CHAPTER SIXTEEN

MICHAEL

This was why Michael didn't drink. After spending the entire day at Donovan's, the bar outside town, he'd stumbled home, lost all control, tripped, and fallen onto the dry grass in the backyard.

He hadn't felt much at the time. That had been the point, hadn't it? But now he was fairly conscious, and the prickling sensation of so many dry blades at his skin was unbearable. If he tried to move, it made matters worse.

"You were wrong, Mama," he whispered, staring up at the stars. Was she actually up there, in heaven, or was that just as much a lie as everything else?

Even as he thought it, he heard his mama's voice in his head. *You can do* anything *you set your mind to, Michael, you hear me?*

But she was wrong.

He could never be a husband to Vanessa. Not like she deserved. Not like he longed to be.

Of course when he'd told Mam she was wrong back then, she just shook her head. He'd barely been able to see her, he'd been crying so hard.

She'd been sick from the Xterminate virus for months and it was close to the end. They both knew it, no matter how much Michael kept trying to pretend she was going to turn the corner and start getting better any day.

He was a twenty-two year old man, but in that moment he felt six, helpless and wanting his mama to just take him in her arms and tell him everything was going to be okay. That she could make it all better.

"You're stronger than you think, baby. I've done you wrong, letting you shut yourself completely off from the world like you have."

"No, Mama, no." A tear dripped from his cheek onto her hand on the bed. It was the closest he could come to touching her. The thought only made him cry harder. More than anything he wanted to hold her in his arms. To comfort her like she deserved.

She just nodded. "It's true, though. There was no reason for you to stop going outside. To stop seeing people. Having friends."

"I have friends. I have a ton of friends online. They'll fix the power grid any day now and I can go back to—"

"Stop!"

Michael was taken aback by her sharp tone. And he felt terrible for making her upset when it was followed by a hacking cough. Especially when he saw blood trickling out of the corner of her mouth.

"Mama," he whispered, feeling more terrified than ever. He reached his hand toward her, stopping only inches from her face.

Godfuckingdammit! He couldn't even comfort his own mother! What the fuck use was he?

"Promise me, honey." As weak as she was, her bloodshot eyes were no less commanding as she stared him down. "Promise me." She gasped for breath. "One bite at a time." She broke into another coughing fit.

"Hush, Mama. Shhh, it's okay. You don't have to talk anymore. I'll be fine."

He held the glass with a straw to her mouth. Thank God he could stand touching glass—as long as it was perfectly smooth

She took a sip and then coughed more.

With every cough, Michael's chest tightened like the crank of a vice was being cinched tighter around his ribs.

"Promise," she wheezed as soon as she could talk again. *"Never give up. No matter—" Gasp. "How scared. One bite—"*

"I know, I know. The only way to eat an elephant is one bite at a time. I promise, Mama, I won't give up," he said, if only so she'd stop trying to talk. It exhausted her.

She relaxed at his words, sinking back against her pillow. *"Gonna hold you to that,"* she breathed out. *"From beyond the grave. Gonna hold you to it."*

Michael lifted a hand to swipe at his eye.

God, why was he thinking about all this right now?

For a long time, he thought he'd done his mama proud. She'd passed away only a few days after that conversation.

He still remembered it like it was yesterday.

There was no more food. He had one gallon of water left, but none after that. He'd faced a choice.

Either he could take the bottle of pain killers upstairs and join Mama in the afterlife.

Or he could open the front door and step outside for the first time in years.

Into the chaos he and Mama had been listening to for months. Gunshots. People screaming. It had died down a little in recent weeks, but Michael didn't have any illusions.

The world out there was scarier than it had ever been. And Mama expected him not only to walk out there, but to survive?

He went upstairs and stared at the bottle of pills for an entire day. He took the pills to bed with him and woke up and stared at them some more.

Then he thought about his promise to his mama.

He went to his closet and looked at the stacks of silk jerseys she'd stockpiled for him. She'd even found a silk backpack somewhere.

She knew this day would come and she'd been preparing for it all along.

And she'd believed he could do it.

It was that belief more than anything that had helped him take that first step. And the second, and the third.

One bite at a time, right?

It was probably a good thing that he hadn't had any clue just how gigantic the elephant would turn out to be.

But he'd done it. He'd survived. He'd made his way south from Dripping Springs, wandering for a few weeks, sticking close to the river so he'd have clean water. He was starving when he'd heard about the settlement in Jacob's Well from a family headed there.

Everything was terrifying.

Walking through the woods was torture—it was almost impossible to make it three steps without getting scratched at by some bush or bramble. So he stuck to roads. But those were dangerous because of highwaymen so he could only travel at night and he was constantly on edge listening for approaching footsteps or vehicles because his white clothes provided zero camouflage.

There wasn't a single part of it that wasn't horrible. Sleeping on the ground. The noises. Animals. People especially.

But even little things, like flies or other insects. He once had a full-blown freak out panic attack that had him in the fetal position on the side of the road for over an hour because a fly kept landing on his arms.

He'd survived it all, though.

He'd gotten to Jacob's Well.

He'd gotten a job at the paper even though it meant constantly going out into the world. Interviewing people. Being around crowds at events.

But he'd done it.

And sometimes he even felt *almost* normal. Okay, that was a lie. He always felt the gaping distance between him and everyone else.

Always on the outside looking in.

But when he won the marriage raffle and Vanessa talked to him afterward, he thought maybe, just maybe... Maybe he could be part of a family again.

"Fucking idiot," he whispered hoarsely.

There were some elephants that were just too big to eat.

Michael was both relieved and humiliated when the back door opened, and he heard everyone coming toward him. They were interchangeably murmuring things like, "How do we move him?" and "What the hell happened?" He had answers for both, but it was too humiliating to respond.

Vanessa squatted beside his head and whispered, "Oh, Michael."

He opened his eyes to half-mast, made contact with hers, then blinked once. She let out a sigh.

"Can you get up on your own?" she asked.

A useless question if he'd ever heard one. It wasn't like any of them could help him up if he couldn't.

He closed his eyes and powered through. Pushing onto his hands and knees and then to standing. He could feel how much Vanessa wanted to help him. The others, too.

"Stay back," he said, his voice rough and scratchy. He put his hands out at his sides to keep them all at bay as he took a few staggering steps.

He didn't want to feel anything more than what was absolutely necessary.

Of course, that's what the liquor had been for.

And look how well *that* had worked out.

He certainly felt things now. He felt the pounding of his head behind his eyes. He remembered every inch of the humiliation and shame of this morning—Vanessa innocently running into him and his terrible overreaction. The things he'd yelled at her, his *wife*.

It was too much. On top of everything else.

At first, it had been enough to enjoy private talks with her, not to mention his bird's eye view of her climaxing as the other men took her there, the way her eyes fluttered, and her mouth opened; how her neck arched, and how she responded to his encouraging words, and even more to his dirty talk.

He'd tried to pretend it was enough.

But he was a man, goddammit, the same as any other.

He was her husband and he wanted the things a husband wanted. *He* wanted to suck on her lips and pull groans from her throat. *He* wanted to feel her small hand wrapped around his shaft. *He* wanted to sink his cock into her tight cunt.

And he wanted *them* all to watch, just as they all made him watch, night after night after torturous night.

Because watching wasn't enough.

Not anymore.

And Michael was done pretending.

He'd come to a decision somewhere between his fourth and fifth drink, and that had made him order even more.

He thought, maybe, if he dulled his senses well enough, he wouldn't act like such a freak when Vanessa touched him. Maybe, if he was smashed, he could even stand letting her kiss him.

"Phew!" Riordan said, covering his nose.

"Jesus, Michael. You reek of a distillery."

"Let's get you inside," Logan said. "Ross, I think this calls for a pot of coffee?"

"On it," Ross said.

"Maybe fry up some pork, too," Logan added.

Pork? Michael lifted his head and swung it toward Riordan.

"You picked a hell of a day to pull a disappearing act, man." Riordan shook his head.

And then Michael found himself suddenly walking—on a fairly straight path—with Vanessa and Logan at his left and right. They each stayed several feet away, giving him his space, though. He gave a short, bitter laugh. Story of his life. He gave the phrase *keeping people at arm's length* new meaning.

It took some effort, but eventually he was in the bedroom. Logan ordered him to undress and the twins brought in bucket after bucket so he could take an actual bath. He felt slightly normal after that, and the smell of fried pork fat coming up through the window from the backyard was life-reaffirming.

Logan didn't take the time for Michael to find another set of clothes. Instead, he made Michael sit, with just his silk boxers on—on the chair in the corner of the room. He and Vanessa sat next to each other at the foot of the bed and faced him.

"Okay," Logan said. "Let's hear it."

Michael hung his head. "Do I really need to explain?"

Logan made a low grumbling sound in his chest. "The twins told you what happened while they filled the bath, right?"

Michael nodded, swallowing hard. He couldn't believe everything they'd told him. Everyone's lives had been in danger. And he'd been throwing himself a pity party down at the bar. He felt like a giant asshole.

"Our entire clan was threatened. Any one of us could have lost their lives. Puts some shit in perspective. And you better fucking believe things are going to start looking different around here. Like this morning. You were upset? You should have brought it to the clan, not gone off on your own without telling anyone where you were."

Michael lifted his head and swallowed hard.

Logan continued. "Then we come home to find you putting your *own* life at risk. So, yes, *damnit*. I would like an explanation."

Michael nodded, eyes back on the floor. The words came slowly. Quietly. "Isn't it obvious?"

"No," Vanessa whispered. "Tell me what's wrong."

Michael shook his head. He couldn't look at her. "It's not fair to you to have a husband who can't...be a husband, and—"

"If this is about sex, I've had plenty—"

Michael's head jerked up abruptly and his fists struck his knees. "I know!"

Vanessa clamped her mouth shut.

"You don't think I know how well *serviced* you are? Fuck! I've had to watch all of it. *All of it!* Do you understand? It's not enough anymore. If it ever was."

He got up and started pacing, sobering quickly. "And then you accidentally run into me and touch my arm like anyone normal would have, and I *scream* at you? You deserve better than a freak like me. *I* deserve better. But only one of us can get what we want. If you want me to bow out... Maybe the Commander can put someone else in my spot."

"No!" she said, standing up too, taking a step toward him before stopping short several feet away. "What are you even talking about? No!"

"Absolutely not," Logan agreed.

"You aren't hearing me." Michael sat back down on the chair. How could this announcement be a surprise to either of them? "There are just some things I'll never be able to do."

"I won't pretend to understand what you're going through," Logan said, "but I get what it means to have doubts. This has been a hard time for all of us—learning to live together, to care about each other, to make a family together. And that's what we are. *A family*."

"That's rich coming from you," Michael said bitterly.

Logan's jaw tensed. "I'm not saying I haven't made mistakes. I'm trying to fix those now. I've let you down as much as I have Vanessa. But let's work together."

Logan leaned in, elbows on his knees. "What would make it easier? Sleeping in a separate room? I would have thought having you in the room would make you feel better connected, but if it's making it worse..."

Michael shook his head. The only thing worse than being there and not participating would be standing outside the door and feeling his exclusion made all the more obvious.

Logan nodded as if he could read his thoughts. "Well, alcohol isn't the answer. But maybe other things? Like, I don't know... meditation?"

"Mumbo jumbo," Michael said. In truth, he'd tried everything: herbs, yoga, homeopathy, the all-broccoli diet... He had spent his whole life searching for something to bring him relief. Why did people think they were going to suddenly come up with something he'd never thought of?

"Well what if I described what it all felt like as it was happening?" Vanessa asked. "So then you'd be hearing and seeing."

"What?" he asked.

"You know... Like blind people have things described to them so they get a fuller experience. Engaging more of the senses you *do* have access to, since you can't touch."

"You want your *other* husbands to audio describe what it's like having sex with you?" Michael asked. Then he laughed humorlessly. God, the thought of Cam giving him a play-by-play sounded like pure torture. Okay, so he might be getting an erection just thinking about it. But that was just because he was imagining the little sighs Vanessa made whenever any of them finally sank inside her.

Vanessa must have read Michael's smile wrong, though. She must have thought he was into the idea because she leaned back on her elbows and let her knees fall apart.

"What are you doing?" he asked warily. There was no way in hell she was going to give him a sample of her new fucking-terrible idea.

"He slides into me," she said, smiling coyly, "All along his cock he's feeling the *hot...wet...silkiness...*"

Michael froze, his mouth dropping open.

No. It couldn't be that simple, could it?

He looked down at the spot on her jeans where she was teasingly running her fingers.

"Say that again," Michael whispered.

"Um..." Vanessa said, her eyes darting sideways to Logan. She was obviously confused by his sudden change in manner but he just waved his hand at her.

"Say it again."

"...feeling the hot, wet, silkiness?"

Michael turned to face Logan, his expression questioning. "Does it really feel like silk?"

"Holy shit," Logan whispered, and Michael saw his own epiphany written in Logan's wide eyes.

"What?" Vanessa asked, sitting up a little.

Logan's eyebrows shot up even more. "Do you think it would work?"

"Would *what* work?" Vanessa asked.

"I want to try," Michael said. "I have to try."

"Would someone please tell me—"

Logan held up his hand to quiet her, and she frowned. "She's grabby," he said. "She claws and scratches when things get intense. Should we have the others help... Hold her arms?"

"Yeah," Michael said, standing up and looking around. Now that the idea had been raised, he needed to test it out as soon as possible. He had to know. "But not in here. I'd need to stand. She'd have to be on something higher than the bed."

By now, it had dawned on Vanessa they were talking about sex. "Really? Are you serious?"

Her voice was hopeful and it made Michael's cock stiffen even more. She wanted it. She wanted *him*.

"But why now?" she asked. "Why all the sudden do you think you'd be able to—"

"Silk," Michael said.

"That's what you are, baby," Logan offered. "Just like you said. Liquid silk."

"That's the only thing I've been able to endure one hundred percent," Michael said. "If I don't touch you in any other way, if you don't touch me... If it's just that one point of contact between us..." He'd still want more, but this...if it worked...it would be more than he could have dreamed of.

"You think you can do it?" she asked. "If you can, no more talk about being replaced?"

"If this works," Michael said, "you won't be able to get rid of me."

CHAPTER SEVENTEEN

MICHAEL

Michael couldn't get to the kitchen fast enough. He didn't know if this would work, but God, if it did...

Vanessa walked in front of him and she stripped off her clothes as she went. Her shirt first. Then she reached around to undo her bra.

She tossed it to the floor and spun to look at Michael, taking the last few steps into the kitchen backwards.

Michael's chest heaved as he watched her small, pert little breasts bounce with her every step. She backed up all the way into the kitchen table and her hands immediately went to her belt buckle and then the button of her jeans. In the blink of an eye, her pants and underwear were on the floor and there she was, standing before him naked and unashamed.

Fuck but she was glorious.

Michael wasn't the only one who noticed.

"So this is new," Cam said, palming his cock through his jeans. "But I approve."

Michael growled, about to tell him to step the hell back, but Logan was already there, moving in front of Cam.

"You and the twins are just watching tonight."

"We are?" This from Riordan, as he and Ross came in from the living room.

"Oh come on, man," Cam said. "You already had her out in the—"

"Not me, dipshit," Logan growled. "Michael's finally going to have his turn."

"Michael?"

Michael ignored Cam's shocked question. He only had eyes for Vanessa as she hopped up on the table and stretched out, leaning back on her elbows. Her eyes met Michael's and the fire he saw there had his cock pulsing. He was so fucking hard. God, he didn't think he'd ever been so hard in his whole life.

The table was higher than the bed, and perfectly aligned with Michael's hips.

"Ross, Riordan, hold her arms," Logan ordered. "Cam, help me hold her knees. For this to work, she needs to stay perfectly still."

Vanessa rolled her eyes as Logan ran his hand down her thigh and took her left knee, Cam taking her right.

"This isn't necessary," she groused. "You don't have to hold me. I can control myself. I won't touch him."

"The scratch and bite marks you gave me earlier say different, baby," Logan said.

Vanessa made an outraged noise, but she was biting her lip and arching her chest as Logan and Cam stretched her legs wide.

Damn, she was so flexible. Michael had a thousand fantasies about her flexible little gymnastic body.

This won't work. You'll make contact with her body and no matter how 'silky' she's supposed to be, you'll fall apart and throw a shit fit like the little bitch you are.

"Let one of us get her ready first, Michael," Logan said.

Michael nodded shakily.

"On it," Cam said. He reached between Vanessa's legs and swirled his finger gently over her clit. She squirmed and her stomach flattened.

"That's it, sweetheart. Let's see that honey start to flow."

Michael took another step closer to see better. God, he'd never been this close when— Logan wasn't wrong about how wild Vanessa could get in bed. Michael always stayed by the wall to make sure he was well clear of any flailing limbs when they were—

But with everyone holding her down, Michael ventured closer than ever before, and holy God, her pussy, it was beautiful and complicated and even as he watched, wetness began to glisten on Vanessa's swelling petals.

He glanced up toward her face but leaned over like he was, he couldn't see because the twins had leaned over to suckle at her breasts. Already she was liquefying over Cam's fingers.

"Oooooh," she gasped.

Michael knew that noise. It meant she was getting close to coming.

No surprise with Cam playing with her clit and the twins at her tits.

It was a hot fucking scene, there was no denying it: Vanessa spread out on the table like a feast the five of them were ready to devour.

But Michael was ready to do more than just watch.

It was now or never.

He shoved down his silk boxers and stepped forward the last foot until his cock bobbed only an inch away from Vanessa's entrance.

Michael's heart started beating so fast he could hear it in his ears.

"Please, Michael," Vanessa whined. "I need it so bad. Please."

Michael could see the evidence too. Wetness seeped down from her pussy to her ass.

Holy fuck.

"Hold her steady," Michael said, voice shaky.

And then he grabbed his shaft and took that last step.

He couldn't help the "Fuck!" that escaped the second the tip of his cock made contact with the lips of her sex.

"Oh God, Michael," Vanessa cried. "I'm sorry, am I hurting you?"

"No," Michael shook his head so fast he thought it might give him whiplash. "No. God no. It feels—"

He pushed in another inch. "*Ohhhhhhhh.*"

He couldn't describe it.

Oh God, it was— She was—

Silk was the wrong word, though.

Better. She was better than silk.

It was like this was the place his cock had always meant to be.

Vanessa was made for him.

His wife.

He was fucking his wife.

Oh fuck, that thought did him in—he shoved all the way home, burying himself to the hilt.

And Vanessa gasped—she made *the* gasp, the one she made when any one of her husbands penetrated her. Because Michael was as much her husband as any of them now. He could give her everything.

He pulled his hips back and then pushed back in.

Michael had only ever watched, but he picked up the rhythm quickly enough. And with every thrust and Vanessa's every little pleasured cry, he felt more and more like a whole man.

And when they climaxed together, her amazing, perfect pussy clenching on his cock and driving him over the edge, he swore there was nothing he wouldn't do for this woman because she had given him everything.

CHAPTER EIGHTEEN

VANESSA

Were people really allowed to be this happy?

It didn't seem real. Every day Vanessa awoke, surrounded in their huge oversized bed with her four gorgeous husbands, and Michael over in his smaller bed off by the wall, she did more than count her blessings.

She clutched onto them. Literally, more often than not. Finding an eager wife wrapped around them was a fact her husbands were more than happy to take advantage of. Especially considering the morning wood that was always on hand.

She smiled even as she walked down the street toward Shay's house, running her hand from her cheek down her neck.

There'd certainly been plenty of wood this morning—enough to light a bonfire. She'd been burrowing into Cam's arms when he woke up, already stiff as a fire poker.

Logan wasn't far behind. He was at her back and as Cam started kissing her, hands wandering to her breasts, Logan began thrusting his rock hard erection against her ass.

That man was endlessly fascinated by her derrière. Her ass cheeks clenched just at the memory.

The fact that she had a training plug currently wedged up her backside? Well, that only made her cheeks flame hotter as she hurried down the street through the already steamy Texas heat.

The anal plug was a surprise for her clan. She hadn't told any of them she was preparing for... that.

The only reason she had the toy in the first place was because she and Shay had been getting closer lately. Vanessa had just straight out asked her some very frank questions when they'd gotten together to do laundry last week.

Shay was the least shy person Vanessa had ever met. She gabbed about her sex life like she was discussing the weather. And ever since Logan had stuck his finger... *up there*, something he'd done several times since, Vanessa had been curious. So she'd asked Shay about the whole thing and boy did Shay have a lot to say on the topic.

Apparently *anal* was a thing guys were really into. And Shay just happened to have an anal plug still in its packaging that was on the smaller side, perfect for training. Lube too, although apparently various types of oils could get the job done just as well. One of Shay's husbands had picked it up for her—he was the trade secretary and could get his hands on all sorts of things, apparently.

So every chance she could steal alone, Vanessa had been, well, experimenting. Stretching herself. Following Shay's instructions and wearing the plug for extended periods of time.

Because the thing was, as amazing as life was, there was always that niggling voice at the back of Vanessa's head—*are you doing enough? Are they getting bored?*

Stupid. She was being stupid.

Probably.

But every day she spent with her husbands, the more she saw how amazing each of them was.

Like Cam. He put on such bravado but every now and then she saw beneath it. There was a core of vulnerability he never showed anyone. Except her.

Occasionally, and it had only happened a handful of times, but sometimes when they made love, she'd look in his eyes and see... well, she couldn't even really describe it.

But it was like he was finally letting her see *him*. The real him, beyond the smirk and the cocky attitude.

Then there was his skill as a doctor. He'd never let anyone call him a doctor—he insisted he was only a *physician's assistant*—but she didn't know why. He'd forgotten his lunch the other day and she'd dropped it by the clinic only to walk in on him stitching up a little boy's knee.

He was telling a funny story to distract the boy from what he was doing. The tear tracks were still wet on the little boy's cheeks, but he was watching Cam's animated face with wide eyes. Because that was just who Cam was—magnetic. Whenever he was in the room, you wanted to be there too, even if it was to just stare and share in the special.

Compared to that... who the hell was she?

Just some chick who happened to survive Xterminate. That was literally the only notable thing about her.

She'd been a no one in the world pre-Fall. Barely anyone even knew her name back in school. She wasn't bullied or anything. That would have meant she registered on people's radar. And she just... didn't. She showed up, went to classes, did her work. She had acquaintances, she hadn't taken a vow of silence or anything. But there was nothing special about her.

Nothing like Cecily, Dad's other daughter. Unlike Cecily, Vanessa didn't sing or play an instrument in band. She was a straight B student and was too small to play team sports, so she'd stuck to track. But even with that, her legs were too short to be competitive. She could run for a long time but she wasn't any faster than anyone else. Gymnastics might have been good but they never had much money so apart from one summer program when she was a kid, it was nothing she could really pursue.

In short, she was nothing worth sticking around for.

She wasn't the kind of girl who got the guy.

Much less *five* of them.

Hadn't she learned the hard way that happily ever afters were never real?

"Oh, hi, Vanessa!" Shay opened her front door, looking surprised when she saw Vanessa standing there. "Why didn't you knock?"

Vanessa blinked. She hadn't even realized she'd walked all the way to Shay's house. Even up onto her porch.

"I was just heading over to pump some water." Shay held up a water bucket. Then she leaned in. "Okay, truth? Sophia and Drea are getting into it again, and I'm sneaking out for a little escape."

"Oh God, what about this time?"

"They're arguing about what it means to be a feminist in a post-Fall world."

"Look at that," Vanessa looked down at her wrist even though she didn't have a watch on. "I'm suddenly in the mood to help you carry that bucket of water."

Shay smiled. "Thought you might be."

They started across the yard. There was a communal pump at the corner of Oak Street, several yards away.

"How's the sculpture coming for the President?" Vanessa asked. Shay was a talented artist. After a national newspaper did a piece on a sculpture she'd done for the Commander, she'd been commissioned to make a bust of President Goddard.

Shay's smile dimmed. "Fine."

Vanessa frowned. Was it just her or was something suddenly off with Shay?

Before they'd made it three steps, though, the front door slammed behind them. Vanessa looked over her shoulder to see a red-faced Sophia storming down the porch steps, bucket in hand.

"That woman is the most annoying, *infuriating*— Oh, hi Vanessa."

"Lemme guess," Vanessa said, "You had a sudden, unquenchable thirst?"

Sophia huffed, blowing a lock of dark hair off her face. "I swear she makes a sport out of getting under my skin." Sophia stomped past Vanessa and Shay. "Can you believe my dad's actually thinking about taking her *with* us on the delegation to the capital in a few weeks? He says she won't let up until she meets with the President herself! I say the best way to shut her up is to take her to the edge of town and boot her in the—"

"Sophia," Shay chastised.

Sophia's mouth pursed as she obviously bit back whatever else she'd been about to say. It worked for about two point three seconds. "I'm sorry, but that woman never has anything helpful or kind to say. She's a total witch. We save her, my dad takes her in, feeds and clothes her, and what's her thanks? Badgering him every single day—" She cutoff mid-sentence and took a deep breath.

Then she looked over at Vanessa. "God, here I am obsessing about her when I'm not even in the *room* with her anymore. Vanessa, tell me about you. How's your week going?"

Vanessa fought to hold back her smile.

"Oh, guys," Sophia stopped, slinging the bucket up her arm so she could grab both Vanessa and Shay's arms. "When we get back inside, make sure to try to be extra cheerful. Audrey got her period again and she's trying to pretend she's not upset."

Shay's brows drew together.

Sophia rambled on. "She wants a baby so bad. I shouldn't have let Drea draw me into a fight. We really need to be focusing on Audrey right now. She's hurting."

Vanessa looked Shay's way, but Shay was staring steadily at the ground, an unreadable expression on her face. For as open as Shay was about some topics, sometimes her face would go so distant she seemed as unreachable. The only time Vanessa had asked about her past, Shay had changed the topic quicker than a hummingbird's heartbeat.

Sophia's voice dropped as they reached the water pump. "Okay, I have a secret, but swear you won't tell."

Vanessa looked back to Sophia who was barely holding back a grin. "What?"

"Well, I overheard Nix talking to Dad last night. He was asking about getting time off to take Audrey away for a couple of weeks before we all go to the capitol. To take her on the honeymoon they never got. Isn't that romantic?"

Vanessa nodded, smiling at the thoughtfulness of Audrey's husbands even though most of her mind was still caught up on the previous topic.

Babies. Pregnancy. Periods.

And the fact that she hadn't had one in seven years.

She was still thinking about it an hour and a half later when she was heading home after a good time visiting with her friends.

She'd laughed and joked along with everyone. Gone along with Sophia's cheer-Audrey-up agenda. It was good to see everyone. Kylie was fun to hang out with and it was good to get a chance to spend more time with her.

But Vanessa's mind was only half present.

She'd never told her husbands about the no-periods thing.

How did you bring up the fact that you couldn't perform one of the —according to Sophia "primary functions of being a woman?" Child-bearing. Vanessa had certainly heard Sophia and Drea argue about it often enough.

Sophia could go on and on about how it was a woman's main purpose in life. Of course, Sophia was a healthy, vibrant nineteen-year-old. Still, what did she know about it?

Vanessa hadn't given it much thought when her periods first stopped. She'd remembered from school learning it could happen if you were an athlete or got too skinny. If you had less than a certain percentage of body fat, blah, blah, blah.

She remembered being relieved, back when it stopped. It was one less hassle when every day was a struggle to survive.

But now...

What if she'd screwed up her body permanently by all those years living on the edge of starvation, barely surviving?

And of course her husbands would want children. So when they realized she couldn't...

God, there was even that provision in the Marriage Rottery law. If a woman couldn't have children, she was allowed to stay unmarried.

Because no one would want a barren woman, right?

The more Vanessa thought about it, the tighter her chest cinched. So tight that by the time she got to her own yard, it was difficult to draw in breath.

What if she told them and they decided they didn't want her anymore?

No. They wouldn't do that. They I—

... They really like *you.*

They liked having sex with her anyway. That she felt confident about. Well, she was pretty sure, anyway. Ever since the expedition to go out after the twins, when Logan had come back to them and started directing things in the bedroom again, the sex had been off the charts. At least it had been for her.

But would good sex be enough long term? If she was... broken? Didn't every man want to pass on his legacy? God, it was more important than ever these days. Cam had talked about it once. Something about warrior babies...

Her heart beat a mile a minute as her panic ramped up with every new worry.

She couldn't lose them. She couldn't.

She couldn't be left behind.

Not again.

Oh God, not again.

She skirted around the house to head in the back door. She didn't know who was home, but she couldn't handle seeing anyone right now. She needed to calm down first. If she just sat for a little while on the back swing, maybe she could get her shit together.

She couldn't let them see her like this. She had to be perfect. Cecily had been perfect. If she could just be per—

"Vanessa? Are you all right?"

Vanessa's hand flew to her chest in surprise at Ross's voice. He was sitting on the back step, coils of rope piled around him on the porch.

"God, you scared me," Vanessa said, letting out a skittish high-pitched laugh. "What are you doing out here?" It was probably around eight o'clock, so the sun was lower in the sky, but it was still hot enough to have her cotton dress damp with perspiration just from the walk home.

"Oh." Ross's face was a little pink but Vanessa swore his cheeks reddened even more at her question. "It's stupid."

Well that had her curious. And curious was good because it was distracting her from her panic. She took a deep breath and then went to sit down beside him on the step.

"I highly doubt it's stupid. Tell me."

He glanced furtively at her. After all they'd shared, the fact that he could still be embarrassed around her was pretty dang adorable. "Well, I know it's dumb, but I always wanted to be an Eagle Scout."

Vanessa scrunched her brow. "Like... Boy Scouts?"

Ross's hand went to the back of his neck. "Yeah. Dumb, right?"

"No, not at all. So what's this? Practice for something? What did they call them? Patches?"

"Merit badges. You have to master a dozen knots to be an Eagle Scout."

Vanessa glanced around them. She didn't know one knot from another, but there were definitely more than twelve.

Ross smiled. "Yeah, I was always sort of an overachiever. I'm trying for forty."

Vanessa's heart melted.

It wasn't just Cam who was special. Every single one of her husbands was such an amazing puzzle, each one presenting never-ending facets to discover.

And just like that, the panic came back.

Because again, compared to them, she felt like an uninteresting, ugly, half-plucked sparrow.

Sex.

That was her one trump card.

They couldn't get it anywhere else, so, as long as she kept things interesting in the bedroom...

Vanessa's eyes flicked around to all the ropes and intricate knots as sudden inspiration struck.

"Ross," she lowered her voice and trailed a finger down his thigh, "you're so good with that rope and those knots. You wouldn't like to try... maybe tying me up?"

CHAPTER NINETEEN

RIORDAN

Riordan ripped his gloves off and threw them in his bag, wiping his forearm across his forehead for the millionth time and flinching.

Jesus fucking Christ, he was going to kill whoever'd stolen his hat.

Eight fucking hours in the Texas heat picking fucking corn without a hat and he was sure he was roasted worse than a damn Thanksgiving turkey. He was Scotch-Irish for fuck's sake. He got a sunburn if he walked from the front door to the mailbox and back.

He'd taken a nap during lunch and when he'd woken up, the damn baseball cap was gone. It was an orange UT cap which wasn't as unique as you'd think considering they were twenty minutes outside what used to be Austin. Plenty of guys had them. And some son of a bitch had stolen his.

To make it worse, that bastard Sandoval had gotten promoted to Shift Supervisor even though Riordan worked twice as hard. Riordan had put in for the position, but *noooo*, he was only nineteen, he had to put in his time first.

It didn't matter that he was smarter than half the bastards working these fields. Or that he'd always done passably well in school all those years. None of it fucking mattered.

There was no more *career path* or getting ahead. No pulling yourself up by your bootstraps. The truth was there were a thousand bastards fighting for every job.

And no way for a man to stand out and make a name for himself.

Not in a nowhere, shit little town like this.

You should have gotten out when you had the chance.

His jaw tensed as he stomped down the street toward his house. It wasn't the first time he'd had the thought.

Vanessa was awesome. More than that. She was amazing. Being with her made Riordan feel— Well, it was really, really good when he was with her.

But days like this?

It was hard not to think about the what ifs.

What if he hadn't stolen the lotto box and it had just gone off like normal? Odds were, his name wouldn't have been called. Or what if he'd just hightailed it way before it even got to that point? Why hadn't he taken off six months ago? Or hell, a year ago?

What the fuck had been tying him to this town? Because it had been so important to his mother that he got that fucking laughing-stock piece of paper claiming he'd 'graduated'?

Yeah. Fat lot of good that so-called education was doing him while he spent all day shucking fucking corn. And as good as his time with Vanessa was, he always had to share her. He barely ever got to spend any time with her, just the two of them.

And sure, she liked him. But would she really notice if he wasn't there? He was just part of the group. He wasn't a Logan. Jesus, even Michael found ways to connect with her that Riordan couldn't—

He shook his head. He could have been halfway to California by now. Having adventure. Seeing if he really had what it took to be the sort of man that could make his mark on the world.

Sweat rolled into his eyes and he wiped his head, wincing again from his sunburn.

He finally got home and stalked around to the back porch. They kept a barrel of water back there. He was so hot, he might just dump the whole damn thing on his head. Steam from his sunburn would probably be enough to fucking cook supper.

But as soon as he kicked open the gate to the back yard, he heard a cry.

A female cry.

What the—

He started running, tossing his bag to the side. He sprinted around the side of the house and shoved the gate to the back fence open.

And then he came to a stop so suddenly he almost fell over.

Jesus fucking *Christ*.

Not ten feet away, Vanessa was strung up from the beams of the roof on the back porch by rope artfully knotted all around her body. And Ross, he was fucking her and she was groaning like it was the best goddamned thing she'd ever—

Riordan's cock stiffened even as his stomach bottomed out.

Because here was his fucking twin, managing yet again to do what Riordan never could. Stand out. Shine brighter. Make Riordan the spare. Unnecessary. Extraneous. Superfluous. See, he'd paid attention in fucking English. Not that all his vocabulary or the fact that he'd read every history book cover to cover would ever matter for fucking *shit*.

Not when Ross or Cam or Logan was in the room.

He was just about to spin around and get the hell out of there when Vanessa looked his way and their gazes locked.

"Riordan," she called. "Come join us."

Ross paused, looking his direction and jealousy burned through Riordan's gut.

"Yeah. No thanks." Riordan didn't bother hiding his bitterness as he waved at the elaborate rope harness. She was strung up by both her wrists and her legs—not just her ankles, no, that would have been too simple. Instead, Ross had done some crazy, complicated pattern looping the rope around her bent legs like she was a macramé bowl, spreading them open so her pussy was on dripping display when Ross pulled out to turn Riordan's way.

Riordan took a step back. "I don't need to butt in on my brother's Eagle Scout project fuck. Y'all have fun now."

He spun, ready to get the hell out of there when Vanessa's snapped retort had him stopping.

"Don't you dare walk away from me, Riordan Washington."

He turned around only to find her imperiously glaring at him. An impressive feat considering she was still strung up like something in the butcher's poultry case.

"Why not? You don't need me." He waved at Ross. "There's nothing I can give you that Ross can't. Or Logan or Cam. Fuck, even Michael now." He huffed out a bitter laugh. "Give it a week. If I left you wouldn't even notice I was gone."

"How can you—" she cried out, and Riordan was taken aback at the anguished emotion in her voice.

She took a deep breath like she was trying to get herself under control. "Would you come closer so I'm not yelling halfway across the yard? I want to tell you something."

Riordan's jaw set and he stared at the ground in front of him. He didn't want to listen to what she had to say. She'd try to say he was important to her, that every person was a special snowflake in their own way, yada, yada, yada. She'd just try to say the shit people always said, but she couldn't understand.

She didn't know what it was like to live in someone else's shadow her whole life. And now that shadow was bigger than ever because it wasn't just his brother anymore.

When he didn't move, after several seconds, Vanessa took a deep breath and continued anyway.

"I have a half-sister. And my father loved her more than me."

Riordan's head jerked in her direction and their gazes locked.

What? She had a sis—

"Everyone always says that parents don't pick favorites. That parents always love their children equally. But it's not true. My father loved her more."

Ross took a step forward and put a hand on her waist. "I'm sure that's not true."

Vanessa didn't move her gaze from Riordan as she answered Ross's assertion. "It was true. Still is, I'm sure, wherever he is."

"Vanessa, no," Ross tried again, but Vanessa cut him off.

"He left us when I was three to start another family. He had another daughter, just a few years younger than me. He lived with them in the same town as me. I spent my whole life watching him go to her soccer games. Her band performances. Her dance recitals."

Her voice was unflinching. "And when Xterminate hit and neither me or Cecily got sick, he made the ultimate choice. He took her and ran. He left me behind, all alone, during the Death Riots while he took her to safety."

"Oh Jesus, Vanessa," Riordan said, hurrying forward up the stairs of the porch. He was an asshole. A young, petty, stupid asshole.

He'd let himself get so wrapped up in his own shit. His mother paid more attention to Ross, sure. And yeah, he'd been a solid B student while Ross had been their sixth grade Valedictorian, something both their parents had gone on and *on* about endlessly. But Jesus, it was nothing to what Vanessa had gone through.

"I'm so sorry." He went up to her, needing to touch her, to hold her.

But there she was, her legs spread, pussy glistening. His cock had already been stiff but as he wrapped his arms around her and pulled her close, he couldn't help his hard-on becoming like granite. He tried to hold his hips back from her as he hugged her and quickly let her go.

She must have misunderstood the quick embrace, though.

"Don't you dare think you aren't special to me. *You*. You're brash. Adventurous. You do everything balls to the wall. I love that."

He scoffed, shaking his head as he looked down. Even though she understood better than he could have imagined, it didn't just magically change everything. "I work in the *fields* every day."

"For now!" Vanessa exclaimed. "That's the other thing I l—" she cut off abruptly and looked down, "the other thing I like so much about you. You're never satisfied."

"Yeah, yeah," Riordan swallowed hard. It was hard to hear the same failings his mother always harped on coming out of her mouth. "Mom always told me I should learn to be satisfied with what I had instead of having my head in the clouds."

"No, it's a good thing not to be satisfied," Vanessa said. "It means you'll never stop fighting for what you want. You'll never give up. You'll never settle for mediocre. Don't you get it, Riordan? You're bound for an extraordinary life. And I feel so honored that I get to be a part of it."

Riordan blinked hard. "You really—" His voice came out a little choked and he had to swallow hard before continuing. "You really believe all that? About *me?*"

"Of course I do," she said, like he was crazy to think anything different.

Riordan just stared at her.

She really did.

She really believed in him. She thought he'd have an extraordinary life. No one ever thought of him as anything other than Ross's brother or one of those twins. But this woman, this goddess of a woman, she—

He lunged forward, gripping the back of her head and pulling her in, kissing her deeper and harder than he ever had before.

She kissed him back with just as much need and fervor.

He thought his cock was hard before? He growled, half in lust, half in pain at how his jeans restricted his dick. He reached down to undo the button and zipper because it hurt too much not too.

But when Vanessa looked down and saw what he was doing, her nostrils flared and her eyes went bright with desire. She pulled her head back from his lips.

"Do you want to go on an adventure with me right now?" Her chest heaved up and down with her every word. Considering she was still strung up like a prize bird in a shop window, Riordan had an idea what kind of adventure she meant.

And he was all fucking in.

"Hell yeah I am, babe." He shoved his jeans down his legs and kicked them off. Damn was he glad for the privacy fence around the back yard.

When he looked back to Vanessa, she was glancing between him and Ross. Her gaze had gone suddenly shy, cheeks pink as she whispered, "If my hands were free, I'd pull it out myself. You see, I've been, um, preparing..." She glanced down.

"What is it, honey," Ross asked. "You can tell us anything."

She lifted her eyes, gaze meeting Riordan's straight on. "I've been preparing to take two of you at once."

Holy shit, was she saying what he *thought* she was saying?

"So if you, um," her eyes flicked down and up again, "Well, there's a plug I've been using to stretch and it's…"

Riordan knew his eyes were wide as they shot to Ross's, who's expression he was sure mirrored his. Total shock and lustful hunger at the thought of what Vanessa was offering.

"Riordan, will you pull it out?" she asked, her delicate voice all breathy with need like it got when she was turned on. "And fill me up with you instead?"

CHAPTER TWENTY

RIORDAN

"Will you pull it out? And fill me up with you instead?"

Well that was a request that no man in history would ever fucking say no to.

Riordan's cock bobbed heavily as he walked around Vanessa's body. And holy fucking shit, she wasn't lying.

There, nestled between her ass cheeks right at her anus, was the stopper of a small flesh-colored plug.

"Jesus," Riordan hissed. His hand dropped to massage her perfect ass, curving down to the plug. The rubber was so hard compared to her luscious, soft skin.

"Pull it out," Vanessa said. "Please. I want to know what it feels like to have you inside me there, Riordan. What it feels like to have one of my husbands take me there for the first time."

Riordan almost lost his shit at her words.

He'd be her first.

The first to take her ass.

Something none of the rest of them would ever have. It would be *his*. His alone. Forever he'd be her first.

He wedged his fingers around the rim of the plug and slowly started pulling it out.

When she started making the sexiest fucking throaty groan Riordan had ever heard, he wanted to yank the damn thing out and shove his cock in without preamble.

But no.

He'd make this a first she remembered.

He'd make it *extraordinary*.

So he teased Vanessa with the plug as he pulled it out. Sometimes pushing it back in and giving several quick thrusts before continuing to remove it.

And watching her ass expand and contract around the toy was. So. Fucking. Hot.

Finally the plug came all the way free. Riordan's hand shook as he took a step to set it on the porch railing. Because as cool as he was trying to play this, holy shit, holy shit, holy *shit*.

He was about to be treated to the fucking ultimate—what guy didn't secretly dream about anal?

Riordan had seen some porno magazines once where a guy was doing it to a chick and ever since... But Riordan never thought a good girl like Vanessa— Not in a thousand years...

His hands were still shaking as he came back around to her backside. Ross had strung her up at the perfect height for fucking.

Of course he had—the perfect height for Ross to fuck her was the perfect height for Riordan. And hey, at the moment, he wasn't complaining. Vanessa might have just found the one activity in the world he didn't mind sharing with his brother. Riordan smirked. As long as he got to claim the important *first*.

"You should dip inside her pussy first," Ross said, coming back to stand in front of Vanessa and dipping down to kiss her breast. If he had any issues with what Vanessa was proposing, he sure wasn't letting it show.

And not to be an asshole, but Ross was a pretty simple guy. He was never any good at hiding his emotions or what he was thinking. So he was probably exactly as into this as he seemed. Who wouldn't be, considering how hot as fuck their wife was.

Their wife.

Shit. Riordan didn't let himself think of Vanessa by the title much. But she was. She was his wife. This was his life, and maybe not all of it was everything he wanted it to be, but it was a fucking good one.

And he was about to pop his wife's anal cherry.

Fuck yeah.

Riordan took Vanessa's hips and swung her around. The ropes twisted easily and soon she was facing him.

He kissed her deep again and slowly, achingly fucking slowly, he aligned his cock with her dripping pussy and thrust in.

She groaned into his mouth and her flesh clenched around his shaft.

Jesus, her body was fucking *heaven*.

He only allowed himself a few thrusts, though. He was way too turned on and he *had* to get to that ass. If her pussy felt this good, what would her ass feel like? It took everything he had not to come just at the thought of it.

He pulled out and gave her one last lingering kiss. He paused, looking her in the eye. "Are you sure, honey? You ready for this?"

There wasn't even a waver in her gaze. "Yes. I want this. I want it with you, Riordan."

She was trying to fucking kill him, wasn't she?

He leaned in again to taste her lips because he couldn't fucking not. And then he let the rope unwind, swinging her so that her gorgeous ass was back in front of him. He squeezed her cheeks, loving the way they looked in his hands.

His cock was wet with her juices.

Jesus fuck but it was the hottest thing he'd ever seen.

Well, aside from actually seeing himself penetrating her *there*.

He sucked in a breath as he lined himself up. He was so fucking big. At least twice the size of the plug. Maybe three times.

He'd always suspected he was a respectable size. But it wasn't until he'd seen the other guys' cocks on the wedding night that he'd known for sure. He and Ross were the biggest ones there, and not by a little. They were longer *and* thicker.

But Vanessa was still trusting him with this.

"Any time you need me to slow down or stop, you just say the word, okay, babe? I don't want to take you anywhere you aren't ready to go. You promise you'll let me know?"

She nodded but he needed to hear the words.

"Let me hear you promise."

She looked over her shoulder. "I promise."

"Good girl." He grinned and gave her ass a quick smack.

She sucked in a breath and bit her bottom lip as her head dropped slightly back. Oh fuck, she liked it.

He did it again and the pleasured groan that came out of her throat was the final straw.

No more waiting.

He took her hips and held her still, then started pressing in.

Nothing happened at first. He wasn't going anywhere and for a panicked, disappointed moment he thought he was just too big. He wouldn't fit.

But then the head of his cock popped through the rim of her hole and holy fucking Jesus Krishna God *FUCK*—

"So tight," he gasped, wrapping his arm around her waist like a handlebar. "Jesus, honey. I never— You're—" He pressed in another inch. "Awww *fuck*."

He dropped his forehead down to her shoulder blade if only because he needed something to fucking ground himself.

It felt like he was pushing his cock into the tightest fucking glove that had been created perfectly for his shaft. And in truth, he was.

Vanessa.

She was perfect.

And the fact that she was giving him this— Giving him *her*—

"Ross," he growled, "hurry up and get your dick inside our wife. Let's make her fantasy real. Both of us at once."

Vanessa panted and hissed air through her teeth. Riordan felt the instant that Ross started penetrating her because the vice grip of Vanessa's ass around Riordan's cock grew impossibly tighter.

Riordan dragged his hips backward, the friction the most incredible fucking thing he ever could have imagined.

He glanced over Vanessa's shoulder and saw the veins in Ross's neck raised and straining. Then Vanessa leaned forward and kissed Ross, their mouths a hot tangle.

Riordan waited for the jealousy to hit.

But it... *didn't*.

He blinked in confusion.

Of course he didn't *want* to feel jealous, but he always had. Every single time they'd been forced to share something, Riordan always came off feeling like he got the short end of the stick.

But now, here, with the most important thing they could ever share... Riordan only felt satisfaction that Vanessa was getting exactly what she'd fantasized about.

And even as he paused thinking about all this, Vanessa pulled back from Ross and turned to look over her shoulder, eyes dark with lust. It was obvious she was seeking a kiss. From him now.

Because she honestly didn't like Ross *better* than him, but as much as.

He'd never believed the bullshit about it being possible to love two people equally. He thought it was just lies parents told to try to make themselves feel better about the fact that they loved one kid more than another.

But what if Vanessa... What if in this one case it *was* possible—

"Riordan," Vanessa whimpered, the need in her voice so fucking hot, Riordan immediately thrust back in again.

It just happened to be at the same time that Ross did the same.

Vanessa's eyes went round and she gasped. "So *full*." And then her eyes went pleading. "More. Please."

Riordan looked over her head to his brother.

"Together?" They both asked the question at the same time, and then gave each other mirroring grins.

And then, in unison, they fucked their wife.

Riordan kissed Vanessa deep and then passed her back to Ross, who kissed her just as voraciously. They plunged in together and

Vanessa's mouth dropped open wider and wider with each stroke, a high-pitched cry coming from her throat.

Instead of loosening, her muscles only clenched tighter around Riordan's cock. From the look on Ross's face, she was doing the same with her pussy.

Riordan made it way longer than he would have imagined. Maybe ten minutes? Ten minutes of agonized ecstasy, especially toward the end, fighting the knife's edge of tipping over and coming but not wanting to give in.

Just a little longer, he kept telling himself. Just one more thrust. And then one more. Okay, *this* would be the last one.

But fuck, she felt so good. And he'd never get this first again. So he'd grit his teeth and hold off again.

There came a time, though, when no gritting of teeth or reciting old Civil War generals was going to cut it.

And that was because their gorgeous, perfect fucking wife was coming like a goddamned earthquake.

Her orgasm rippled up and down Riordan's cock and that was it. He was fucking done. He was—

He roared Vanessa's name as he shoved in to the root and cum pumped out of him, deep into his wife's darkest, most forbidden place.

And he knew that she might just be right—life with her, this astounding woman, could be the greatest adventure of his life.

CHAPTER TWENTY-ONE

LOGAN

One Month Later

Logan pulled yet another box out of the back corner of the closet as he hunted for the pair of boots he knew was back there somewhere.

Jesus, they hadn't lived here long enough to accumulate all this crap. What was even in all these boxes?

Probably Cam's shit.

Logan would bet he'd just shoved these boxes back here when they'd moved in and never given it another thought. Or thought about what a pain in the ass it would be for anyone else in the house to dig through when they needed to get at something *they'd* boxed up.

Logan shook his head as he went to lift another box. His back immediately felt the strain and he stopped lifting.

Jesus Christ, what was in the damn thing? Bricks?

"Logan?" he heard Vanessa's voice distantly call.

"In here," Logan replied, "I'm in the closet."

After Logan found these damn boots so he wouldn't have to fumble for them in the morning, he was going to make Vanessa a romantic meal he'd been planning all day. It was a rare occasion to get alone time with her, much less an entire night.

But Michael was out at the paper burning the midnight oil on a story he was trying to get in tomorrow morning's edition, and Cam had the night shift at the clinic. Then the twins had both picked up extra shifts doing night irrigation for some extra script. Vanessa's birthday was coming up in a couple months and they wanted to get her something special.

Now, if only Logan could just find these damn boots for tomorrow, then he could get back to the slab of deer meat he had marinating. Ross and Riordan weren't the only ones who could do something special.

He repositioned the oil lamp on the stack of boxes he'd made to his left and yanked on the top flaps of the heavy cardboard box to open it and look inside.

"Logan, wait!"

Logan only registered the panic in Vanessa's voice as the flaps flipped open. He looked down in bewilderment and then up at Vanessa standing in the closet doorway.

"Logan!" Her chest heaved like she'd just run a marathon. She met his eyes and then her gaze dropped to the box at his knees. She didn't look surprised to see it.

"What the hell, Vanessa?" He reached down and pulled two of the probably thirty or forty cans stacked in the bottom of the box. Along with, shit, was that jerky? And several fat, ten pound bags of cornmeal.

Vanessa backed up. "I'm sorry," she whispered.

What the fuck was going on here?

Logan dropped the cans back in the box and followed Vanessa out of the closet. "Did you steal these?" he demanded.

"What?" She blanched. "Of course not!"

"Then..." Logan frowned.

She stared at the ground, arms tight across her stomach.

"Tell me," he demanded, probably too harshly, but fuck, she'd been hiding something from him. Something big, by the look of guilty dread on her face as her eyes flashed back up at him.

"I lied, okay?" she whispered.

Logan didn't like the trickle of unease tickling up his spine. "About what."

She gestured at the box. "I lied when I said I wanted to pick up the rations for the clan every day because I wanted to be helpful."

Logan stared at her in bewilderment. "So, what? You volunteered so you could stash some of it away up here? But why?"

She let out a huff of air through her nose, nostrils flaring. "A person can't just..." she snapped her fingers, "*change*, just like that. I spent years—years—never knowing where my next meal was going to come from. God, there were bad days—bad *months*—where I'd think about eating grass I was so hungry."

She shook her head. "And every day you didn't eat made it that much harder to get food the next day because you were weaker. So if you found a place to get food, you have to be smart about it. You always prepare for the bad days."

What the—

"But you aren't out in the fucking wilderness anymore!" Logan couldn't help his voice rising. Did she not think he could provide for her? That he and the clan would take care of her?

"Don't you know how worried we've all been about you not gaining weight? And the whole time you've been stashing food instead of eating it? Jesus Christ, Ross and Riordan went out hunting and almost *died* because they were so worried—"

"I know," she whimpered, hands going to her head. "Don't you think I know that?"

Logan flung his arms out. "So why the fuck do you still have this box up here?"

"Because what if I need it again?" she shouted.

Heavy silence hung in the air between them after her heated declaration.

She thought she might *need it*...?

She was hoarding the food because she thought—

She thought that at some point she'd be alone again.

She believed it enough to continue starving herself for months after she'd come to the safe haven of Jacob's Well. Did she even eat dinner on the nights they weren't all together? Or did she just skip any meal they weren't there to watch her? Jesus *Christ*.

"My whole life I've been left behind," she whispered. "Not wanted. Not loved."

"Vaness—" he started but she talked over him.

"The only man who ever wanted me wanted me because he thought he could get top dollar for my virgin pussy at a slave auction."

Her words sliced into Logan like a branding iron.

"That's not fucking true. We want you. We're your *clan*."

But again, she was shaking her head. "Maybe you want me for now. But eventually you'll realize I'm not what you *really* want. Someday you'll want someone who will— Someone who can—" her voice broke and she looked away from him toward the wall. "I just need to know I'll be able to survive if the bad days come again."

Her gaze had gone distant, like he wasn't even there with her. Which pissed him the fuck off.

"Don't you dare try that," Logan stalked across the room to where she stood and took her arm. "Not with me. Not now. You don't get to shut me out."

Her eyes flicked back his way but only landed on his face for a second before shifting away again. She waved a hand and let out a short, bitter laugh. "I've told you about my luck. How long can this all last?" She shook her head. "People don't get to be this happy. Not people like me."

Jesus Christ.

"We made vows, Vanessa," he growled. "We promised to protect you."

Her spine stiffened and Logan couldn't say he wasn't glad to see it. He'd been wondering where her fierce warrior spirit had gone.

"Almost every one of you had half a foot out the door from the very moment they called your names for the lottery." There was accusation in her eyes and it hit its mark.

Fuck.

No wonder she hadn't felt secure.

She was right. In the beginning, he'd been running as hard and as far as he could without actually being absent.

So of course she'd been making contingency plans. She hadn't survived the harsh Texas summers and bandits and smugglers for nothing. Her survival instincts were honed.

And Clan Washington had not felt like a safe bet.

Because Logan had failed her.

"Oh baby," Logan said, crossing the last couple of feet between them and pulling her into his arms.

She was stiff at first. Resistant. She'd reverted to survival mode, but Logan was done letting her down. He knew the only thing that would convince her was time, but he'd show her he was a sure thing.

"I'm not going anywhere, baby. *Ever.*" Even as he whispered the word, his heart lurched. After losing Jenny, he'd sworn, *sworn*, he'd never promise forever to anyone again.

But he hadn't counted on Vanessa. She might be the one person in the world he'd push aside his worst fears and all those clamoring demons for—no matter how much taking that leap fucking terrified him.

He'd failed Jenny, but he wouldn't fail Vanessa.

Not again.

Not ever.

"I swear it," he whispered into her hair.

"What?" she asked, pulling away just far enough to look up at him.

And what he saw on her face fucking gutted him.

Fear. She was still afraid to believe in him. Fuck, he had so much to make up for. So much to prove to her.

But there was hope in her eyes too. Christ, he didn't deserve her.

He didn't answer her, he just cupped her face and then kissed her. Kissed her and kissed her and kissed her.

They shed their clothing as he walked her backwards toward the bed.

And then he made love to his wife, trying to prove with his body what words couldn't—that he would never leave her, never forsake her, and always, *always* provide for her every need.

He genuinely believed it, too, even as they both slowly drifted off to sleep. He held that thought all the way up until the town's alarm sirens started screaming in the middle of the night, and he heard the best and worst news of his life.

CHAPTER TWENTY-TWO

LOGAN

The town's alarm sirens blasted through the night.

"What the fuck is going on out there?" Logan demanded as he pounded down the hallway, dragging on his jeans as he went. Vanessa was right on his heels. They'd been sound asleep when the town's alarm sirens had started blaring.

"It's Colonel Travis's soldiers," Michael said, coming through the front door and slamming it behind him. "They have Jacob's Well surrounded."

"Oh my God," Vanessa gasped from behind Logan, reaching forward and grasping his hand.

Logan's face snapped toward the window. "But I don't hear anything. No bombs or shelling."

"That's the weird thing," Michael said. "They aren't attacking. They're just... standing there. They have been for over an hour now."

"What does that mean?" Vanessa asked.

"I have to go down to the Security Squadron Headquarters. With

Nix at the Capitol with the delegation, I'm the Senior Commanding Officer."

Vanessa was already nodding. "I understand. Go. I'll be fine."

Logan growled. She was doing it again—assuming she didn't take priority in his life. He leaned down and kissed her hard, only pulling back when the front door opened. It was the twins and Cam.

"We just came from the square," Riordan explained. "They're asking for all able-bodied men to help defend the perimeter. But we had to make sure Vanessa was safe."

Logan nodded even as Vanessa pulled out of his hands. "I'll be fine. You go. The town's more important—"

"Shut up with that crap," Logan snapped.

Vanessa looked his way sharply, eyes wide with surprise and hurt at his tone. Shit. He was already fucking this up.

He took her cheeks in his hands. "Baby, you're the only important thing to me. To all of us. You won't be alone. None of us would be any use to anyone out there if we were worrying about you."

He turned to the others. "I have to go, so who'll go with Vanessa to the shelter? Two to stay with her, two to go defend the perimeter."

"I'll stay," Riordan said at the same time Ross said, "I'll go."

The two looked at each other and without a word, gave a quick nod.

All right, not the way Logan would have guessed that would play out, but okay.

Logan looked toward Michael and Riordan. "Riordan, you know where the Glock is?" It was a rhetorical question since obviously Riordan had stolen it for his ill-fated hunting adventure.

Still, Riordan gave a nod, and Logan could tell he was proud to be trusted with the gun. Logan's trust only went so far, though. "Good, then go get it and give it to Vanessa. We all know she's the most lethal one in this room."

He'd forced her to eat some of the jerky she'd been stockpiling after they'd made love earlier, so she should be in good shape.

He pressed a kiss to her forehead. "Stay safe."

She clutched his waist. "You too."

He had to force himself to pull away, otherwise he'd never leave.

Outside, it was mayhem. People ran every which way by the light of the full moon, dragging suitcases, carts, anything and everything they could carry. Kids wailed as terrified looking parents carried them down Main Street toward the shelter. In case of emergencies like this, civilians were supposed to gather in the school. At least the damn siren had finally turned off. Everyone had gotten the message by this point.

Logan spent the next few hours running himself ragged, prepping the town's fortifications.

They were working blind. Usually they had an infrared satellite feed —their system was one of the only, if not *the* only one besides Fort Worth that did.

But the technology officer who'd taken over for the usual tech, Graham Hale, while Clan Hale was in Fort Worth—well, it turned out he was a spy for Colonel fucking Travis.

And the bastard had taken a sledgehammer to the computers before they'd apprehended him.

So yeah. They were fucking blind.

They only had a few pairs of infrared binoculars and they weren't showing shit. Right when the siren had been sounded, Travis's troops were within visual contact. Not just soldiers, either. Tanks, too. Even one fucking Patriot *missile launcher*.

By the time Logan got on scene, though, they'd all pulled back. There weren't any heat signatures in sight of the binocular's range, but that wasn't saying much since they only had a range of a little over a quarter of a mile.

Clouds started settling in, obscuring the light from the moon, and even when Logan sent scouts as far as a mile and a half out, they *still* reported no sign of troops.

"Well where the hell did they go?" Logan shouted when he got the latest scout report. "Are they fucking ghosts?"

He would have doubted they'd ever been there in the first place if there hadn't been so many eyewitnesses who claimed to have seen them.

Why had they shown themselves only to pull back? To scare the shit out of everyone in Jacob's Well, that was clear.

But why give away their position like that when they had the element of surprise? It didn't make any sense.

And where had they pulled back to?

He was sending his scouts farther and farther out every hour and they still weren't seeing them. Things like tanks and portable missile launching vehicles weren't quiet. If the damn alarm hadn't been going for so long, they might have heard the soldiers and had a clue which way they'd gone.

As it was, they were both figuratively and literally in the fucking dark.

Was Travis waiting for dawn to attack?

That was the only thing that made sense, but something didn't feel right. *At all.*

"Sir!" Juan, one of Logan's lieutenants, ran into the strategy room of the Squadron Headquarters. "We have movement! A huge column of troop busses headed our way from the north."

Logan frowned even as he jogged for the door. "North?"

Travis Territory was southeast of them. And the earlier eyewitness reports hadn't said anything about *busses* before. Travisville was only fourteen miles away, an easy enough distance to travel by foot if Travis had his spy hiding the satellite imagery.

"I'm just reporting what I heard."

Logan shoved open the door to headquarters just in time to hear several people on the street shouting, "Look!" and pointing upwards.

Logan's head jerked upward. When he first saw the bright flare of light in the sky, his stomach dropped.

Oh God, no. They've shot a missile.

But then he saw a second light and, after a long pause, a third. Followed by a fourth and fifth in quick repetition.

"Hold your fire," Logan shouted, running toward one of the Security Squadron's three trucks. "Hold your fire, send the command down the line. It's Nix!"

Cheers sounded all around Logan at the news as he and Juan hopped in the four-by-four and he shoved the keys in the ignition.

They met Nix up near Jacob's Well—the actual well the town was named for—right as dawn broke.

"Goddamn is it good to see you," Logan said, embracing his friend when Nix hopped down from a troop truck at the head of the line of armored busses.

"That damn Travis spy busted our satellite phone," Logan said. "Finn said he tried to get a mayday call off to y'all in Fort Worth, but he couldn't hear anything on the other end so he didn't think it had gone through."

"We got it," Nix said, somber.

"What the hell is all this?" Logan asked, laughing as he waved to the line of busses that trailed off as far as the eye could see.

Nix wasn't smiling though. "Goddard sent five thousand troops to take Travis out once and for all. Well, about three thousand here and another two following on foot."

"Great," Logan said. "Let's teach that fucker a lesson he won't forget."

But Nix was already shaking his head. "Logan, Travis's army is long gone. There's no one here. Scouts on motorcycles have gone thirty minutes down the road. There's nothing."

What? Wait... Oh shit, that meant—

"We were a decoy," Logan said. "A distraction. But from what?"

"I don't know. I was just about to call the Commander and see what the hell's going on back at the Capitol. But brother," Nix put a hand on Logan's shoulder, "after I do, you and I need to talk."

From the grim expression on Nix's face, it couldn't be good. Not surprising considering the shit storm Travis was trying to stir up, but there was something about the way Nix was looking at him— It sent a cold spike shooting all the way down Logan's spine.

Nix let go and went to make his phone call and what they found out from the Commander was bad. Really fucking bad.

Logan was right. Travis having troops show up at Jacob's Well was a distraction. One they all fell for hook, line, and sinker.

The five thousand troops Goddard had sent to help Jacob's Well was only a tenth of his fighting force, but General Cruz was famously vigilant—him being absent from the capitol had meant it was more vulnerable than ever.

Which was right when Travis struck.

The President was dead.

Assassinated.

They didn't have all the details yet. Travis had somehow framed the delegation from Jacob's Well, but that barely mattered.

Travis was trying to stage a coup and take the presidency for himself.

And while the attack last night hadn't been real, the first place that would have a giant target on its back after Travis finished taking Fort Worth?

Central Texas South and Jacob's Well had been a constant thorn in Travis's side.

He'd come for them.

Anyone in leadership positions would be targeted first. And the women. None of the women were safe.

There was no choice but to evacuate.

Nix even had a place to go. It was just a matter of getting Vanessa and the rest of the clan packed up and then they could—

"Wait," Nix said as Logan grabbed his service weapon and moved toward the door of the strategy room.

"No time. Gotta get my clan prepped—"

"You need to hear this, brother."

It was the finality in Nix's voice that stopped Logan in his tracks.

"What the fuck, man?"

Nix took a deep breath and ran a hand through his hair. He had dark circles under his eyes. Damn, when had he last slept?

"You look like shit, man. Come on, whatever it is, you can tell me on the way down to—"

"Would you just shut up for one goddamned second?"

Logan raised his eyebrows at Nix's sharp tone, lifting his hands in a whatever-you-say gesture.

"Shit," Nix dragged a hand down his face. "I'm sorry. This day." He shook his head but then steeled his jaw and looked over his shoulder.

"Finn!" Nix snapped his fingers. "Bring over the pack we confiscated."

Finn was standing by the armored vehicle Nix had stepped out of and he nodded, jogging over with a large, overstuffed pack.

"On our way south, we ran into some smugglers. We thought they might be Travis's spies so we flushed them out and they started firing at us. I don't think they had anything to do with Travis. We *interrogated* the one that was still breathing after the firefight was over. Especially when I found a certain item in his pack."

Ah. Logan knew just how persuasive Nix's interrogation procedures could be. He'd witnessed them firsthand enough times.

"Did he talk? What was it that had you so determined, anyway?"

Nix took a deep breath and that icy feeling Logan had earlier came back twice fold. "He had medical supplies on him. Pills, packs of unopened syringes. That sort of thing. And this. I think he was using it as a sleeping mat."

Nix grabbed the pack from Finn and pulled out a rough, black cloth. "He said he stole the shit off a few groups between New Braunfels and the caves at the north of San Antonio. He died of his wounds before he could tell us any more."

Logan frowned. He wasn't following. What did he care about some random fucking smuggler? They were at war. And why the fuck was Nix acting so weird?

Nix held up the black cloth. Okay, there was a hood on it, so it must be some sort of cloak. Like Little Red Riding Hood's, but black.

"I don't get it," Logan said. "What's with the cloak?"

"It's a Mexican widow's cloak."

And? But fine, Logan would humor him. "How can you tell?"

"The color mostly, and the size," Nix answered. "My grandmother was from Mexico and she made one after my Grandpa died. I was looking at this pattern along the edge when I saw it." Nix turned the cloak the other way around, then pulled back. "Maybe you should sit down first."

"Jesus Christ, just show me," Logan said impatiently, grabbing for the fabric.

Almost as soon as he did, his eyes landed on the linen label stitched into the inner seam.

And Logan's entire fucking world tilted upside down.

Because as he looked back down at the garment in front of him, he read not only the letters that were still legible:

J NY WA NG N

but also the letters that were no longer there.
Or...at least...could have once been there...

JENNY WASHINGTON

No. No, he refused to believe it.
Jenny?
After all this—?
Could she actually be... *alive?*

CHAPTER TWENTY-THREE

ROSS

Ross pushed through the people clogging the streets to get home.

People had cheered when the President's army battalion first rode down Main Street, but the truth of what was happening in the capitol quickly spread.

President Goddard had been assassinated.

Colonel Travis was staging a coup.

The soldiers only moments before welcomed as liberators were suddenly a liability. Travis had always had beef with the Commander, everyone knew that. So that was bad enough. But if you added in the fact that Jacob's Well was housing a whole battalion of thousands of troops who might stand against him?

They might as well paint a target on their foreheads.

The entire town had erupted in chaos.

Just like back during the Death Riots.

Ross had only been ten at the time. But he remembered. He remembered the sounds of the crowds outside. The noise of men shouting, pierced every so often by a shrill female scream.

"I'll be fine, Louise," Dad said, putting a hand on Mom's shoulder. "Don't worry. I have to get more food for us. If we're going to hunker down to ride this out, we have to have food. Now, you and the boys stay down in the basement and don't you open the trapdoor for anyone, do you hear me?"

Mom looked so afraid. Ross hated her looking like that. His stomach hurt and not just because he hadn't eaten anything more than peanut butter and stale crackers for the last three days.

"Don't go, Dad!" Ross flung his arms around Dad's waist.

"Let us come with you, Dad," Riordan said, standing beside them. "You taught me how to shoot last year. I could help—"

"No," Dad said sharply, peeling Ross's arms off him and stepping back. "Now you boys have an important job. I need you to stay here and look after your mother." He put a hand on each of their shoulders. "You're the men of the house while I'm gone."

"But Dad—" Ross tried again to protest.

"Enough."

Ross bit his lip, trying to fight back tears. He wouldn't be the baby Riordan was always accusing him of being.

He'd be what Dad said. an of the house. He'd be strong. Dad never cried. He knew how to do everything. You didn't get to be the Head Scoutmaster for two counties without knowing your stuff.

Ross wanted to be just like him when he grew up.

So Dad would be fine, no matter what was out there.

But Dad wasn't fine.

And he never came back.

They only learned what happened a week later when his Uncle Chet came to get them. Dad had been part of a group of townspeople trying to restore order in the little East Texas town where they lived.

He was trying to ration out the remaining food. But some maniac with a machine gun shot at the crowd and Dad was one of the people killed. He'd died a hero.

Ross tried every day to live up to his Dad's example.

But the immediate danger was past and now his place was at Vanessa's side.

He jogged down the street the last block to the house, shoving the front door open. He needed to know she was safe.

He wasn't expecting to walk in on her crying, reaching out to Logan, who pulled away from her touch. Michael, Cam, and Riordan stood in the living room in various postures, but all of them were strained.

What the hell?

"I only came to say goodbye," Logan said roughly.

"What's going on?" Ross demanded, throwing the door shut behind him.

When Vanessa looked his direction, the devastation in her eyes had his stomach feeling as sour as it had the day his father left and never came back.

"What?" he asked, but this time it only came out as a whisper.

"Logan's wife might be alive," Michael said. "His first wife, I mean."

Ross's head jerked Logan's direction but the older man wasn't giving anything away on his face. His eyes looked as remote as Ross had ever seen them.

"What makes you think—?"

"This," Cam said, lifting a bundle of rough black fabric. "He thinks it belonged to her."

"Thinks?" Ross questioned.

Ross was still shaking his head in confusion when Riordan grabbed the cloth out of Cam's hands and stalked over to Ross with it.

"See?" Riordan pointed down at a small label sewn into the hem of the hood. "These are the same letters as in her name."

Ross reached out and ran his hand across the scratchy fabric to read the handful of scattered letters.

J NY WA NG N

"But lots of names start with J," Michael said. "You said it was a Mexican cloak. Juanita. Jacinta. Jimena."

"Was your wife Mexican?" Cam asked. "Why would she even have this?"

"No, she wasn't— *Isn't*, I mean—" Logan broke off, pain straining his face before his jaw locked and he looked at the wall.

"You can't just go off on your own, Logan," Vanessa said, her voice pleading.

Ross's eyes shot open wide. "What?" but Vanessa was already continuing.

"You heard Nix. He said a bunch of the families are heading south to those caves. Natural Bridge Caverns. The smuggler said he stole the supplies off groups all between here and the caves. So we go and look for Jenny along the way. *But we do it together*."

Logan was already stubbornly shaking his head.

And Ross was ten years old again.

Watching the man he admired and respected most in the world preparing to walk out the door. For what might be forever.

"No!" Ross shouted, moving to block the doorway. "I won't let you. You don't even know if it's her! Come on, what are the chances that it's Jenny?"

"He has a point," Riordan said, leaning over and pulling the cloak into his arms. He lifted it close to his eye. "What kind of fabric is this anyway? Where would she get something like this? You already said she didn't have it back when you were together."

Ross nodded. Riordan had never been exactly the attention-to-details kind of guy, but Ross would take all the back-up he could get.

Cam stepped forward and rubbed his thumbs over the nubby weave. "It's rough. Not burlap exactly... Wool maybe?"

Michael gave a little shudder.

"Is there a yarn rougher than wool?" Riordan asked.

"Let me feel it," Michael said.

Everyone's head swung his direction.

Ross had only briefly touched the cloth but it had felt rough and scratchy to *him*. And Michael could barely handle the silk clothes he wore touching his skin.

But Michael's jaw was clenched in determination.

"Michael." Vanessa reached up toward him. "You don't have to."

"No," Michael said. "Let me. I'll tell you what it's made of."

No one questioned him. His sensitivity meter was through the roof.

Michael brushed his index finger over the fabric tentatively. Then he squeezed his eyes tight and sucked in a deep breath. His whole arm shook and sweat sprouted at his temple as he turned his wrist and took another pass with the back of his hand.

Then he stumbled backwards, breathing as hard as if he'd just finished sprinting a mile.

"Michael," Vanessa cried.

"It's wool," he said through gulps of air. "But not sweater wool. It's coarser." He shook his head, eyeing the cloak like it was poisonous. "Like woven sandpaper. Why someone would wear something like that..."

"There's more than one type of wool?" Riordan asked.

"Yeah." Michael gestured with his chin toward the fabric in Cam's hands. "That's like... the kind of wool they use in carpets. Probably from a llama."

Logan's mouth popped open and he took a step back like Michael had just slugged him in the gut.

"What?" Vanessa asked, moving like she was going to comfort him, but Logan held up a hand and shook his head.

Vanessa stopped in her tracks and Ross didn't miss the flash of devastation that crossed her face at Logan's rejection.

No, no, no. This was all wrong. They were a family. They were—

"Our neighbors..." Logan finally managed to choke out. "Back in Austin before the Fall... They were of Mexican descent. The wife had a little farm, raised chickens and llamas. She sold eggs and spun wool for a farmer's market every weekend."

The group let that sink in. Cam turned away from where they were all gathered, walking to the window.

"Could still be a coincidence," Ross said feebly, but not even he believed it. He watched Logan's face. Whereas when Ross had come in he was stoic and blank, now every emotion flashed on his features: grief, terror, guilt...*hope*.

"Jenny's alive," he said, his voice little more than a strained whisper. "She made it back to Austin. And I wasn't there."

"You don't know that, man," Cam said, turning around from the window.

But Logan just shook his head. "She was strong," Logan said, finally looking at Vanessa. "Just like you. If she survived long enough to make it back from San Angelo, then to keep on going, she's alive. I can feel it."

"So what does this mean?" Ross asked, and his voice broke on the last word before he cleared his throat.

"It means I have to go," Logan said. "With war breaking out... I have to find her and make sure she's safe. I failed her once. I can't do it again."

"What about Vanessa?" Ross cried. "So you're just going to fail her instead?"

Logan flinched at Ross's words but Ross didn't take them back. He couldn't believe the things Logan was saying. Especially after Vanessa had shared her past with him and Riordan. This had to feel just like her father choosing her half-sister over her during the Death Riots, all over again. *Worse*, because Logan was her *husband*.

Logan finally crossed the space between him and Vanessa, bowing his head and pressing his forehead to hers. "I'm so sorry, baby."

"You promised," she whispered brokenly. "Last night you promised me forever." Her bottom lip trembled as she looked up into his eyes.

Logan looked gutted by her words.

And Ross saw it clearly on his face.

Logan loved her.

He loved her as much as Ross did. Ross hadn't said it out loud because, well, none of them had. He didn't know why. But he figured he should take his cues from Vanessa and Logan because he didn't know anything about women or romance.

He saw now that had been the wrong move. He should have told Vanessa he loved her every day since the wedding. He should have shouted it from the rooftops. Whispered it in her ear while they made love. Written poems and sang songs to her letting her know in a thousand different ways.

Ross should have done anything and everything so that when Logan pulled away from Vanessa yet again, there would have been some buffer from his continual rejection. So that Vanessa would have known, deep down to her soul, that she was loved.

But he hadn't, and he could tell by the look on her face that she didn't know. She couldn't even believe it was possible.

"This is something I have to do by myself," Logan said. "It's too dangerous for you all to spend any more time than necessary on the road to the caves. I'll try to meet you there... eventually."

But Vanessa was shaking her head.

She swiped angrily at the tears that streaked her cheeks. Then she glared at Logan, fire burning away the despair that had been there only moments before.

"We are Clan Washington. We're strong together and weaker with any one of us gone. We're *family*. If you go, you take our head. If you go, you take our *name*."

Logan threw his hands up. "What do you expect me to do?"

"I expect you to take us with you," Vanessa snapped. "We do this together. Or not at all."

"No." Logan's voice was adamant. "I refuse to put you in that kind of danger."

Vanessa's chin ticked a notch higher and her eyes went icy with determination. "Well then I guess it's a good thing we aren't children who have to wait for your permission. Wherever you go, you can bet your ass your family *will* be following. Go ahead. Try to ditch us. I've tracked prey far scarier than you."

She stepped forward until she was chest to chest with Logan. "You really want to keep us safe? Travel with us. But we're coming. End of story."

"Boys," she said, eyes still locked with Logan's, "start packing our gear."

CHAPTER TWENTY-FOUR

VANESSA

That first day, they hiked for six hours, not including breaks. They walked in pairs, separated by rugged terrain, but always remaining within earshot of each other. Vanessa always made sure to pair with Logan, thinking that maybe during the hours on the trail she could get through to him.

A switch had been flipped when he tried to leave them earlier. She knew the situation they found themselves in was difficult. Impossible even, maybe.

But she refused to let Logan go without a fight.

After all the weeks—months—of feeling so unsure of herself, Logan had promised her he'd be hers always. And damn it, she was claiming him.

Screw the universe. Screw fate.

Maybe the only way you got anything in this life was by fighting tooth and nail for it. She hadn't escaped Lorenzo Bernal, the most ruthless flesh trader in all of the Republic by just sitting back on her laurels and hoping fate would set her free.

No. She watched and waited and taken her chance. She'd taken down Jack. She'd stolen their truck after Lorenzo shot her. When the truck ran out of gas, she'd dug the damn slug out of her thigh and patched it up by cutting up the seatbelt and using it as a bandage.

Then she'd kept running, or well, *hobbling*, but she hadn't let it stop her. She managed to make it to the river and threw herself in it with what felt like the last of her strength. She rode the current until she was miles and miles downstream from where she'd ditched the truck. And then she'd dragged herself up the muddy banks, nothing but her captor's knife to her damn name, and kept on fucking surviving.

Because she was not a goddamned quitter.

As for all the other conflicting emotions and questions warring inside her chest... Did she want Logan to find Jenny?

She was terrified that she didn't want that—terrified of what kind of person that would make her.

Because she loved Logan. Why hadn't she ever told him? They'd whispered about forevers but not once about love.

And if she said it now, it would sound like a plot to manipulate him.

But she did.

She loved him.

And that meant she wanted him to find Jenny. Because she saw how it was tearing him apart. Thinking he'd failed her. If he never found her, Vanessa wasn't sure he'd ever stop tormenting himself.

So she wanted him to find his first wife.

But what would it mean if he did?

Luckily the hike itself soon became too strenuous to keep obsessing. It was all she could manage to keep one foot in front of the other.

If she had to guess, she would have said the hiking boots Ross found for her weighed nearly as much as she did. But maybe that was normal. She'd never been much of a hiker. Once she found a place that felt safe, she tended to hunker down. That's what she'd done in Marble Falls where she built her first shelter, and then later in the cave near the Pecos River. Come to think of it... That's what she'd done in Jacob's Well.

These beautiful men—*strangers* just two short months ago—were now her safe haven.

Ross, Riordan, and Logan had looked at the map and set out their course before they left this morning.

It was going to be a long trip, and it was more than just the fifty-miles of winding paths toward San Antonio. There was also a wide band of hilly, overgrown land to cover. There would be doors to knock on, and random abandoned houses to explore.

While it would take Nix and the other Jacob's Well clans only days to get to the caves, it would probably take Clan Washington weeks. Maybe months before they found Jenny—or before Logan gave up and mourned her all over again.

They had the ATV but it was loaded with supplies so, at most, only two could ride on it. The rest of them walked. At least it turned out all those hoarded food supplies were good for something after all.

They passed a few dilapidated farmhouses and Vanessa hid while they inquired after Jenny. No one knew anything about her or any of the groups the smuggler had mentioned.

At nightfall, they reached their planned meeting spot. The twins had gone ahead on the ATV to set up camp and Vanessa was relieved to find the twins *not tied to a tree*, and with the canvas tent standing upright and a welcoming campfire snapping in the twilight.

They'd also cooked polenta with some wild greens and a bit of smoked meat left over from the hog.

"That smells like heaven," Vanessa said, dropping onto the ground and unlacing her boots. Oh God it felt good to pull them off. She yanked her socks off too and grabbed her flip-flops from her bag. Texas grass was always full of burrs so you could never just walk around in your bare feet, but she didn't even want to *look* at those freaking boots again until she absolutely had to tomorrow.

She dropped her face into her hands.

God, would tomorrow be any better in terms of getting through to Logan? Because today had been an absolute disaster.

Every time she tried to broach the subject of Jenny, he shut her down. He didn't want to talk about the possibility of bringing her into their clan, should they find her. He didn't want to talk about how Vanessa would be *totally fine* if he wanted to be married to two women.

This strange new world is all about changing the rules, she'd said. *We'll figure something out.*

She meant it, too. She didn't know exactly how, but she'd do anything not to lose Logan.

He'd only ignored her, though.

He said he didn't feel like talking about it and then started walking faster. She had no chance of keeping up with his long legs. He'd stop every so often so she could catch up but only so he could take off again.

Even now he took his soup bowl and walked to the furthermost edge of the light the fire cast. He sat down to eat, his back half-turned to the rest of them.

Enough.

This was bullshit and she was going to call him on it.

Camp was set up for the night. There was nowhere for him to run.

She grabbed her bowl of polenta and marched right up to Logan, plopping herself down on the grass beside him.

"You can stop with the martyr act any time now," she said acerbically. "You're not the only one this is happening to, you know?"

He winced at her words but she didn't take them back.

"I don't know why you won't at least *talk* to me about it. Let's figure this out."

With every word, she felt him shrinking further and further inside himself, though. She wanted to shake him until his teeth rattled and he stopped being so goddamned stubborn.

"I wasn't just saying shit earlier when I said we could find a way to make it work. It's not a crime to love both of us."

She only realized what she'd said after the words were out of her mouth, but Logan's head jerked up to face her.

Shit. Shit shit shit.

Every impulse in her shouted at her to take it back. To sputter that she meant "love" as a euphemism or metaphor or some other b.s.

But this was a fight for her life.

Time to put all her cards on the table.

So she squared her shoulders and looked him in the eye. "I love you, Logan. Maybe you don't feel the same for me yet, but if you just gave it time, I know—"

"Stop," he said, voice thick with anguish as he pulled her into his arms. The weight of relief that swept through her body at feeling his strong arms around her—God, she thought she might choke with sheer happiness.

Turned out she didn't know happy because the next words that fell out of his lips topped her all time moment of favorite moments in her life:

"Of course I love you, Vanessa. I wanted to make you mine from almost the first moment I laid eyes on you. I love you more than words can say."

Did he— Had she just heard what she thought she'd heard?

"Logan—"

"No. Let me finish. This isn't about love. It doesn't matter if I love you. You're too young to understand, but—"

"Don't do that." Her throat was thick as she said it. For him to tell her he loved her one moment and dismiss her the second, it was almost more than she could bear.

"I wouldn't make you choose," she said, swallowing hard and trying to keep her shit together. "Believe me, I understand more than anybody what it's like to love more than one person. It doesn't mean that love is any less real."

She took a deep breath because the next part was going to be hard to get out but she'd decided if it meant keeping Logan, she'd make any sacrifice. "And if you feel like it's what you'll need to honor your marriage vows to her, I'll give up my claim on your body."

He expelled a harsh breath at her words. Good. Maybe it meant she was finally getting through to him.

"But I will never," she grabbed his arm, "never, do you hear me, give up my claim on your heart."

The haunted look in his eyes didn't change though. If anything, her words only made him look more tormented as he pulled away from her, shaking his head.

"I don't deserve your loyalty." He stood up and backed away from her. "You're young. You don't know what you want. Or what's good for you. I'm not it. But you have four men that are."

"Logan," she cried, unable to fight the swell of tears.

"I'm gonna go for a walk."

And all she could do was watch his back as he disappeared into the darkness.

CHAPTER TWENTY-FIVE

CAMDEN

Cam heard every word between Vanessa and that stupid son of a bitch motherfucker. There she was, the most beautiful, sweet, goddess of a woman in the whole goddamned *world*, pouring her heart out, begging to be loved— And what did that fucker do?

He threw it back in her face and walked away.

Cam seethed about it until he couldn't stand it anymore. Vanessa was remote and withdrawn all through dinner and cleanup. They were all exhausted from everything that had happened that morning to the long day's hike, so they all climbed into the tent not long after the dishes were done.

Even Logan, who'd come back from his "walk."

He was sleeping at the far end of the tent and for all Camden cared, he could be sleeping outside. Maybe the world would do them a favor and a bobcat would come in the night and they'd be done with the big bastard.

Thinking about Vanessa's drawn face throughout dinner had his blood heating all over again.

Cam shoved Ross out of the way and took the spot on the spread out sleeping bag beside her. He needed to be beside her. To protect her from Logan hurting her any more. To somehow make her feel better.

She'd stripped down to just a camisole and underwear, it was so hot, even during the night. Cam and the others only had on their boxers—all except Logan who still had his damn jeans on.

Cam looked at Vanessa lying beside him.

She wasn't sleeping.

Over the past months he'd spent so much time watching her. Studying her every move, her every sound.

When she was sleeping, she'd breathe in this calm, steady way, occasionally with the cutest little snore.

Cam hadn't known snoring could be cute. And he'd never imagined that lying next to a woman while she did it could be so... peaceful. Especially after they'd just fucked. She was almost as bad as a guy, often falling asleep within minutes after.

Then again, they sure used her up every time, all four or even five of them having her in one night sometimes. He couldn't imagine how she managed it—how she managed *them*. She not only put up with all of their bullshit but she kept it from tearing them apart.

It was because of her they were a family.

He didn't know family could be like this.

You sad sack of shit, do you know how bad it makes me look when my own son *can't pass his MCATs on his first try? You made me look like a fool today! But then, I don't know why I expected any different from such a disappointment like you. I'll swear to my last breath that your mother whored herself out and you're some other man's bastard because you're certainly no son of mine.*

Jesus, hadn't they resurrected enough ghosts today?

He leaned his forehead against Vanessa's shoulder blade. Her slight jump at the contact gave away even more that she wasn't sleeping.

Was she running Logan's rejection over and over in her head the same way Cam's dad's seemed to spin on an endless loop in his?

Cam pressed a kiss to her back, right between her spine and her shoulder blade. Instead of stiffening, she relaxed back against him.

Atta girl.

The next second, though, she was trying to squirm away.

No. Please.

Because the truth was, he needed this as much as she did. For all the facades he tossed up, for all his fucking posturing...

It was all bullshit.

He was a fraud.

And a hypocrite.

Because what Logan had said to Vanessa outside tonight? It was no worse than Cam had said to her the day they met.

But it was time to tell his truth.

He smoothed his hand through her hair and then whispered in her ear from behind, "You're beautiful, do you know that? God, the first time I saw you up close, you scared the shit out of me."

His body was cemented so close to hers, he felt her little jolt of surprise at his words. But he didn't let up, he just caressed a hand down the front of her body. Down her neck to the valley between her breasts. Then back up again.

He had a hard on, he usually did whenever Vanessa's body was anywhere near this close, but this wasn't about that. Or well, not just about that. So he shifted his hips back even while continuing to hold her tight.

"All that time I'd waited and then there you were, beautiful and wild and glorious and I was scared shitless."

She tried to turn her head to look back at him but he just hugged her tight to him from behind, notching his head in between her shoulder and neck. He needed to tell her his truth, but part of that truth was that he was a fucking coward. And he wasn't sure he could get this out if she was looking him in the eye.

"So I did what I always do. I tried to push you away first before you could realize what a fucking useless, spineless waste of space I am."

No matter how tight he held her, though, she twisted out of his grasp and rolled them over, pinning him to the ground on his back.

Her breaths came in quick pants and even though it was almost pitch dark in the tent, when Cam felt the wetness splash on his cheek, he knew what it was. Fuck. He'd made her cry.

"Don't cry," he whispered. "Never fucking cry for me."

He dragged her down and kissed her tears away.

And then he spoke his final truth. The truth that had changed everything. The truth that had changed him and was changing him still every day.

"I love you, wild woman."

She let out a choked cry.

If anyone had been sleeping, they weren't now.

The twins helped Cam pull Vanessa's camisole and underwear off and Michael whispered words of love, too, and the twins, as one after the other, they made sweet love to their wife.

Halfway through, Logan shoved the tent flap open and stormed out but Cam only took Vanessa's face in his hands and kissed her to bring her back into the moment with them.

Logan could go fuck himself.

Tonight was about cherishing Vanessa.

Afterwards, they all fell into a sweaty, exhausted sleep. With Cam's last conscious moment, he intertwined his hand with Vanessa's, toying with her fingers and he thought, *this, this is what I want for the rest of my life*.

But in the morning, when he woke up, his hand was empty.

"Where's Vanessa?" Cam asked groggily, scrubbing at his eyes as morning light illuminated the tent.

"Hmm?" Riordan asked, eyes still closed. He didn't offer anything else and Cam rolled his eyes. Fucker was probably already asleep again.

Logan was also nowhere to be seen but that was hardly surprising. Bastard had probably slept outside on a cactus rather than be warm and cozy next to their wife.

Cam unzipped the tent flap, still scrubbing at his eyes.

But then he looked up and what he saw turned his blood to ice.

The camp site was a mess. The cookfire hadn't been started yet, but a bag of cornmeal was half spilled on the ground, along with several cracked eggs and an upturned pot.

Fresh eggs were like gold. No one was careless with them.

But the thing that really had Cam's heart stopping in his fucking chest was the single flip flop flung haphazardly at the edge of the campsite.

Flung... or lost as the person wearing it was dragged away.

"Get up!" Cam shouted, reaching for his boots and shoving them on. "Get the fuck up! Something's happened to Vanessa."

CHAPTER TWENTY-SIX

VANESSA

One Hour Earlier

Vanessa woke when the tent was barely lit with the light from the burgeoning dawn. She looked around. Her fingers were still entwined with Cam's. Everything he'd confessed last night—finally busting down all his walls and baring himself completely like that—

She bent down and kissed the back of his hand with the barest whisper of her lips. She didn't want to wake him. When she peeled her fingers away from his, he stirred but then when she froze, he settled back in to sleep.

Beautiful man.

All of them.

Her gaze swept across the tent. She grinned seeing the twins, Riordan's arm slung across Ross's face. And Michael on his mat covered in a silk sheet at the bottom of the tent.

And Logan's sleeping bag... wait, where was Logan's sleeping bag?

All her warm, fuzzy feelings dissipated.

He must have come in after they'd all fallen asleep and taken it so he could sleep outside. Her chest tightened, but she swallowed her emotions back.

As quiet as she could, she unzipped the tent, slipped on her flip-flops, and climbed out.

She expected to see Logan asleep on his bag near the fire ring. The fire itself had burned down to coals but still. He might not have needed it for warmth but he knew the dangers out there as well as she did. This was bobcat territory. If you camped, you stayed in a tent or close to a fire. Even when she'd lived in the cave, she'd set up a series of traps and alarms to alert her if anything big was coming through the entrance.

But wait, seriously, where *was* he?

She turned in a circle. They'd stopped on the edge of a clearing, and looking out, she didn't see him. She glanced behind her at the woods. Why would he take his sleeping bag into the woods...

Her eyes widened as she realized what he'd done.

That *bastard*.

He'd called her bluff.

She'd talked so big about how she could track him anywhere but it was mostly b.s. Yeah, she was a passable tracker. But a man like Logan knew how not to leave a trail.

When she went over to the ATV and found his pack gone, she knew it was true.

He'd left.

Probably in the middle of the night so he could get far enough of a head start that they couldn't catch up with him. Well one or two of them could with the ATV—

But she shook her head and looked east toward the sunrise.

She couldn't force Logan to choose her.

To love her.

Just like she couldn't force Dad.

She swallowed hard and tried to push that thought away. No, one had nothing to do with the other. She even tried to believe it.

If Logan's ghosts were going to haunt him to the ends of the earth, no matter much how she might want to follow him... Well, last night had been a powerful reminder that there were four other people in this marriage who needed her just as much.

She'd never give up on Logan.

Never.

But maybe loving him right now meant letting him get lost in the wilderness for a little while. And trusting that in the end he'd come back to her. To them.

She looked again toward the sunrise and took in a breath that filled her chest until it felt full to bursting.

And maybe, *finally*, her ability to feel whole didn't have to depend on whether someone else loved her or not. She'd given as much love as she could and maybe that was enough. Maybe that was the answer she'd been seeking all this time.

And a small smile curved her lips right as the sun broke over the horizon.

Because a man like Logan Washington would never stay lost for long.

She was still smiling as she reached into the plastic cooler that held the last of their perishable food, taking out several eggs, some corn-meal, and a pot.

She'd have her guys waking up to breakfast already well under way. Start the day off right. If they pushed it, they could make it to the caves in three days.

"Well, look at how pretty you are when you smile, birdie."

Vanessa gasped, dropping the eggs and pan in shock at the voice she'd prayed to never hear again.

Oh God. No. He couldn't be here.

All this happened in just a split-second and right as she opened her mouth to scream for her husbands, a dirty hand clamped over her mouth and nose.

CHAPTER TWENTY-SEVEN

VANESSA

Vanessa blinked awake, her tongue feeling swollen and her mouth so dry it was like she'd swallowed sawdust.

Ow, her neck hurt.

She blinked more and the room around her came into focus. She jolted all the way awake, sitting up straight on the wooden chair and *ow*—

Oh shit. Oh shit oh shit oh shit.

Her arms were tied behind her back. And both her arms and legs were tied to the chair she was sitting on.

And she was in a room she'd never been in before.

Where the fuck was she? And how had she gotten here?

But even as she asked the questions, she knew the answers. Deep down, she knew.

It was Lorenzo.

Lorenzo Bernal.

"Looks like my little birdie's finally waking up. I told Jack not to put so much in the vial, but what can I say, he's not exactly in his right mind when it comes to you."

Vanessa didn't look toward the sound of his voice. Instead she looked around the room. There were two windows and it was light outside. She wracked her brain but couldn't remember anything from when she'd been taken. Maybe she remembered waking up and heading outside the tent? Looking for Logan because he'd slept outside? The memory loss was no doubt due to whatever had been in that damn syringe.

The view out the windows was blocked by a few short, scrubby trees, so that was no help for clues. How long had she been out for? Had Lorenzo taken her back to Hell's Hollow or were they somewhere closer to the campsite where he'd grabbed her? Was it even the same day?

The room was as nondescript as they came—cream colored walls, beige carpet. No furniture. Nothing on the walls. It was an empty bedroom in any cookie cutter ranch house, could be anywhere.

"You knew I'd always come for you." Lorenzo stepped closer. "You were the one that got away."

He touched her cheek and she jerked back. His touch was repulsive after months experiencing her husbands' loving caresses, and her response was instinctual. She spit in his fat, jowled face.

SLAP.

The explosion of pain across her cheek dazed her for several moments. The chair rocked on two legs from the force of the blow but settled before toppling over.

Lorenzo was shouting, but Vanessa could barely make out the words. She didn't care to, either.

All she could think about was her clan. What would they think when they woke up to find her gone? Would they think she'd left to follow Logan? Because small details were trickling in from the morning. How she'd stepped outside the tent at dawn and found Logan gone. Along with all his belongings. He'd left them. She'd started cooking breakfast.

The pot! She'd dropped the pot, hadn't she? And maybe some eggs?

So they'd know something was off. They'd be right on Lorenzo's tail to rescue her.

Lorenzo's loud laughter startled her out of her thoughts and she looked up at him. The satisfied smirk on his face couldn't be good.

"You're thinking your 'friends' are going to come and save you?"

She firmed her jaw and tried hard not to let any emotion show on her face one way or another.

Had he done something to them after knocking her out? Because so help her God, if he'd so much as touched a hair on—

"It's so sad," Lorenzo went on, a devilish glint in his eye, but I think they'll find that four-wheeler hard to run with four flat tires."

Vanessa felt her hope deflate with his words.

Foolish. So foolish to think a happily ever after was ever in the cards for her. No, this is exactly the sort of story the Universe would have written for her. Fate let her get a glimpse of her perfect life—at the center of a family who loved her—only to snatch it all away the very moment she began to fully appreciate all she had.

So you're just going to give up?

The voice in her head sounded like Cam's. She could imagine his face. The sarcastic tilt to his eyebrow as he shook his head at her. *I expected more, wild woman.*

And then Ross's voice, coming right on the heels of Cam's. *Remember the knots.*

Vanessa swallowed, her throat still feeling like a desert and spoke in a croak. "So, what? You going to sell me at the auction in Nuevo Laredo?" She coughed but forced herself to continue. "Is that still your plan?"

"Oh birdie, catch up, catch up." Lorenzo laughed again.

Lorenzo snapped in front of her face. "That plan's old news. I couldn't get shit for you now. It's only the virgins that bring top dollar."

Vanessa's blood went cold. "I am," she said automatically. The only reason Lorenzo and his gang hadn't raped her during her weeks of captivity with them was because she was a virgin. And it had been a near thing at the time before he realized that she was. But if he found out the truth now, oh God, all bets would be off.

Lorenzo laughed that fucking demon laugh again and then called out, "Jack, get your one-eyed ass in here."

Oh shit. *No.* Not Jack. Anyone but him.

But even as she shook her head, Jack shoved the bedroom door open and came in. The same one-eyed man who'd captured the twins in the Neutral Zone.

She knew not killing him that day was a mistake.

A mistake that might just cost her her life.

Was she wrong and Jack had still been working for Lorenzo all along? Or had Lorenzo taken him back in after he'd gone and tattled about where Vanessa was?

She'd told herself she could forget about the threat Lorenzo posed, even if Jack had reported back about her. She was safe in Jacob's Well. Besides, what, had Lorenzo and his gang just hung around outside Jacob's Well waiting for the one day she happened to leave? That was insane...

Unless he'd overheard the plans for Jacob's Well from his pal Colonel Travis.

So he'd known *exactly* when she'd be fleeing.

God, had he really wanted revenge that much? She was just one woman. Why the hell couldn't the obsessive bastard forget about her and move the hell on?

"Jacky here has been *especially* looking forward to this reunion."

Vanessa's air caught in her lungs as she looked over at the one-eyed man. Unlike Lorenzo, Jack didn't seem amused in the slightest to see her.

Today he didn't have the patch over the eye she'd stabbed out. It had healed badly. It was basically a gaping, raw, red hollow. It didn't look like anyone had even attempted to sew the eyelids shut.

He glared her down with his one good eye.

She flinched and tried to look away but Jack stomped across the room and grabbed her chin in a crushing grip.

"Look at it!" he shouted, spittle flying. "Look at what you done to me, you fucking bitch!"

Jack had been terrifying before. He was a goddamned cannibal, after all. And not just because he was starving and there were no other options. No. Human was his preferred meat.

Vanessa's entire body shook and she knew she wasn't managing to keep the fear off her face.

Jack leaned in and staring her in the eye, he licked up her cheek.

She wanted to head-butt the disgusting motherfucker just like she had the first time she'd stolen his knife.

But this time it was Logan's voice in her head that stilled her. *Keep calm. Keep steady, baby.*

So she sat still and clenched her eyes shut as Jack's foul breath washed over her and his filthy tongue licked all the way from her chin up her cheek to her temple.

"You're no virgin," he whispered in her ear.

"Yes, I am," she said through clenched teeth.

The next moment, Lorenzo was back in front of her, and shit—

SLAP.

She coughed and spit up blood from her split lip.

She blinked, the room going in and out of focus.

Steady.

Knots.

Wild girl.

"Tell that to the five men who were fucking you last night in that tent," Lorenzo sneered. "Or maybe it was just four. That one big guy did look pissed when he stormed out of the tent right as you really started moaning like a whore."

Vanessa flinched at the mention of Logan. She couldn't help it. Where was he now? Off looking for his first love, no doubt. Was it better or worse that he didn't know she'd been taken? It was one less thing to torment himself over, but then again, eventually he'd show up at the caves and the others would tell him what happened to her.

Because odds were, she was never getting out of here alive.

At least he'd have Jenny to get him over any grief or remorse he felt.

Ironic, since she'd done the same for him to help him get over Jenny. Talk about karmic payback.

"Her cunt's probably a saggy, old tuna taco by now if she's being pounded like that every night, huh, Jack?"

Jack didn't say anything. He just kept glaring at Vanessa.

Lorenzo let out a sigh. He always did love being dramatic.

"I guess there's no way to know unless we investigate for ourselves." Lorenzo started unbuckling his belt.

"No," Vanessa whispered. Not that it would matter to this monster. But no, this couldn't be happening. The blows had all certainly felt real, but please, please, could this just turn out to be an especially realistic nightmare?

She didn't care if fate or the universe had it out for her. She didn't care if karma felt like evening out the scales.

She wanted to live. She and her clan had come too far. Maybe in the end she hadn't been able to get through to Logan, but Camden, and Riordan and Ross, and Michael—

"I'd let you go first, Jack," Lorenzo said, turning to the other man, "but I doubt they'll be much left of her once you're done. Speaking of, why don't you give her a play by play of your plans? I do know you love that."

Jack's beady eye was still boring into hers. "I'm gonna fuck you till your insides bleed. Then I'm gonna cut off your leg and fuck you while it roasts on the spit. Then I'm gonna fuck you while I eat your calf off the bone like it's a fucking turkey leg. The hamstring is a little chewy, but once you get past that, if you spice it right, the rest is nice and juicy—"

There!

The knot in the rope tying Vanessa's wrists together behind the chair finally came free.

It was a trick Ross had taught her.

While he tied her up that day that Riordan found them on the porch, she'd asked him all about the knots he was tying. And boy did he have a lot to say. Not just about tying knots either.

He had all sorts of know-how about how to get stubborn knots *untied*.

For example, the simple knot these fuckheads had tied, like the kind you do when you're tying your shoe before you make the loops, just tying and knotting the rope several times, then pulling tight?

Even the tightest of those knots could be worked loose, according to Ross. All you had to do was grab the bulbous parts of the knot and twist them back and forth, then gently tug. Twist and tug. Twist and tug. It could take time and you had to be patient, but even the most stubborn knots could be worked free.

And it had worked.

She unlooped the rope from around her wrists but didn't let it drop to the floor. She didn't want to alert Lorenzo or Jack that her hands were free.

Because as much as it felt like a victory, there was still the not-unimportant fact that her leg remained tied to the chair. And the little detail of how there were two of them and one of her.

"Boss, it's fine if you fuck her first," Jack whipped out a switchblade from a sheath on his belt. "But let me have a little fun. Don't affect her cunt none if I cut off an ear or two."

Lorenzo laughed.

If it was the last thing Vanessa did, she was gonna stab that bastard in his throat and cut out his voice box so he could never laugh again.

"By all means," Lorenzo said, moving out of the way so Jack could advance. He came toward Vanessa with his knife upraised.

Steady.

Wild woman.

Closer.

Closer.

She only had one chance to use the element of surprise. She couldn't waste it. Jack's unwashed scent filled her nostrils as she took a deep breath, filling her lungs.

He grabbed her ear.

Lifted the knife.

And that was when she struck.

She whipped both arms around, lightning fast. With one hand she gripped his wrist and jerked it sideways, just hard enough to loosen Jack's grip on the knife.

She twisted her other hand to grip as much of the knife's handle as she could from underneath and then in one motion wrenched it up and stabbed it toward his good eye.

The gush of the blade sliding into his eye was familiar, but unlike last time, Vanessa didn't let go of the knife. No, she screamed in feral rage as she shoved the knife in even further. Up through the eye socket and into the brain.

She wasn't the only one shouting though. Lorenzo was yelling for his henchmen.

Vanessa yanked the knife out of Jack's head, ignoring the spurting blood and bending over to saw at the rope around her left ankle.

The rope wasn't thick and the knife was sharp. She cut through it without much difficulty but right when she was turning to cut the other, Lorenzo came at her.

He shoved her so hard the chair toppled backwards. Her head cracked on the floor but it was carpet, so she was scrambling to get away the next second. She only had one foot attached to the chair so she was able to crawl a little with it dragging at her like an anchor.

She didn't get far, though, before Lorenzo was on top of her.

He shoved her on her back and then his hands were around her throat.

Couldn't breathe. Oh God. Needed air. She grabbed his wrists and fought to get him off of her but he didn't budge.

"You fucking bitch!"

His face was red and for once he wasn't laughing.

"I'm *Lorenzo fucking Bernal*. Men all over the Republic piss their pants in fear of my name! You think I'm gonna let some stupid little cunt bitch make a fool out of me? Think again, birdie."

He squeezed even tighter.

Spots danced across her vision.

Couldn't—

She gasped but there was no air.

Needed—

If only she could—

The spots became a block of darkness as her vision blinked in and out.

This was *really* the end.

No!

She struggled even harder.

But her limbs were weak. It was like she was fighting through water. She couldn't move. Couldn't fight.

Couldn't—

Michael.

Riordan.

Cam and Logan.

Ross.

They needed her.

They—

The darkness crept closer.

And then the light blinked out.

CHAPTER TWENTY-EIGHT

VANESSA

Heaven was like a dream.

And in her dream, everyone she loved was there, surrounding her on all sides.

Cam hovered over her. Logan was beside him, his fingers in her hair, caressing her scalp. And Michael stood behind all of them, eyes wide as he looked down.

She couldn't tell for sure, though. Their shapes warped like they were standing in front of funhouse mirrors and their voices were muffled like they were shouting at her through water.

Then Cam leaned over and he was kissing her.

Except—

It wasn't a kiss.

He blew air into her mouth and she felt her chest rise.

That was a neat trick.

After a few seconds, he did it again.

But then she coughed and when she blinked, suddenly the warm blanketing haze she'd been floating in was yanked sharply away.

She sputtered and then Cam and the others moved her so that she was sitting up.

"That's right, baby," Logan said, rubbing circles on her back. "Thank God. Baby, thank God."

He sounded like he was crying.

What was—?

OW. Everything hurt. She swallowed and it hurt so much she let out a pained croak. She tried to lift a hand to her throat but her arm weighed a thousand pounds so she let it fall limply to her side.

"Water!" Cam snapped. "Get her some water."

What was going on? Where was she?

She turned her head the slightest bit and through the small sliver of space between Logan and Cam she saw Lorenzo. Lying in a pool of his own blood. Half his head was blown off. A shotgun was propped against the wall near the door.

The thought distantly registered that she should be more disturbed by the gore. Instead she turned her attention back to Cam and Riordan and the rest of her clan.

Were they... really here?

Was this *not* a dream? Not heaven?

Because as Cam asked her question after question, and Riordan held a canteen of water to her lips, and Ross held her head to help her tip it back, it all felt very, very real. In a surreal way. So surreal it had to be real.

Because frankly, she wasn't this imaginative. Not even in her wildest dreams could she have conceived of such an outpouring of love, devotion, and concern as she was receiving right now.

"How?" she croaked, swinging her head to look around at them all.

Every moment, they came more and more into focus. Cam's bright blue eyes. Logan's cleft chin. The thick, vibrant auburn of the twin's hair. The furrow in Michael's brow as he hovered right behind the others.

"I'm so sorry I ever left," Logan said, reaching down and clasping her hand in his, bringing it to his lips and grazing a kiss over her knuckles. "I turned back after a couple of hours but when I got to camp—"

"And found us going crazy," Riordan took over. "We knew you'd been taken but the tires on the four-wheeler were slashed. We found tire tracks but we couldn't follow until we fixed them."

Again, Vanessa could only manage a single word, "How?"

Ross grinned. "See, I told you my merit badge training would be useful." He shook his head at Riordan.

"Hey," Riordan said, holding his hands up, "I've never been so happy to be proven wrong."

"There's an automotive maintenance badge," Ross said, as if that explained anything.

"*And*," Cam said, reaching over to smack him on the back of the head.

Ross shot him a quick glare but then explained. "Patching tires was part of what I learned. If you slash a regular car tire in the sidewall you can't repair it, but ATV tires are different. It took a while, but eventually we got all four of them patched and then came after you as soon as we could. This cabin was only about twenty miles away, so three of us rode the first time, then Riordan took the ATV back for Michael and Ross."

"I'm so sorry we didn't come for you right away, baby," Logan said, looking haunted as he glanced past her to where Lorenzo's and Jack's body's lay on the floor. "There were six guards, and I didn't want to risk failing just because I was too impatient for the rest of the clan to get here."

Vanessa lifted a shaky hand to his face. "You did right," she whispered. Even getting the three words out hurt her raw throat, and she couldn't help dropping a hand to her neck. She winced as soon as she made contact.

Logan's jaw locked with anger. "This should never have happened to you."

She reached over and took his hand. "I'm fine," she rasped.

He gave a nod but she could tell he was still castigating himself. Just one more thing to add to his supposed list of sins. She sighed, giving his hand a squeeze. When would he learn that the entire weight of the world didn't rest on his shoulders?

Then his eyes came back to hers, and it was like he'd made some decision. There was a purpose and intensity to his gaze.

"It's time to get you home. Time for all of us to go home. Our new home." He glanced over at Ross. "How long do you think it will take us to make it to those caves?"

Wait. Did he just say *us?*

"But... Jenny?" she asked.

Logan's intense brown eyes came back to hers. "Baby, you are my only priority."

She blinked.

He'd picked *her.*

For once in her life, she'd been picked first.

She couldn't help the tears that started rolling down her cheeks.

"Sweetheart," Cam said, wiping her tears away with his thumbs. "Don't cry."

She nodded but continued blubbering, finally managing to get out, "Let's go home."

CHAPTER TWENTY-NINE

LOGAN

Logan felt at peace the next few days as they traveled south. It was a foreign sensation. But it was as if, for the first time in he didn't know how long—almost a decade?—he didn't feel like there was a constant war going on inside him between his guilt and the human desire to be happy.

It helped that the days were full of simple, hard work.

They'd wake up, scramble together some sort of meal, then set out to cover as many miles as possible. They stopped at Canyon Lake in the middle of the night to refill their canteens and bathe but they didn't stay long. It was right on the Neutral Zone between Central Texas South Territory and San Antonio Territory.

Before they'd left, Nix had gotten intel that San Antonio Territory had been taken over by the Black Skulls, a brutal MC that was allied with Travis.

Nowhere was safe.

Logan had come too close to losing Vanessa once. He wouldn't risk her again.

After another day of hiking, Vanessa riding the ATV the whole time, they had to finally abandon the vehicle. They were nearing San Antonio and it was too dangerous to bring any attention to themselves. The caves—Natural Bridge Caverns—were on the northernmost edge of the city.

They slept during the day and traveled all the next night.

It was coming up on dawn, the sky just beginning to lighten when they came across what looked like a rock bridge stretched across a natural sinkhole.

"Do you suppose this is it?" Michael asked.

They stood in a kind of ravine, scattered with rocks and spiked with a few crooked trees. Above their heads, a sixty-foot jagged slab of rock stretched from one edge of the bank to the other. It wasn't a slab that had been lain there, but rather the remnants of what had once been an entire rock ceiling.

"Looks more like a 'natural bridge' to me than anything else we've seen," Cam said. "We must be near the caverns."

"But it doesn't seem like there's anyone here," Vanessa said. She sounded worried.

"If they're here, they'll be deep inside the caves," Riordan said.

"But shouldn't they have sentinels watching the entrance?" Ross asked. "Even if we can't see them, *they* should know we're here."

Cam pointed to an opening in a rock wall at one end of the sinkhole, and the group stepped closer to the apparent entrance.

They were only a dozen feet away when a chorus of high-pitched screeches tore through the air.

Vanessa threw her hands over her ears and Logan didn't blame her. Fuck, it sounded like someone dragging a metal fork down a blackboard.

Logan looked up to see a whole flock of sizable roosting birds. Then, out of his periphery, came a flash of gray.

"What the fuck!" Riordan cried, jumping back.

Two large birds dropped from the bridge, landing on Riordan's back. They pecked and shrieked, clucked and squawked like hell's own chicken coop. It inspired those birds still in the trees to do more of the same, making an intense racket.

Cam only laughed and swatted at the birds on Riordan's back until they alit back to the bridge. "Guinea hens," he said. "Nature's best security alarms. Meet Nix's sentinels. Anyone who's here will know we've arrived."

And sure enough, they weren't more than five feet from the wide entrance when they were confronted by Danny, Gabriel, and Rafe, each holding a torch.

"*Dios Mio*," whispered Gabriel, as the three men stuttered to a stop. Their eyes were wide.

"Logan," Danny said, somehow managing to sound both panicked and relieved. "Thank God you're here. We didn't expect you so soon..."

"What is it?" Vanessa asked. "Is something wrong?"

"Follow us," Rafe said. "And hurry."

They followed them into the caverns. It was dark and cool inside, and the temperature dropped with every step they took. The limestone walls were wet, in some places dripping. Under each drip, small round calcium deposits looked like fried eggs on the damp floor.

"What is it?" Logan asked as he braced himself against the wall, then ducked through a low passageway. "Where are you taking us?"

He'd been expecting to be greeted with hugs and excitement. What the fuck had happened now? He just needed to get Vanessa somewhere safe.

The next room of caves looked like a gothic cathedral with tall broomstick stalagmites growing up from the floor, and drapery stalactites spiking down from the ceiling.

"Logan?" Nix looked up from a bucket and pulley contraption.

But then he was echoed by a much higher, feminine voice. "Logan!"

Logan's head jerked to the left.

And he blinked in shock to see Jenny walking toward him after getting up from a camping chair near the wall a few feet from the cavern's entrance.

She was skinnier than he remembered and her face pale and gaunt, but it was Jenny. His wife.

"Jenny," he whispered, too shocked to even process what the fuck was happening.

She threw her arms around him.

And kissed him.

He didn't kiss her back.

All he could think about was Vanessa watching this from behind him. Oh God, after all she'd been through—

Jenny pulled back from him, and then, before he could get his bearings, she slapped him so hard the sound of it echoed off the cave walls.

"You son of a bitch!"

And then her face went even paler and she fainted dead away in his arms.

CHAPTER THIRTY

VANESSA

She was beautiful. Jenny. His wife.

Vanessa could only watch on with a sort of numb fascination as they entered the cavern and Jenny threw herself into Logan's arms. And then as she kissed him on the mouth.

You're his wife too.

But Jenny was first. His first love. Grief over losing her had made him Ghost. Eight years he'd mourned for her. And even then, as soon as he heard there was even a chance she was alive, he'd dropped everything—even in the middle of a *war*—to go search for her.

Vanessa would never inspire that kind of devotion.

Logan had called Vanessa his priority, but she'd been hurt, and he was a good man. He had a strong protective streak. It was what made him agree to marry her in the first place. Her getting captured by Lorenzo had only triggered it again.

And that was before Jenny was here, in the flesh.

Still, it had been nice to believe... even if for just a few days...

She looked away from the happy couple, only jerking her head to look back when Logan started shouting, "Cam! Jesus, Cam! What's wrong with her?"

Vanessa's hand went to her mouth when she saw Jenny on the floor, cradled in Logan's arms.

Vanessa took several running steps forward. Oh God. *Logan*. She ran to him, but then stopped short. He probably didn't need her right now. In fact, she was probably the last thing he needed. And besides, Cam was there. He'd know what to do.

Cam bent over, ear to Jenny's chest even as she started to rouse the next moment, lifting a hand to her forehead. She was wearing a long-sleeved shirt but Vanessa caught sight of her wrist and a little bit of her forearm.

Holy shit she was skinny. And not just like Vanessa was skinny. There was little more to her than flesh covering bones. She was either starving or she was...

Sick.

Cam looked up at the same moment and his eyes locked with Vanessa's.

Oh shit, *no*.

But her suspicions were confirmed by the expression on Cam's face. Jenny was sick. Maybe even very, *very* sick.

Vanessa's gaze shifted to Logan, who looked down at Jenny with such worry in his features. And her heart broke for him.

Her attention went back to Cam but she didn't get any more clues from him as he went through what looked like a normal diagnostic routine. Jenny didn't seem interested in what he was doing. She only had eyes for Logan.

And for the first time, Vanessa thought about what it must have been like for Jenny.

Vanessa knew what it felt like to love Logan, then lose him for days. Jenny had loved him, then lost him for *eight years*. Even the thought of the unimaginable pain of that kind of loss sent a sharp, stabbing pain through Vanessa's guts.

Only to find him again after all this time—*You son of a bitch!* Vanessa winced remembering Jenny's accusing words. Nix and the others had been here for how long already? Several days at least?

The way they'd all been greeted, Nix must have figured out who Jenny was. She'd known they were eventually coming. Did that mean she also knew Logan had remarried? And about the, er, circumstances of the marriage?

Cam and Logan stood, helping Jenny up off the floor.

Logan swept her up into his arms and Vanessa couldn't help the pain that sliced through her chest at the sight. She was jealous. It was petty. But she couldn't help it.

When Vanessa was a kid, she and her half-sister Cecily had gone to the same elementary school. Vanessa was in sixth grade and Cecily had been in fourth.

Dad had come for field day that year. But not to see Vanessa. He'd come for Cecily.

Cecily fell over during the three-legged race and skinned her knee. Dad ran out on the field and swept her up in just the same way, holding her to his chest with such love and concern. Vanessa had imagined all the little assurances he must have whispered as he took her to the car. The way he kissed her forehead. How he probably told her silly jokes to distract her while he put on the bandage.

Vanessa turned away so she couldn't see Logan with Jenny anymore.

"It doesn't mean he doesn't love you."

Vanessa jumped at Michael's voice then offered him a wobbly, unconvincing smile. "Sure. I know. It's a brave new world and all that."

Michael frowned. "Just give him time. He would never hurt you."

Vanessa let out a mirthless laugh. No, Logan would never hurt her. If he did, he would hate himself for it.

And that thought hurt her worse than anything.

Because she loved him.

She didn't want him to be tormented anymore.

She wanted for him to be at peace. She wanted that more than anything.

And if being at peace means him being with Jenny?

Vanessa swallowed hard, wincing because her neck and throat were still sore from Lorenzo's strangling.

But maybe loving him meant taking on a little of his torment for herself. Absolving him and setting him free.

She wouldn't have to bear the burden alone. Ross and Riordan moved closer to her and she linked her arms with them, relaxing against the warmth of their bodies.

"Let's go find a place to rest," she said, not bothering to hide the exhaustion in her voice.

And that's exactly what they did.

CHAPTER THIRTY-ONE

LOGAN

"I'm so sorry," Logan whispered to Jenny as he laid her down on the cot in the cavern where Nix had directed him. "I'm so sorry." It was all he could say. Over and over again. He was sorry for so many things.

"Jesus, you sound like a broken record," Jenny wheezed. "Stop with all the sorrys. I haven't dreamed of seeing you for eight years just to hear you," she took a short breath, "parrot the same thing over and over."

"I'm sor—" He cut off when he realized what he was saying.

Jenny laughed, but it turned into a cough.

Logan's chest clinched at the sound. She barely weighed anything now. Back when Logan had known her, she'd never been short on curves. Now she was just skin and bones.

"Jen. What's going on?"

She waved a hand. "Nothing. So tell me."

"What?"

Her eyes searched his face and she lifted a wan hand to cup his cheek. "Everything," she whispered.

Logan couldn't hold her gaze. He looked down. "I tried to find you. Please know how hard I tried to find you."

Her hand dropped from his face and he glanced back at her.

She was nodding but her jaw was working in that way Logan recognized. Christ this was such a mindfuck. She seemed like a stranger and at the same time, like the same Jenny who'd busted his balls every day of his life after they met in high school. And that look she had on her face now—she got it every time she was firing up to get good and pissed.

Logan braced for it but didn't say anything. He deserved whatever she had stored up to throw his way. Would she ask about Vanessa? Nix and the others had been here for a while now. Had she talked to them. Learned about the lottery?

"Why the *fuck* didn't you wait for me?" she finally asked.

Logan's mouth opened, but then he closed it again. "I " he started but then stopped. "It was chaos out there," he said. "As soon as I was better, I tried to find you. You wouldn't answer your cell phone and I—"

She shook her head, biting her bottom lip like she did when she was trying to bite back angry words.

But Logan didn't want anything left unsaid.

"What?" he asked gently. "You can say whatever's on your heart."

She glared at him. "What's on my *heart* is that you're a fucking idiot. You knew cell reception was spotty during the Death Riots. People were sabotaging cell towers, breaking all sorts of shit. Why couldn't you just have *trusted* me? For once? I told you I'd come back after I got the penicillin."

"And I told you not to go." Logan couldn't help his own temper flaring. "I told you to give the tea a chance to work. Do you know what it felt like to wake up and find you gone?"

"Because you couldn't even walk!" her voice went shrill. "I was afraid you were going to die from that infection and I would have just sat around and done nothing. What do you think *that* would have felt like for me?" She jutted her chin out. "I did what I thought had to be done."

"And how'd that work out for you?" Logan regretted the sharp words as soon as they came out of his mouth. "Shit. I'm sorry." He dragged his hands through his hair.

"Jen." He leaned over and took her hand. Fuck, it was so cold. She was in rough shape. Did she have pneumonia? Jesus, being in this damp cave couldn't be helping things. He needed to get her warm. He put his other hand over it and rubbed hers between both of his. "I don't want to argue. I'm here now. That's what's important."

But Jenny just shook her head, tears gathering in her eyes. When she next looked at him, they crested and spilled over her cheeks. "It's too late."

Ice spiked through Logan's heart at her words. Especially when she had a coughing fit that seemed to last for minutes.

"What do you mean? Jen, what's wrong?" He clasped her hand even tighter between his.

She rolled her eyes as the fit finally died down. "Isn't it obvious?" She waved a hand down her body. "I'm dying."

"No," Logan choked. "No. You're not."

Her smile was watery as she looked back over at him, more tears streaming down her eyes. Logan wiped them away, but more fell as quickly as he could swipe at them.

"How long did you search for me?" she whispered.

"Jen," he said, his voice thick. "You're not dying. Why would you say you're dying?"

"How long did you search?" she asked, louder, coughing again.

"Months," he cried. "I followed the trail to San Angelo." He shook his head, remembering the horrors he'd seen there.

Her eyes went distant and she swallowed.

"I found the guy. The dealer you'd talked to. He said he was out of penicillin but that he'd sent you to Pflugerville."

She nodded. "I went there. And I got it. Enough to save you." Her chin wobbled as her eyes met his again.

Logan choked on a sob as he went on. "I was on my way there when the bombs dropped. Between that and Xterminate, I thought there was no chance— Jesus, Jenny, I'm so sorry."

She looked away from him, throat working like she was fighting back another coughing fit. "I would have been in Austin if Daniela hadn't helped me get out of town. Her church was evacuating all the healthy women who were left." She shook her head. "Austin was a war zone by the time I got back. The Death Riots— I went back to the house and it was trashed and looted. You were gone and I thought— I thought—"

Oh God. She thought the house had been looted because he'd died. She must have assumed they'd dragged his decaying body out into the streets for the burn crews or something.

"So I went with Daniela. A week later Austin was bombed."

Logan squeezed his eyes shut against the images. Jenny fleeing with the crowd of refugees in the chaos after D-Day when the bombs had dropped. The EMP strikes had happened simultaneously and all electronics were wiped out. Cars, phones, all communication lines, shut down, just like that.

She must have been so scared. All the while thinking he'd died.

He opened his eyes. "All that's in the past. Jenny, you're sick. What's wrong?"

"The past is my present," she whispered.

Logan frowned. What did that—?

"I got sick. I *wasn't* one of the lucky ten percent," she whispered. "I *wasn't* immune, Logan. Turned out, there was an even smaller percentage of us who got sick but survived it."

Logan felt his eyes go wide with surprise. He didn't even know that was possible.

"Daniela nursed me through it. She was immune. And somehow, I survived." She shook her head. "But it took its toll. I've never been the same since."

"What do you mean? How?"

She laughed humorlessly, ending in a coughing fit. It took several minutes before she could talk again. "Scar tissue everywhere. My lungs. But mainly my heart." She sucked in a breath. "I shacked up with a group that had a doctor for a while. Well, he was a pretty shit doctor. But even he knew enough to recognize congestive heart failure."

"What's th—"

"My heart's giving out," she coughed. "I've already," *cough*, "made it longer," *cough*, "than anyone thought." The last few words came out on a wheeze.

Logan's lungs hurt just listening to her.

He bent over the cot and cradled her to his chest. "Jen. Oh God, Jen."

He wanted to tell her she was wrong. That they needed a second opinion. That Cam would examine her and tell her she was wrong. That it was just a bad case of pneumonia... that she'd had for eight years...

He held her tighter to him. This was the girl he'd taken to prom. The first girl he'd introduced to his parents. She was the second girl he'd ever kissed but the first girl he'd gone all the way with.

She'd been his best friend.

They stayed like that for a long time, clinging to each other. Maybe half an hour. Logan thought Jen had fallen asleep but when she finally spoke, she didn't sound sleepy at all.

"I want to meet her."

Logan pulled back and looked down at her, not following.

"Your wife. I want to meet your other wife."

CHAPTER THIRTY-TWO

VANESSA

"You don't have to do this." Logan sounded more than anxious as he walked with Vanessa down the cavern passageway to where Jenny was staying. "I'm not sure what she wants and you don't have to—"

"Logan." Vanessa stopped and put a hand on his shoulder. "It's all right. Whatever she has to say to me. It's going to be okay."

He looked so worried and haggard. He had ever since they'd arrived yesterday. Vanessa lifted a hand to cup his cheek. "Stop worrying so much about me. I'm a big girl."

She dropped her hand down to his chest, settling it over his heart. "And I'm so, so sorry that Jenny is so sick."

It was true, too. Because she saw how much Logan was hurting, she genuinely wished they'd found Jenny healthy and whole. "Come here, hon." She wrapped her arms around his chest and pulled him in for a hug.

"There are no expectations here," she whispered. "I'm not mad at you for loving her." His body started shaking at her words. "It's gonna be okay." She rubbed his back, fighting tears knowing how deep his hurt was. "Don't worry about me on top of everything else, okay? Promise me?"

He nodded his head. He was so tall, she just felt his chin moving on the top of her head. She squeezed him even tighter. "I'm here for you. No matter what. We all are, okay?"

She finally pulled away and looked him in the eyes. And God, but she'd do anything to get rid of the tormented shadow she saw lurking there.

She offered a smile. "Come on, handsome." She reached out a hand to him and he took it, squeezing like she was his lifeline.

Soon, maybe before Vanessa was fully ready, they reached Jenny's cavern. The cave system was insanely extensive. It went on for miles and miles. There was one cavern as big as a football field and lots of little ones like this that made for perfect little private rooms. An oil lamp burned at the foot of Jenny's cot.

She didn't look good. In the light of the single lamp, her face looked even more gaunt, her cheekbones standing out in sharp contrast. She was covered in blankets even though there was only a slight chill to the cave air.

She blinked and moved her head slowly when Logan and Vanessa came in. A wan smile tilted her lips at seeing Logan. Her eyes flickered Vanessa's way but then they quickly went back to Logan.

"I brought you some hot broth," Logan said, kneeling beside the cot with the bowl and spoon.

Jenny nodded before succumbing to a coughing fit.

Logan put the bowl on the cave floor and helped Jenny sit up and sip some water after the fit passed.

"Leave us," Jenny said when she could finally speak. "Vanessa," she paused, wheezing for breath, "will help... with the broth."

Vanessa nodded, stepping forward. "Of course. I'd be happy to."

Shit. That probably came across too eager. She just wanted to show Logan she could be totally cool with this. She didn't want to give him any more reasons to stress. She'd keep her mixed feelings about this whole situation to herself. It was the barest of sacrifices she could make.

"Are you sure?" Logan's brow furrowed as he looked back and forth between his two wives.

Vanessa nodded emphatically. "Of course. Go. You haven't slept since we got here."

"Or bathed," Jenny said, nose wrinkling.

Vanessa couldn't help her bark of laughter. "Well, I wasn't going to say anything, but yeah, you are getting a bit ripe."

A smile broke across Logan's face as he looked back and forth between Jenny and Vanessa. It was the most beautiful thing Vanessa had seen, and it let her know she was doing the right thing.

So she moved behind Logan and gave him a shove toward the curtain that had been hung across the 'doorway' to the cavern. "Go. We'll be fine. I'll come find you later so you can come back and spend the afternoon with Jenny."

Logan turned to look over his shoulder. Checking with Jenny.

It hurt a little, but not too bad. Nothing Vanessa couldn't stand, anyway.

She helped Jenny sit up, and she fluffed the pillows behind her back. Only when Logan could see that she was comfortable did he finally leave.

Then...silence. Vanessa wasn't gonna lie, it was awkward.

"So," she finally said. "Should we try the broth?"

She knelt down and picked up the soup Logan had deposited beside Jenny's cot.

"Look," Jenny finally said, coughing a little. "I don't have time to beat around the bush." She sucked in a wheezing breath. "I got shit to say. So you listen. Agreed?"

Vanessa felt her eyebrows go up but she nodded and set down the bowl. Then, for the first time, she lifted her eyes and met the gaze of the other woman Logan loved.

"You seem nice," Jenny said.

"Thank y—"

"Logan doesn't need nice." Jenny struggled to lift a hand in the direction of Vanessa's neck. Toward the ring of bruises from where Lorenzo had strangled her. Vanessa swallowed but didn't pull back, and eventually Jenny's arm dropped back to the bed.

"He doesn't need," Jenny took another gasping breath, "a victim either."

What the fuck?

"I'm not a victim." Vanessa couldn't help the bite in her response.

"Damsel in distress. Whatever."

Vanessa crossed her arms over her chest. So this was how it was going to be?

"I was captured by a flesh trader and his crew. One of whom was a cannibal."

Jenny rolled her eyes. "Shit's hard these days. *Wah.*" She took a deep breath. "You think I'm gonna leave Logan with some chick who's always getting herself in trouble? With that man's savior complex?"

Ah. So she wasn't trying to be a bitch.

"Hmm," Vanessa half-laughed. "Didn't know I'd ever find anyone who could worry about that man as much as I do." She looked Jenny straight on, ignoring the slight discomfort it gave her to know Logan had loved those eyes, this woman, for years and years with a single-minded devotion.

"He mourned you for almost a decade," Vanessa said gently. "He tortured himself over it. Wore his wedding ring until about a month before I met him earlier this year. They called him Ghost. Because he all but stopped living after he lost you. He became a shell of a man."

Jenny sucked in a breath and for once, it didn't seem like it was because of her illness. Neither did her watery eyes.

"Fucking tear ducts," Jenny growled, swiping at her eyes. "No fucking control over them anymore."

"I won't say I don't need Logan's protection," Vanessa said. "But I can take care of myself in a fight. I've killed men. More than I would have ever cared to. The world out there is fucking scary and it's getting scarier every day."

Vanessa leaned in. "But I swear to you I'll protect Logan as much as I hope he'll protect me. And it's not just the two of us. We're a clan. We're a family. I'll protect him from the monsters outside and from his own demons inside. With everything I have in me."

Jenny nodded, her bottom lip quivering. "He needs a strong woman to keep him in line. He's stubborn, self-righteous, and prone to..."

"Chronic bouts of moodiness?" Vanessa suggested.

Jenny smiled, then coughed. When the fit was done, she wheezed, "Not to mention he's gonna get a collapsed spine from carrying the weight of the world on his shoulders."

"That's why he walks so stooped?" Vanessa joked.

"That man..." Jenny said, shaking her head. She blinked rapidly then reached out and grabbed Vanessa's wrist with a surprisingly strong grip. "Be good to him. Love him. And," her voice trembled, "if it's not too much to ask, don't let him forget me."

"I promise," Vanessa said, reaching out and squeezing Jenny's other hand.

Out of all the things Vanessa could have expected... She'd never— God, life wasn't fair. This woman was— Well, it was no wonder Logan loved her.

"I swear it. None of us will ever forget you."

CHAPTER THIRTY-THREE

VANESSA

Jenny lived for another six weeks. The entire clan got to know her and her cavern was never empty. They made sure the end of her life was filled with laughter and love.

Vanessa got closer to Jenny than she ever could have imagined. And every time Logan walked in to find Vanessa reading a book to Jenny, or Jenny telling Vanessa an off-color joke, that weight on his back seemed to ease up just a little bit more.

He was with Jenny the night she died, cradling her to his chest as she wheezed and gasped and breathed her last breath.

He'd cried plenty throughout the six weeks, though he tried not to do so in front of Jenny. She didn't like it when he did. But at nights in the cavern with Vanessa and the rest of the clan, he let it all out. And Vanessa was the one to hold *him*.

They didn't sleep together, out of respect for Jenny. But Vanessa found every excuse possible to touch him. To hold him. To do everything possible to infuse him with her strength so he'd have what he needed to bear up as Jenny grew weaker and weaker.

After that last long night, Logan emerged from the cavern where Jenny slept and said simply that she was gone. He didn't cry.

His face was... blank.

Vanessa had looked around at Cam, the twins, and Michael, and they'd all looked worried, but Cam had whispered they just needed to give him time. That everyone grieved differently.

Jonas performed a small ceremony in the caverns and then the clan men hurried to take Jenny's body to bury her outside before the sun came up.

When they came back, Logan's countenance hadn't changed. He seemed just, *gone*. Vanessa didn't know how else to explain it.

"Logan," she said, touching his arm when he and the others walked back into the main cavern.

But he just pulled away. "Need to go wash," was all he said. He walked off without another word and when Vanessa looked to Cam, he didn't offer any reassurance.

"He just needs time," Ross said. "He's barely gotten any sleep the past few days, he's been staying up with her."

Vanessa nodded. That made sense.

And after cleaning up, Logan did sleep.

He slept. And slept. And slept.

"Hey man," Ross said, shaking his shoulder after he'd slept for almost twenty-four hours straight. "You gotta eat something."

Michael paced along the cavern wall. Nix had found a mid-sized cavern for them. They used their sleeping bags and had found comfortable enough places on the ground to set them up. Still, comfortable enough to be out like a light for a whole *day*?

Logan just pushed Ross away.

He eventually woke up and ate.

But that was all.

No matter how hard they tried to engage him in conversation, he barely spoke two words, and they were always monosyllables.

Vanessa had known in theory that he used to be called Ghost, but now she finally understood what it meant. It was terrifying to see firsthand.

Vanessa put up with it for exactly one week.

She came back in the cavern after helping with the afternoon meal. The amount of mouths they were trying to feed had recently grown to insane numbers. As big as the caves were, they were almost at capacity.

But she couldn't even think about all the crap going on with the war, or with Travis or with any of the rest of it.

Her entire focus was zeroed in on the big lump snoring in the corner of their cavern. He was taking *another* nap. In the middle of the day. *Again.*

"Enough," Vanessa whispered.

Then she turned on her heel back the way she'd come. She stomped all around the huge cave system until she'd located all of her clan and dragged them back to their cavern.

"I don't see the point," Riordan complained. "He's not going to do anything other than lay there and stare at the wall like he's a coma patient."

"Shut up," Ross said. "He just needs time—"

"Bullshit," Vanessa said. "He's running. He's running from what he feels. Trying to hide behind this bullshit coping mechanism."

She shoved the curtain back when she got to the cavern. Logan hadn't moved. He was still snoring away in the corner.

"Enough," she shouted.

He stirred slightly, but then settled back in.

Son of a—

She reached over into their pack and grabbed their camping pot and a spoon. And then she started banging them against each other.

"Wake up!" she shouted. "Time to wake up!"

"What the fuck!" Logan yelled, sitting up and looking around.

"So good to see you conscious," Vanessa said in a peppy voice. "Now, it's time to fuck."

Logan's face blanched and then he grabbed his pillow and turned toward the wall, laying back down and giving them his back.

"Michael," Vanessa turned to Michael. "You're up first."

Vanessa reached down and grabbed the hem of her shirt and then ripped it up and off over her head. Her bra was next.

Michael already had his shorts down by the time her bra hit the floor.

Vanessa grinned and pulled Michael's silk covered sleeping bag right beside Logan. She lifted her hips and pulled her jeans and underwear off, then her socks.

She hiked her ankles up and held her arms underneath her knees to make sure she wouldn't touch Michael anywhere else than... well, the most important place.

"God, I've missed this," Michael groaned as he sank down to his knees in between Vanessa's spread legs.

Since she hadn't been having sex with Logan and they all shared a cavern, well, no one had been getting any. It just hadn't felt right.

But now, God, Vanessa couldn't wait to get Michael's cock inside her. Michael must have felt the same because he wasn't wasting any time.

He grabbed his shaft, positioned himself, rubbed his tip up and down Vanessa's lips several times in a way that made Vanessa's stomach clench in pleasure, and then he plunged in.

"Oh fuck," Michael hissed, and Vanessa had to agree.

"You didn't get her wet enough," Cam said but Vanessa just shook her head.

"Feels so good," she gasped, her fingernails digging into the flesh of her knees. She wasn't as wet as she sometimes got, but she was plenty wet enough. And feeling Michael's sizable cock stretching her after going so long without, oh *God.*

"Deeper," she begged. "Go deeper, Michael. I need to be filled all the way up."

"Goddammit," Logan growled from beside them, shoving to his feet and moving like he was going to storm out of the cave.

"Cam, Ross, Riordan, don't you dare let him leave."

"On it," Ross and Riordan said at the same time.

They grabbed Logan on either side and tackled him to the ground. As two of the few people in camp who were bigger than Logan, they were able to hold him down.

"Keep going, Michael," Vanessa said, clenching her pussy around him and looking up to look into his eyes. It was the only way she could ever touch him and she wanted to make the most of every moment.

"God, your cock feels so amazing fucking me. I love every inch of you."

Michael sucked in a huge breath, his chest expanding as he pulled out and then thrust back in.

"Oh God, yes. *Michael. Yes.*"

Those were the magic words, apparently, because Michael just lost his damn mind fucking her then. He rammed in and pulled out and rammed in again. Her pussy squelched with every thrust and she didn't bother quieting her escalating cries. She wanted Logan to hear every goddamned moment and she didn't care if everyone in the caverns around them were getting an earful too.

"Oh. Fuck, I—" Michael's words cut off in a strangled gasp as he thrust in and held. Vanessa felt his cum spurt inside her and it triggered her orgasm that had already been on the edge. She screamed out her release, watching the wrecked pleasure on Michael's face.

"I love you," she whispered after the spasms finished shaking her body. She squeezed around his cock again. "I love you, Michael."

His deep brown eyes went so warm, Vanessa's belly went liquid all over again. "Love you, too."

They stayed there for another long moment before he pulled out and gestured over to the others.

Vanessa was satisfied to find Logan staring at her, slack jawed. He averted his face the second she caught him watching.

Stubborn ass of a man.

That was okay. She'd promised Jenny she'd be more stubborn. She wouldn't let him withdraw into himself or accept him living as only half the man he could be.

She walked over to where the twins held Logan down, swaying her hips sensuously and trailing her hand down from her neck to circle her nipples.

Then she bypassed Logan and walked over to their pack. When she bent over, she made sure to sway her ass in their direction.

When she glanced over her shoulder, all eyes in the room were zeroed in exactly where she meant for them to be.

She chuckled and stood up holding the small plastic bottle.

"What's that?" Cam asked, breathing hard like he was winded. No doubt he'd seen the small plastic nub of the plug she had buried up her ass. Exactly like she meant for him to. For all of them to.

The twins were the only ones who'd she'd shown it to before. The question was, had Logan seen it, too?

"Cooking oil," she said with a smile. "I traded for it."

When she came over and crouched over Logan to undo his jeans, she found his eyes laser focused on her ass.

So he *had* seen it.

Good.

"Oh, big boy." Vanessa's smile grew even wider when she found Logan fully hard as she tugged his jeans down. And was it just her or did he lift up slightly to assist her in getting rid of his pants?

When she grabbed Logan's shaft and jacked it up and down, rolling her thumb over the small bit of precum that had gathered on the tip, he gave a desperate moan.

His stomach hollowed out when she leaned over, tongue out.

"Do you want me to..." she trailed off, teasing her tongue just an inch away from the crown of his cock.

His whole shaft jumped but she moved back. "Ah ah ah," she shook her finger at him. "You have to ask."

His chest heaved up and down. "Goddammit yes, I want it."

She immediately obliged. She didn't need him begging. Just willing.

She swirled her tongue all the way around his crown, then popped the entire tip in her mouth, humming around it when he groaned in satisfaction and one of his hands came to her head.

That's right, baby, she silently encouraged. *Take what you want.*

But the next second, his hand disappeared.

Fine.

Maybe she'd make him beg after all.

She bobbed off his cock, looked up his body through her lashes and found him watching her.

He looked away the second their gazes connected.

Goddammit, he needed to quit that. She moved her lips back and let her teeth graze down his cock until his eyes jerked back to hers.

That's right. They were playing by *her* rules.

She moved down, swallowing him as deep as she could down her throat.

She watched his nostrils flare with lust and swore she felt his cock swelling in her throat. She grinned, well, as much as she could with a throat full of cock, and then came back up, letting go with a wet *pop*.

She twisted so that her ass faced Logan and then she looked over her shoulder at him. "Pull it out. I want you to fuck me there."

He swore but it looked like he'd stopped fighting her, at least for the moment. The twins let go of his arms and he reached forward.

He wasn't gentle as he worked his fingers around the rim of the plug and yanked it out.

"Oh," Vanessa gasped, her entire body rocking and her sex clenching. Jesus, she needed to be filled. She needed to be filled completely.

But there was time for that later.

First things first.

She reached back to hand Logan the bottle of oil. "Get me ready for you. Stretch me out and get me slick."

He all but ripped the bottle out of her hands. She heard him pop the top and then he poured liquid down the crack of her ass.

And his *fingers*. Oh God, his fingers.

With one hand, he grasped her hip roughly, and with the other, he shoved two, maybe three fingers up her anus.

He wasn't gentle. No, there wasn't anything gentle about Logan tonight.

His demons needed a playground.

And Vanessa would give them one—her body.

He stroked his fingers roughly in and out of her ass and poured more oil until it was dripping down her pussy and to the smooth cavern floor.

Then he shoved two fingers of his other hand up her pussy.

"Logan," she cried out, bowing her head down to the floor, shoving her ass even further toward him.

His hands were merciless. She didn't mean to come. Not until he was inside her.

But it was clear he'd turned the tables.

She wasn't in charge anymore.

So she came with a screech, biting down on her forearm so people in the caverns around them didn't think someone was being murdered.

But, oh *Jesus*, she didn't know she could be brought so high— With just his *hands*.

Logan wasn't done, though. Not even close.

Both of his hands grasped her hips, and he turned her to face him. Just in time to see him drizzling oil all down his huge cock.

Vanessa swallowed, panting. This man had her panting for him. God, she was going to be the one begging if he didn't hurry up.

His eyes burned with intensity as he yanked his shirt off over his head. In seconds, he had her straddling him. There was no Ghost in sight.

She was confused because he had her facing him. Did he want to fuck her pussy first? And then he'd turn her around to take her ass?

But no, he grabbed her hips and pulled her forward until *oh!*

The tip of his cock nudged at her asshole and he lifted up on an elbow to position himself better.

Vanessa breathed hard. This was what she'd wanted. It was why she'd brought the oil. And she'd had anal before. Logan wasn't larger than Riordan, so she couldn't explain the sudden apprehension that took over her. Her ass clenched tight, though, denying Logan entry with her nervousness.

But then both his hands were at her face and his gaze was searching hers.

"Baby. Baby, it's me. I'm here with you. One hundred percent." Then he swallowed hard. But he didn't look away as he whispered his next words. "I love you. I'm so sorry it's taken me this long to say it. I'm sorry I've been such a shit the last week. Shutting down like this. I just—"

"No, Logan," Vanessa shook her head, then leaned forward to kiss him. "You're perfect. And I'll always be here to pull you back if you try to go away like that again." She pressed her forehead against his. "I promise you that."

He sat up further and wrapped his arms around her waist, burying his head against her breasts. "I don't deserve you," he growled. Then he drew her nipple into his mouth.

And just like that, her entire body relaxed. His cock was still pressing at the entrance to her ass and the second her body loosened, his crown immediately began sliding inside.

His face jerked up to look at her and she smiled through cresting tears. She dropped her head to kiss him and he devoured her, tongue plunging into her mouth and taking what was rightfully his.

He shoved his hips upward at the same time and Vanessa groaned long and low as he fed his stiff cock up her ass.

Oh God, there was nothing like that feeling of *fullness*.

Logan kept one arm around her, securing her body to his. But he dropped the other between them and dived three fingers deep inside her pussy.

"*Ohhhhh*," she cried.

"That's right, baby," Logan said, "Give me everything." His voice was dark and demanding and Vanessa couldn't do anything but give in.

She lifted up and down with his motions but even though she was on top, he did all the dominating. His powerful thighs and hips drove into her, thrust after thrust, bucking her up and down on top of him. She clung to his shoulders and held on for dear life.

"Logan," she screamed as the orgasm exploded over her. She dug her fingernails into his shoulders as the spasms wracked her body, head to toe.

"Yeah, baby, that's fucking right. Give me everything."

"I'm yours," she cried, whimpering and gasping for breath as the last shudders of the orgasm finished quaking through her.

"Fuck right you are," he growled.

She blinked up at him. "Did you come?"

He gave her a dark smile. "You think I'm done with your gorgeous ass that quick? Oh, baby. I'm not giving you up that easy."

He reached around and smacked her aforementioned ass and she jumped, clenching around his still rock hard cock. He groaned even as he slipped out of her, then looked up, eyes latching onto Cam.

"Camden. Help a guy out? We need to remind our wife what it means to be the woman of Clan Washington."

"Yes, *sir*." Cam mock saluted but he had an easy smile as he came over and helped Vanessa up and off Logan's cock.

Vanessa couldn't help but whine a little at losing his fullness but Logan just chuckled and gave her ass another little swat. "You'll get me back soon enough, baby. Just you wait. Now jump up and wrap your legs around Camden."

Vanessa's eyes widened when she realized what he meant for them to do and then a thrill shot down her spine.

She bit her lip with excitement as she stepped toward Cam and wrapped her arms around his neck. He'd shucked off his clothes somewhere in the last ten minutes. The twins and Michael, too, all of them with their fat cocks in their hands, watching on with avid concentration.

"You keep biting that lip like that and I'm gonna have to teach you a lesson about what happens to naughty teases," Cam said, gripping her around the waist and slamming her up against his chest.

Vanessa arched her back, rubbing her breasts against the wiry hair of his chest, loving the friction. She sucked even more of her bottom lip into her mouth and batted her eyelashes up at him. "Oh?" she asked in her most innocent voice.

He reached around and spanked her ass—but unlike Logan's light swats, Cam's smack had a sharp bite to it.

And Vanessa fucking loved it.

She moaned and thrust her breasts even harder against Cam's chest.

"Holy shit, she likes to be spanked," Ross whispered, and out of the corner of her eye she saw his hand on his shaft start working double-time.

"I told you," Riordan said, smug.

"That true, gorgeous?" Cam asked, spanking her other ass cheek with just as much force.

Oh *God*. She was so wet she swore she was seconds away from dribbling down her leg. "Why don't you reach between my legs and find out?"

He did just that. But the smirk on his face died away when he felt just how drenched she was. Instead his nostrils flared and his eyes went dark with need.

He gripped her ass and kneaded the flesh in his hands. Then he slid one hand around to jerk her thigh up. The next second, he'd repositioned his cock and then he entered her in one swift, sure thrust.

"*Fuuuuuck*," he swore as Logan's heat came up behind her.

Together they lifted her and just as Logan instructed, she wrapped her legs around Cam's waist.

"Hold her," Logan said.

"I'll help," Ross said, hurrying over to her left and reaching under to support her with his hands on her ass.

"Hey, me too," Riordan said, coming to her other side. It was tight with all of them so close but God, it was perfect, too.

Especially when Logan's cock lined up with the rim of her ass and then he started plunging in too.

"*Ohhhhhhhh*," she cried, leaning her head back against Logan.

So full. Oh God. *Oh*—

She moved one of her arms from around Cam's neck to drape it backwards over Logan's.

He took a small step back. With the twins supporting her, he was able to open up a little more space between him and Cam. Which meant the twins could lean down and suck her nipples.

Riordan's suction was forceful, drawing on her nipple to the point of pained pleasure whereas Ross just teased with his tongue. Until he grazed it with his teeth.

Michael and Logan already had her so primed, she could have come from that alone. Combined with the fullness of Cam and Logan fucking her pussy and ass, she was a goner.

She cried out her release, moving one hand to grab Ross's head and shove him harder into her breast.

"More," she cried as her climax peaked. Both Ross and Riordan sucked and sucked and sucked while Cam and Logan's thrusts grew more fervent.

"Fuck, baby," Logan shouted from behind her. "That's right. Now give us another one. You know you love my huge cock up your ass. Cam, hit her fucking G-spot. I know you know exactly how."

He spanked her ass while he fucked her and Vanessa felt another orgasm rising.

How? She'd just finished. She didn't think she could.

But oh God, here it was. It was coming. It was—

"Oh fuck— Yeah, right there," Logan continued. "That's right. Clench my cock. Fuck. You're like a goddamned vice. Just like that. I said fuck her, Cam! Fucking fuck her."

At Logan's words Cam started hammering away at Vanessa's pussy. Fucking destroying her while Logan did the same to her ass.

And the pleasure. Oh God, the pleasure.

It was almost mystical. She was in her body but where they were taking her— It was like a different plane of existence.

The orgasm rose and rose, impossibly high and it was still growing.

"I can't, I can't," she wept.

"Yes you fucking can," Logan demanded.

"Oh God," she cried. "I— I—"

And the explosion of blinding stars burst outward from her center. Vanessa didn't know if she screamed or wept or how long she held there, suspended in that sublime light of perfection where her lovers had taken her.

She only knew that when the stars finally fell back to earth like dying fireworks finally dissipating, she was clutched between four men who held onto her like she was the most precious thing on earth. Michael hovered just behind Logan, the widest smile on his face, too.

She was surrounded by love.

EPILOGUE

VANESSA

The next couple weeks were the happiest of Vanessa's life. Which had her conflicted, considering the rest of the world had gone to shit.

But in Vanessa's tiny corner of the universe, things were... wonderful. Logan surprised Vanessa every day with his open affection and attentiveness. It was as if that weight on his shoulders had been lifted and it changed everything about him—his posture, his sense of humor, even that constant tension she was used to seeing on his features was gone.

Ross and Riordan's scouting and hunting skills were also improving exponentially. Vanessa worried about them every time they went out but she could tell Riordan was more energized than ever by doing work that really made a difference.

And in spite of limited rations, Vanessa was gaining weight since her men made sure she ate every bite of every meal. Her breasts swelled and her hips rounded. The part she loved best: her dark brown hair grew more quickly than it ever had before.

Today she smoothed out the quilt in the center of her Clan's little cavern floor. She'd laid out a mat underneath it and it made for the perfect rug. Of course they could curl up in it on chilly nights, too.

"That's better," she smiled, looking around the room. She didn't know how long they'd be here, but she'd decided to make it as homey as possible. Women in the cave had taken to spending time together a couple afternoons a week for a quilting circle. It was the first time Vanessa had ever tried her hand at it.

She'd sewn before—it was something of a necessity to repair clothing while she'd lived on her own. But this was the first time she'd done anything remotely on this scale. As for the results... she tilted her head and looked down at the quilted rug.

Well, she was no master quilter and she'd definitely embraced the patchwork nature of the medium, but overall, she was pleased. She'd tried to find as many warm-toned fabric scraps as she could—dark reds, browns, oranges, yellows. Yes, she was quite pleased.

But whew, she'd worked up a little bit of a sweat hustling around the cavern to clean everything up and to make space for the rug. She swept her hair up into a short ponytail and secured it with the elastic she kept around her wrist.

The sound of a low groan behind her made her jump in surprise.

"Seriously," Ross said. "You can't keep doing that."

"Doing what?" she asked, turning around to find Ross and Riordan coming into the room, Logan and Cam just behind them.

"Honey, when you pull your hair up like that, exposing that beautiful neck..." Ross started, "I just want to ..."

"Bite it," finished Riordan.

"Oh stop kidding around," Vanessa said, turning away from them and hiding her smile. Her men were incorrigible.

Logan's arms slipped around her waist and she felt the warmth of his breath against the nape of her neck. Moments later, his lips dropped soft kisses there that sent shivers all the way down to her toes. Then she felt the gentle graze of his teeth.

"Who says we're kidding?"

Her grin grew wider right as Logan hugged her tighter, his chin resting on her shoulder.

"That's pretty," he said, obviously noticing the rug.

"Yeah," Cam said. "But I hope you didn't have to trade half our extra rations for it."

She turned in Logan's arms, looking around at all of them. "I made it. I wanted it to be a surprise." She hadn't told them about the quilting circle—just that she was getting 'together with the girls'—in case hers came out hideous and she wanted to pretend it had never existed.

"It's beautiful," Michael said, eyes soft.

"I don't know about y'all but I think this gorgeous new rug needs to be properly initiated," Cam said, stepping closer to Vanessa.

"Agreed," Ross said.

His expression was hungry, and he blatantly let his gaze move down her body. But when he got to the apex of her thighs, Ross's eyes jerked up to hers, face going deathly pale.

"Vanessa," he gasped. "You're hurt!"

"What?" she asked in confusion right as Ross's eyes rolled back in his head and he went down like a redheaded oak tree. Cam barely managed to catch him before he bashed onto the floor.

"Ross!" she cried, but at the same time she was laughing.

With joy.

Because she'd just looked down and saw what had Ross fainting— she'd finally gotten her period.

She was not a genetic dead end. In spite of the difficult road that might lay ahead, Clan Washington could have a future. It just went to show that with her family by her side, nothing was impossible.

***

Continue reading to enjoy an extended preview of Theirs to Defy, the next book in the Marriage Raffle Series

CHAPTER ONE

DREA

Compared to all the other places Drea had been imprisoned, President Goddard's personal detention center was pretty nice, all things considered.

It was in the basement of Fort Worth's Omni Hotel. He had to have had it built special—a series of ten cells, bars and all. Smaller than you'd find in say a local county jail, but then, these were obviously just meant to hold one person apiece.

Because that wasn't creepy. That the president of the Republic kept his own little jail-slash-torture chamber in the bottom of what was essentially the capitol building.

"Ya know, like you do," Drea whispered under her breath, working her way down the bars, testing each one for weaknesses again. "Not abnormal at all."

She rolled her eyes at herself. It had been a real *genius* move joining the delegation from Jacob's Well coming to the capitol yesterday. She'd been so sure she could convince the President to give her some troops to go back down to the Gulf Texas island, Nomansland, to rescue the women she'd been forced to leave behind three months ago.

Her women. The women she'd promised to keep safe. *Come to this island*, she'd said. *We'll fortify it against the outside world*, she'd said. She'd been so good at making speeches. *Enough of men ruling over us! We'll band tzogether and protect ourselves!*

She swallowed against the bitter taste in her mouth.

Too bad she hadn't been as good at fulfilling all those grandiose promises. Their greatest asset—secrecy—had lasted all of six months. She'd grasped too far, reached for too much. Elena told her not to keep accepting refugees. Elena said they should close their borders, ignore the outside world, become an island unto themselves.

But had Drea listened?

No.

Drea had not listened. Drea said they could still take in women if they were careful. They'd use computer messages and neutral meeting places.

Nothing is safe enough, Elena said. *There's one of us to every ten of them.* Them being men. The Xterminate virus had wiped out 90% of the earth's female population. *It's made them all animals. They'll never stop hunting us.*

Elena was right.

Two months after they opened up the island to refugees, one of their supposed 'rescues' turned out to be bait. The woman had a GPS implant so those watching could see where she was taken. It wasn't the Black Skulls MC's men who first besieged the island, but they took over pretty soon after.

Drea and the women had weapons stockpiled, but they were no match for the all-out assault that lasted for days on end.

In the end, surrender was the only choice if they were to survive.

Though the months of abuse that followed hadn't much felt like survival. More like hell on earth.

The Black Skulls were one of the biggest players in the female slave trade. And they set out immediately 'training' the women who'd first come to Nomansland for shelter and safety.

And *then*, when salvation *did* come? Did it come for the whole island? Oh no, of course not! A group of men came to rescue their wife who happened to be locked in a closet with Drea and they decided, oh look, we'll save this one too.

Her. Drea.

Out of all the women there who actually *deserved* rescuing, they plucked *her* out, the one who'd led all the rest there like lambs to the slaughter.

It had been her hubris and foolish pride to ever think that she could ever—

She growled in furious frustration at herself as she continued feeling along every bar of her cell.

She'd spent every waking moment of the last three months since her 'rescue' trying to get back to them. Trying to undo her wrongs, atone for her sins.

Hence this ill-thought out trip to the capitol.

If the President could have just given her something. Maybe not a battalion of troops, but what about a strike team. A helicopter. *Something*.

But noooooooooo, apparently President Douchie McDouchebag was a misogynistic pig who had a problem with women doing anything with their mouths other than sucking—

Well, suffice it to say, the second she questioned His Almightiness, she'd ended up in this cell.

She shook her head. Hadn't she learned by now that if she wanted something done, she had to do it herself? No more trusting in the inherent goodness of her fellow man. That was a crock of shit. Maybe her fellow *woman*, but definitely not her fellow fucking man.

If she was gonna free her women, she was gonna have to do it herself.

"And hopefully not fuck it up this time," she muttered under her breath. But *no*. She couldn't afford to think that way. She go and get them free or die trying.

She tugged again at the bars. They were steel, she was pretty sure. So bending them and trying to slip through wasn't an option. And the joints and pegs were on the opposite side of the door so she couldn't jimmy those loose. But maybe if she—

"You sure are pretty."

Oh goody, the guard had decided to do rounds again. He sure did them an awful lot considering she was the only prisoner.

She didn't give him the satisfaction of a reaction to his words. He was middle-aged, had hair that was more gray than brown, and a potbelly that hung so far over his belt she imagined it had been half a decade since he'd been able to see his toes.

But he thought she was pretty. Of course he did.

Drea stilled.

"And with all that pretty blonde hair. I bet you could make a fella feel reaaaaaaal good."

Drea breathed out a sharp breath.

Don't lose your temper. Don't lose your temper.

Do use *all* the tools at your disposal. Even if it makes you want to gag on your own dreadlocks.

She slowly crossed her arms over her stomach in a way that propped her boobs up and out. She rubbed her arms.

"Say, it sure is chilly in here," she said, face slightly downturned so that she was only looking at the guard through her eyelashes. "Do you think I could borrow your jacket?" She bit her lip and continued blinking up at him. "I promise I'll be good."

Shit, she was laying it on too thick, wasn't she? He'd see right through her act and—

"Well, I could always warm you up."

Or not.

She smiled and dipped her head. "If it wouldn't be too much trouble, I mean. I know all you men here at the capitol have such important jobs. Working for the *President* and all."

"Aw he wouldn't mind me seeing to the comfort of a prisoner. The New Republic is all about treating folks humane."

"Oh my gosh," Drea said, jumping up and down and clapping her hands—she was just purely channeling Sophia, the Commander's daughter, now.

Jesus, never thought she'd see the day. She might only be eight years older than the nineteen-year-old Sophia, but it felt like five decades separated them.

The guard was just eating this shit up, though.

Men were so fucking easy.

She'd shake her head if she weren't so busy keeping to her act.

That's right, buddy. Reach for those keys.

She fought to keep her eyes on his face while his hand went to the keyring at his belt.

He lifted a warning finger. "Step back now. Don't give me any trouble or you'll regret it." He touched the retractable billy club on his belt.

"Oh no, sir," Drea simpered. "I would never. If I could just have a friend in this cold place, it would mean everything. I'll do anything just to have someone on my side helping me. I'll pay you back however you want."

He grinned lasciviously. "However I want, huh?"

Drea nodded over and over, feeling like a bobblehead. She backed up against the far wall right beside the twin bed, hands up where he could see them.

He reached down and readjusted himself right before sliding the door open.

Patience.

Not yet.

He stepped inside the cell.

Not yet.

Smile. Look innocent and harmless.

She giggled and ducked her head as he shrugged out of his guard's jacket halfway across the room.

NOW.

She struck while his arms were still half-caught in the jacket, yanking and twisting it to trap his arms at the same time she swept his legs with a low kick.

Dad would be so proud.

Right as the guard hit the floor she was on him, yanking the billy club off his belt. Because the other thing Dad taught her?

Hit first and ask questions later.

It was something of a family mantra.

In one swift downward motion, Drea had the billy club extended and she got to work.

The guard was a screamer, so she went for the throat first. One swift hit to his larynx had him grasping his throat and choking.

She *tut tut tutted* at him for being dumb enough to expose himself like that. Because obviously her next hit was going to be to his scrotum.

That was just female self-defense 101.

She struck a few other of the best impact points to make sure he was disabled. One hard blow to the solar plexus, then, when he curled in on himself, a couple of strikes to the kidneys from the back.

He gasped for air and—was he crying?

She shook her head at him. Pathetic.

Let it never be said that she ever behaved like one of those clichéd blondes from old horror movies who always celebrated too early without double checking that the monster was really dead. Drea always made sure that her enemy was *down*.

She raised the club one last time and put all her weight behind a hit to his knee. He howled like a banshee

She reached and grabbed his keys off the floor from where the guard had dropped them, then she hurried out of the cell and locked it behind her.

Only to find the door to the stairs was being pushed open.

Shit.

Of course there were probably cameras on the cells. Someone had seen. *Or heard*. The question was how many they'd sent down to subdue her.

Screw it. She'd come this far.

She raised the billy club and ran at the door, knowing surprise was her best weapon.

"Drea?"

Wait, what?

"*Eric?*"

She was running so fast she couldn't stop herself in time and she collided with Eric. He wrapped his arms around her and together they rammed into the door, knocking it shut.

For a second it was just the two of them, breathing hard, him looking down at her. Wow, his eyes were a really nice gray, weren't they?

Wait, wait, wait.

Record scratch. Back the fuck up.

She hated Eric, *The Commander*, Wolford. He'd founded the new community at Jacob's Well after The Fall and ran the larger territory of Central Texas South.

Okay, maybe *hate* was a strong word. But she strongly disliked him. He was a chauvinist pig who'd come up with the most ridiculous, degrading system of treating the women in his territory. Giving them out as fucking raffle prizes, for Christ's sake. She'd had to lie and say she was a lesbian or else he was gonna try to force that shit on her.

And he too had refused to help her go back to Nomansland even though it had been men from his community who'd taken her from there in the first place.

Drea jerked away from Eric. "What are you doing here?"

He raised his arms in an *isn't it obvious?* motion. "Rescuing you."

Drea huffed out a laugh and then waved behind her at the guard on the floor of her cell. "Thanks but I can rescue myself just fine." She pushed the billy club back into its retracted position and shoved as much of it as she could in her pocket.

Eric crossed his arms and leaned against the wall. "You got out of your cell, but how exactly were you planning to get out of the city in the middle of a coup?"

Wait, what? She couldn't have heard that right.

"A what?"

"A coup. You know, when someone comes in and tries to take over—"

"I know what a goddamned coup is." Drea narrowed her eyes. "What makes you say one is happening here?"

"Oh you didn't hear? President Goddard was just assassinated. About..." He looked down at his watch. "Twenty-eight minutes ago."

Drea felt her eyebrows all but hit her hairline. Shit.

"Even better, they think it was someone from our group. I'm surprised your pretty head is still attached to your neck."

Despite herself, Drea's hand lifted to her throat. As soon as she realized what she was doing, she dropped her hand and glared at Eric.

"And why do they think that?"

He waved a hand to brush her off. "Shay's sculpture *may* have exploded and either someone in her clan or Vanessa's is most likely working for Arnold. Colonel Travis I mean."

Travis.

The governor of Travis Territory who, according to which rumors you listened to, was either a benevolent leader or a power-hungry slave trader. Drea had seen enough in her life to know the second was more likely the truth.

And now he'd assassinated the President.

Fuck. Her. Life.

Drea blinked, thoughts racing a million miles a minute.

Because if her instincts were right and he was a slave trader, he'd have dealings with the Black Skulls. Who were holding her women captive.

And Travis had just become the most powerful man in the country.

Drea's head snapped toward Eric. "And you're so calm about this... *why?*

"Well, it's all finally happening now, isn't it? I've been waiting for the shit to hit the fan for a long time and," he held out his arms. "Shit, meet fan. Now come on. I know where the President keeps his private helicopter."

"Why didn't you fucking open with that?" Drea growled, pushing past Eric.

"You're a very difficult girl to rescue."

Drea pulled the billy club out of her pocket. "Call me a girl one more time."

Eric lifted his hands in a surrender gesture. "I apologize. You're a very difficult... er, *complex* woman."

"And I rescued myself, remember?"

"Ah, but I'm the one with the helicopter, remember?"

————

"You were saying?" Drea put a hand on her hip as they looked out the window of the door that led out to the President's private helicopter pad.

The helicopter pad currently swarmed by soldiers wearing black and gray fatigues.

"Shit," Eric swore. "Those are Travis's soldiers. I thought they were at Jacob's W—" Then he shook his head. "It doesn't matter."

He took Drea's elbow and started pulling her back toward the stairs of the four-story parking garage that was a block away from the Omni.

Drea jerked out of his grasp. "Okay, we tried it your way. Now it's my turn." She strode in front of Eric and started down the stairs.

As she did, she realized this had been her problem all along.

She wasn't the kind of woman who waited for other people to help her get shit done. No, she blazed ahead and did it herself.

Why the hell had she even come to Fort Worth pandering to that asshole of a President in the first place? She should know—you wanted shit done, you did it *yourself*.

Well, lesson learned. How much time had she already wasted? She was going back to Nomansland to rescue her people. Today. Fuck everyone else.

"What are you— You don't even know this city. Have you even been to Fort Worth before?"

She didn't answer him until they got to the first floor of the garage before turning to face him. "No. But I know how to hot wire one of those." She pointed to the Harley she'd seen on the way in. In fact, there was a whole bunch of them lined up. She smiled sweetly and tilted her head at Eric. "Now, you don't mind riding bitch, do you?"

Eric's face darkened as he glowered at her. "I hate motorcycles," he muttered. But he did start walking in the direction of one of the Harleys.

She had the thing hot wired in three minutes flat and she handed a helmet to Eric. "Safety first."

He took the helmet but stared down at the growling motorcycle as she slung her leg over it. "You realize this is most likely a Black Skulls motorcycle."

Drea just grinned. "Where do you think I learned how to hot wire a hog? 4H?"

Seeing how Eric's eyes went saucer-wide almost made the whole shitty day worth it. Drea patted the seat behind her.

"Climb on."

Eric shook his head like he was rethinking his decision to ever come back for her in the first place. But he put the helmet on and climbed on behind her.

And if she noticed how good it felt having his strong arms around her waist? Well, that was just her damn hormones talking.

She turned her head to the side, not looking all the way back at him. "Hold on tight. I'm not gonna take it slow, and if you fall off, it's your own damn fault."

Eric's only response was anxious swearing.

Drea laughed and closed the face visor on her helmet before pulling out of the garage. Having the purr of a big twin engine between her legs felt far better than she'd like to admit. Eric would be in for a surprise when he realized they weren't heading for Jacob's Well.

And as she rode south, the morning sun to her left, she thought, *aw, this might even be fun.*

CHAPTER TWO

ERIC

Eric hated motorcycles. Hated them. He had ever since he was a teenager and his new best friend Arnie had double-dog dared him to steal his dad's motorbike and take it for a joyride around town.

He hadn't even made it to the end of the street before the bike tipped over and skidded sideways. He was lucky he hadn't been going any faster or he would have broken his leg for sure. Still, his leg was ripped up all to hell, almost down to the bone in a couple places. He was out the entire junior season of football.

He hadn't so much as looked at a damn murder-cycle since then.

And here he was stuck on the back of one clinging to a crazy woman with her hand on the throttle.

"Slow down!" he shouted but with the wind screaming around their ears, she couldn't hear him. Or maybe she could and she was just ignoring him. Drea was good at that. Damn stubborn woman.

He glanced over her shoulder and saw another curve in the street coming up. "Jesus," he swore, tightening his arms around her tiny waist. He frowned. She was so small. Was she not getting a large enough share of rations?

She was living at the single female dormitory in Jacob's Well.

Eric hadn't wanted her staying there. Only thirteen women lived there, but the truth was it was the closest thing to a brothel Jacob's Well had.

If a woman was past child-bearing age or decided she'd prefer not to be limited to five men such as the marriage raffle system confined them to—at least in theory, they hadn't had much problem with infidelity under the new system—she had the option to live in the dorm.

Such women generally shared their favors freely and were thus understandably popular and treated like queens wherever they went, no matter their age or looks. But a woman like Drea?

Eric's guts twisted just at the thought of the animals that would be mobbing her door if she indicated interest.

But she wouldn't.

She's a lesbian, remember?

Thank God for small favors—just because she was so against the whole Marriage Raffle thing—that was all he meant. And her being a lesbian exempted her from the lottery, he'd decided.

He'd never been in the business of forcing things on anyone. The Marriage Raffle system had been devised as the way to make the best out of a bad situation and to keep the peace. How else was he supposed to keep a town, much less a territory, of men in line with such limited access to female companionship? Lord knew it had made savages of the rest of the country. The rest of the *world*, whatever there was left of it.

But then, he'd never counted on coming across the likes of Drea Valentine, had he?

If only she weren't so damn stubborn, and opinionated, and—

"Jesus Christ!" he shouted as she took a turn with barely the slightest slow in speed. She leaned and he leaned with her. He didn't care if squeezing his eyes shut made him a chicken. If he didn't, he was afraid he'd upchuck his breakfast bagel all over the inside of his helmet.

"Shit!"

He barely heard Drea's shout above the wind. It was a panicked shout. What could have the badass woman who stood up to world leaders and took out prison guards twice her size sounding so panicked?

Eric's eyes popped open right as the tires locked and the brakes squealed.

Momentum shoved him forward even tighter against Drea's body and she held her own, he'd give her that. She kept the bike upright and they were slowing down.

But not fast enough to avoid the line of spikes that had been laid across the road.

"Fuuuuuuuuuuuuuck!" Eric yelped as the motorcycle skidded straight into two menacing looking spikes.

Then the world was fuck upside down and— He was airborne and—

Holy—

Jesus, he couldn't—

SLAM.

Owwwwww was the only thought he managed before the world went black.

———

"Shit, you think his head got cracked? Y'all both sure went flying. I've never seen anything like it."

"Eric? Eric."

That voice. Eric knew that voice.

"Eric, goddamn you, open your eyes right fucking now, or I swear I'll fucking—"

Drea.

Eric forced his eyes open.

Drea's face was right in front of him. Close. Really close.

Wow, her eyes were blue. Really, really blue. She probably hated that. She was such a badass, he bet being blonde with blue eyes totally pissed her off.

The thought made him smile.

"Eric? Are you fucking smiling? Shit, do you think he has brain damage?"

"Hey dude, can you track my finger?"

Who was she talking to? It was a man's voice. Eric moved his head slightly to the right, following Drea's line of sight and saw a skinny guy dressed in a worn t-shirt and ripped jeans with a bandana on his head.

He was waving his hand in front of Eric's face but Eric was too busy looking at the beat-up truck idling behind him and Drea. Looked like the guy had managed to stop before hitting the spikes.

Shit, the spikes.

"What happened?" Eric asked, trying to sit up and look around. "FUCK!" he yelled as pain screamed down his left arm.

"Shit, what?" Drea yelled. She put her hands on his stomach, feeling up and down his torso. Jesus that wasn't helping.

"His arm's broke," the guy said. "And I haven't seen road rash that bad since my Aunt Patty Mae went ass over ankles on her scooter when she was racing my cousin Grady and me. She—"

"It's definitely broken." Drea's voice was cool and matter of fact.

Billy was nodding. "We should set and splint it as soon as we can. But first we've got to get the hell out of here."

Eric glanced down at his arm and dammit, it was bent at an angle that was *not* natural. Not to mention shifting it even slightly send a blinding pain shooting through his whole damn body. "Mother fucking piece of—" he swore before gritting his teeth.

"Does anything else hurt?" Drea interrupted. "Eric?" She snapped her fingers in front of his face when he apparently didn't respond quickly enough for her. "I said, *does anything else hurt?*"

He wanted to roll his eyes at her, but every little shift of his body— *Ow!* Son of a—

"No," he bit out. Hadn't she fallen off the bike too? Who'd made her inquisitor in chief. "What about you?"

She just stared at him a moment, a look he couldn't decipher on her face. "I'm fine. You broke my fall."

Then she moved back and stood up. "Come on. We need to go. We're just sitting ducks out in the middle of the road like this. Billy, help me get these damn spikes off the tarmac."

Eric struggled again to sit up and Drea shot a short, "Don't move," at him before joining Billy at the edge of the road to drag the strip of spikes off to the shoulder.

Eric ignored Drea's snapped command, gritting his teeth against the pain in his left arm as he forced himself up to a sitting position.

"Little busy over here."

That was when he saw the bodies.

Two of them, blood pooling on the ground beside each.

They were wearing Travis's colors—black camo that was completely impractical in the Texas landscape and heat. It wasn't meant to blend in, only to intimidate. That was Travis's M.O.—make your enemies cower and whimper at your feet. And anyone who didn't play by Travis's rules? He just swept them off the board. Total destruction. The post-Fall world was the perfect playground for such an egomaniacal sociopath.

Eric shook his head as he looked from the two dead soldiers back to Drea and the guy—Billy.

Which one of them had taken the soldiers out? Drea couldn't have had a gun on her. He'd rescued her from prison. She was good but not even she could manufacture a gun from thin air.

That only left Billy. Sure he looked like a happy-go-lucky guy, but anyone who managed to survive The Fall this long and still have access to a truck and a weapon was someone to take seriously.

Eric locked his jaw and forced himself to his feet. Fucking hell, his arm hurt. It was the worst time imaginable to break his damn arm. He briefly glanced skyward. *Really? I can't catch one damn break?*

Then he huffed out, walking closer to the truck. He had to clutch his broken arm to his chest like he was an injured bird but you gotta do what you gotta do.

He climbed up into the cab of the truck. The keys were still in the ignition. Okay, so maybe the guy wasn't the brightest crayon in the box. Whatever, all the better for Eric and Drea.

Eric turned the key and the truck's engine roared to life. Eric didn't waste any time. Drea and Billy both looked up at the noise but Eric had already jammed the car into gear and was speeding toward them.

Billy jumped backwards to get out of the way but Drea stood motionless. Good girl.

Eric stomped the brakes and jerked the wheel, turning with a screech of tires and bringing the truck to a stop so that the passenger door was right in front of Drea. She didn't even flinch as the cloud of rocks and dust was kicked up all around her. She just grabbed the door and hopped up on the benchseat beside Eric.

"Drive," she ordered and Eric was only too happy to oblige.

Problem was, they hadn't gone more than fifty feet before Drea dropped a hand on his uninjured forearm, shouting, "Stop."

Eric squinted at the road. Were there more spikes ahead he wasn't seeing?

"I said, *STOP.*"

Fine, fine. He put his foot to the brake pedal again, slowing their speed. He wasn't willing to stop all the way, though. She hadn't been wrong about the sitting ducks comment. And when those two sentries back there failed to check in? They'd be having company reaaaaaaal soon.

"We have to go back for him."

Eric stared at her, not bothering to hide the fact he thoughts she was nuts. "Are you crazy? We don't know who the hell he is. He could be working for those bastards back there for all we know. A lookout in plain clothes and when you shot—"

"I didn't shoot them," Drea said. "He did. To protect me after he saw the spikes take us out. We were in the middle of the road after crashing. You were unconscious and I was freaking out thinking you were dead when those assholes must have come out from the ditch where they were hiding."

She'd been freaking out thinking he was dead?

"I didn't even see them. They were almost on top of me when Billy shot them. I only turned around at the gun shots and they were right there. Maybe four feet away."

Eric blinked, trying to focus in on what she was saying. Wait. She couldn't mean—

"We have to go back for him," she said. "He saved my life."

"Oh come on," Eric scoffed, shaking his head at her. "I never took you for a bleeding heart. We don't know anything about him."

"I don't leave my debts unpaid." Her face went hard. "Now turn the damn truck around and go back for him."

Eric glared out the front windshield, finally bringing the truck to a stop. Was that why she'd been worried he was dead? Because she considered trying to 'rescue' her a debt she owed him?

"I barely trust half the men in my own camp and you're willing to trust this stranger you just met how many minutes ago? For all we know he put the damn spikes there in the first place."

"Just shut up and—"

"Fine." Eric slammed the truck in reverse and then hit the gas pedal. She wouldn't change her mind. She never did, once she got set on something.

The truck jerked into action. Eric locked his eyes on the rearview mirror and navigated around debris and shit in the road that had been much easier to avoid when going forwards.

"Jesus Christ," Drea swore, her head swinging around to look out the back window. "I don't mean you have to get us fucking killed."

Eric ignored her and kept going, only slowing down when he saw Billy standing in the middle of the road where they'd left him. Billy jumped to the side when he saw the truck heading his direction in reverse.

Eric gritted his teeth against a fresh round of pain shooting up his broken arm as he stepped on the brakes yet again and brought the truck to a stop. He reached over with his good arm to roll down the manual window.

"Get in the back of the truck if you're coming," he yelled.

"Hey, you stole my truck!" Billy said, walking toward them and pointing at Eric. Then his focus shifted to Drea. "And *you* never gave me my gun back."

"Of course I didn't give you back your gun, do you think I'm an idiot?" Drea leaned across Eric to talk to Billy out the window and Eric blinked. Jesus, didn't she realize— Her breasts were almost skimming his—

"Now get in the damn truck bed if you don't want to be left out here to be picked off like road kill."

Eric was too busy trying to remember how to breathe with Drea so close but when she pulled back and he heard a thunk in the truck bed, he figured Billy had gotten on board with her plan.

She was persuasive like that. And hot. Her body he meant. Not like — He just meant that when she'd leaned over like that, the heat of her body had— Jesus, did he have a fever or something? He wiped at the sweat on his forehead with his arm.

"Now you." Drea glared at him when he looked her direction. "Switch seats. The last thing I need is you passing out in the middle of the highway."

Eric punched the gas before she could unhook her seatbelt. "I got it, thanks." He held his broken arm against his chest. Fuck it hurt. He'd need to splint it soon. But he was not giving up this little bit of control.

Drea let out a small, exasperated noise. "You're hurt. What the hell am I supposed to do if you black out while you're driving?"

Eric rolled his eyes. "I broke my arm. I'm not bleeding out. And let's not forget what happened the last time you were in charge of the moving vehicle."

If he thought she'd been exasperated before it was nothing to the offended noise she made at that. "There were *spikes* in the road. It had nothing to do with my damn driving."

"Well maybe if you'd been going slower, we would have been able to stop in time."

"Is that why you're only going fifty-five miles an hour, Grandpa? There is a war just starting. Might be nice to make it out of the area before reinforcements arrive."

"Jesus," he swore, shaking his head as he looked over at her. "I'm trying to conserve gas. Everybody knows you conserve up to twenty percent more gas by going fifty-five rather than seventy-five."

"Yeah well we won't be around to enjoy all that gas we're saving if the bad guys catch up to us because you're driving like you've got a stick up your ass, will we?"

"Fine," he growled, "you want faster, you'll get faster." He pressed harder on the pedal, shaking his head as he looked at the fuel gage that was only slightly above half full.

———

Drea and the Commander's book, Theirs to Defy is AVAILABLE NOW

*Want to read EXCLUSIVE, FREE novellas by Stasia Black and A.S. Green
that are only available to newsletter subscribers?*

To get *Making Waves* by A.S. Green please visit
BookHip.com/FHPQQN

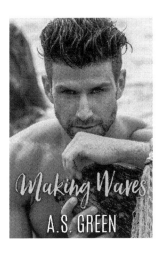

To get *Their Honeymoon* by Stasia Black
please visit
BookHip.com/QHCQDM

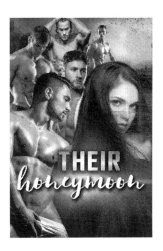

OTHER BOOKS BY STASIA BLACK

MARRIAGE RAFFLE SERIES
Theirs to Protect

Theirs to Pleasure

Theirs to Wed

Theirs to Defy

Theirs to Ransom

BREAK SO SOFT SERIES
Cut So Deep

Break So Soft

Hurt So Good

STUD RANCH STANDALONE SERIES
The Virgin and the Beast: a Beauty and the Beast Tale (prequel)

Hunter: a Snow White Romance

The Virgin Next Door: a Ménage Romance

OTHER BOOKS BY A.S. GREEN

FAE HELL HOUND'S FATED MATES SERIES
Hounded

Guarded

Cursed

ROMANTIC BEACH READS
Summer Girl

Wild Child

ACKNOWLEDGMENTS

First of all, to my PA's, THANK YOU!!! You ladies help me stay sane so I can focus on what I love, the writing, while also still actually communicating with the outside - only possible because you all make it easy and non-stressful. Without you, I would run with my arms over my head and hide under the bedcovers. #introvert

Melissa Lee – ❤ thank you for all your help and mad organizational skillz, gorgeous. My life got so much less stressful since you dropped into it and help keep my head on straight. Thank you!!!

Melissa Pascoe— Thank you for keeping my page and Stasia's Babes a super fun place to hang out with my babes! All the ❤

Christine Jalili – You kick butt at making It's Raining Men the hottest Reverse Harem Group on FB 😃 You're always so on top of the ball, ❤ you!

Aimee Bowyer, my gorgeous beta! Thank you as always for your feedback. Readers can thank you for the Epilogue, lol, cause I was just gonna be lazy author and say The End. You always push me to be my best. Huggles!!!

Bobby! Thank you for everything!

Alana Albertson! Thank you for keeping me sane throughout this one and I'm always here to geek out over covers and gorgeous man candy with you!

ABOUT THE AUTHORS

STASIA BLACK grew up in Texas, recently spent a freezing five-year stint in Minnesota, and now is happily planted in sunny California, which she will never, ever leave.

She loves writing, reading, listening to podcasts, and has recently taken up biking after a twenty-year sabbatical (and has the bumps and bruises to prove it). She lives with her own personal cheerleader, aka, her handsome husband, and their teenage son. Wow. Typing that makes her feel old. And writing about herself in the third person makes her feel a little like a nutjob, but ahem! Where were we?

Stasia's drawn to romantic stories that don't take the easy way out. She wants to see beneath people's veneer and poke into their dark places, their twisted motives, and their deepest desires. Basically, she wants to create characters that make readers alternately laugh, cry ugly tears, want to toss their kindles across the room, and then declare they have a new FBB (forever book boyfriend).

A.S. GREEN is the author of erotic novellas (Real Man, Rough Ride) and new-adult novellas and full-length romances (Making Waves, Summer Girl, Wild Child). She lives in the cold, upper-Midwest with her husband and three mostly grown children, usually hunkered down with a good book. You can find her on the interwebs at asgreenbooks.com and @asgreenbooks. Say hello and follow on Facebook, Twitter, Instagram, Book Bub, Goodreads, etc.

Printed in Poland
by Amazon Fulfillment
Poland Sp. z o.o., Wrocław

25174007R00161